"I don't care about anybody in that ballroom."

Jack further silenced Maggie's protest with a kiss. "If we're going to go back inside that hotel, there's only one place I want us to be—my suite." He kissed her again until she was out of breath.

"Does this mean I'm forgiven?" she whispered throatily.

"That depends."

"Depends on what?"

"On whether you spend the night with me."

She ran a teasing finger along the inside of his collar. "Rumor has it that Jack Brannigan can cruise the university campus and pick up any girl he wants. Why would he want a goody-two-shoes?"

Jack pressed himself even closer to her so that she could feel his desire for her and said, "Because he knows that she can be naughty for the right guy."

ABOUT THE AUTHOR

In just a few short years, Pam Bauer has
soared to the top of her chosen profession,
achieving recognition from both her peers
and her readers. Still, modest Pam is always
surprised when fans tell her how much
they enjoy her work! Pam makes her home
in Minnesota with her husband and
two children.

Books by Pamela Bauer

HARLEQUIN SUPERROMANCE
236–HALFWAY TO HEAVEN
288–HIS AND HERS
330–WALKING ON SUNSHINE
378–THE HONEY TRAP

Don't miss any of our special offers. Write to us at the
following address for information on our newest releases.

Harlequin Reader Service
901 Fuhrmann Blvd., P.O. Box 1397, Buffalo, NY 14240
Canadian address: P.O. Box 603,
Fort Erie, Ont. L2A 5X3

Memories

PAMELA BAUER

Harlequin Books

TORONTO • NEW YORK • LONDON
AMSTERDAM • PARIS • SYDNEY • HAMBURG
STOCKHOLM • ATHENS • TOKYO • MILAN

Published June 1990

ISBN 0-373-70406 - 2

For Chris, Renae, Brenda,
Patty, Jan and Gwen
in celebration of twenty-five
years of friendship
with fond memories of the Cooper
High School Class of '68

PROLOGUE

Twenty years ago

"WHERE'S BOOGIE?" Maggie Stewart asked as she walked to the front of the typing lab and found her best friend sitting in the chair normally occupied by their teacher.

"Probably home in bed. Didn't you hear? She fainted during fifth hour—got the flu or something." Sheila Wilson snapped her chewing gum as she unfolded bits of paper and added them to the small mound in the center of the desk.

"So who's going to count the ballots?" Maggie dropped a stack of books onto one of the typing tables in the front row and draped her navy-blue parka over the back of a chair.

"We are."

"Without our advisor?"

"Relax, Maggie. I talked to Boogie before she left and she told me she trusted the three of us to take care of counting the ballots."

"The three of us?"

"Yeah. Boogie told me to get at least one other member of the coronation committee to make it official. Judy Karner should be here any second."

Maggie frowned. "I thought the rules stated we needed to have a teacher present when we count the votes."

"Maggie Stewart, do you think that just *once* in your life you could break a rule?" Sheila demanded impatiently. "No one's going to know or care who counted the darn ballots. All anyone is concerned with is who gets crowned Snow King and Queen tomorrow morning at the pep rally. And if we don't count the ballots today, we won't be able to tell them. Besides, aren't you dying to find out who won?"

"Of course I am. I'm just surprised Boogie trusts us."

"Trusts us?" Sheila repeated. "You're president of the National Honor Society and I'm the senior class secretary."

Just then Judy Karner burst into the room clutching her schoolbooks close to her chest. "You two are going to just *die* when you hear what's happened!" she exclaimed, rolling her eyes heavenward.

"What? Tell us! Tell us!" Sheila begged excitedly, jumping up from her chair, her eyes widening behind the black pointed frames of her glasses.

Judy glanced from one girl to the other, as though debating whether she should. "If I do, you have to promise you won't breathe a word of it to anyone."

"We won't. We promise," Sheila vowed anxiously.

Judy paused dramatically, then finally said, "Gina Loring's p.g."

"Gina Loring?" Maggie and Sheila echoed in unison, their faces registering their shock.

"I don't believe it!" Maggie exclaimed, tossing her long auburn curls over her shoulder with a flick of her wrist. "It must be a rumor. She doesn't even have a steady boyfriend."

"At least not one who wants to be seen in public with her," Judy added cattily.

As usual, Maggie came to the unpopular girl's defense. "Well, I for one don't understand why not. She's a nice person."

"Nice and pregnant," Judy retorted, which drew an icy glare from Maggie.

"So who's the father?" Sheila asked in a near whisper.

Again, Judy looked as though she were deciding whether or not she should tell them. After a long pause, she took a deep breath and said, "Jack Brannigan."

Two startled gasps were the only sounds heard.

"Now I know it must be a rumor," Maggie declared. "Everyone knows Jack's going steady with Linda Benson."

"Not anymore," Judy announced smugly. "They broke up this afternoon. Linda threw his ring back at him right in the middle of study hall. And guess who was cuddled up next to Jack when he drove out of the school parking lot?"

"Gina." Sheila stated the obvious. "That means he must have gotten her pregnant while he was going steady with Linda. That's disgusting!" She wrinkled her nose distastefully.

"Are you sure about this, Judy?" Maggie asked, giving her a hard stare. "I mean, I know Jack's got sort of a bad reputation..."

"Sort of a bad reputation!" Judy echoed with an exaggerated drawl. "Do you realize how many hearts he's broken in the short time he's been at Jefferson High? I heard he even cruises the university campus looking for girls."

"Which makes it all the more unlikely he'd mess around with Gina. Why would he when he could have his pick of any girl in school?" Maggie reasoned.

Judy dropped onto Miss Boogstrom's chair, her arms folded across her angora sweater. "Believe what you want. Time will tell that I am right."

Maggie looked at the other girl's self-assured face and felt more than a twinge of annoyance. Judy had a reputation herself—of being the school's biggest gossip. And as much as Maggie hated to admit it, she usually did know what she was talking about.

"So now what's going to happen to Gina?" Sheila asked.

"The same thing that happens to all unwed mothers," Judy answered, her face grim. "She'll get sent away—probably to some unwed mothers' home. You can't stay in school if you're pregnant."

"I don't see why not," Maggie protested. "Just because she's having a baby doesn't mean she shouldn't be allowed to graduate."

"I agree," Sheila concurred. "After all, Jack will get to complete his senior year, won't he?"

"Of course he'll graduate. Not only that, he's probably going to be crowned Snow King tomorrow." Judy gestured toward the pile of paper ballots heaped atop Miss Boogstrom's desk.

"Well, there's only one way to find out. We've got to count the ballots." Sheila took charge once more, maneuvering Judy out of Boogie's chair before handing each of them a pencil, paper and a portion of the pile of ballots. "We'll double-check each other's when we're done."

They worked quietly and diligently until the tabulating was complete. Then, with a sober face, Sheila made the announcement.

"It's official. This year's Snow Queen is Diane Robinson and The Snow King is Jefferson High's own expectant father—Jack Brannigan."

"I can't believe he won by only four votes," Judy groaned, unwrapping a stick of gum.

"It doesn't matter if he won by four or forty. The point is, he did win," Maggie reminded her.

"Yeah, but how many kids do you suppose would have voted for him if they had known about Gina?" Judy posed the hypothetical question. "If the balloting were to take place tomorrow, I bet he wouldn't win."

"It doesn't matter how the kids would have voted tomorrow, Judy," Maggie insisted. "He won *today*."

"Maybe we added wrong," Sheila said, double-checking the figures in front of her.

"No one would know if we did." Judy's words were softly spoken but carried an implicit message.

Maggie's eyes widened in disbelief. "You're not suggesting that we fix the contest?"

"I didn't say that...exactly," Judy hedged. "But tell me, Maggie. Who did you vote for? Was it Jack?"

Maggie's ivory skin turned a rosy pink. "All right, so I voted for him. Most of the girls did. He's the cutest guy in the senior class."

"I voted for him, too. What does that have to do with anything?" Sheila asked.

"Because I voted for Jack, too," Judy explained. "And now we're all regretting it. Don't you get it? If the three of us were to change our votes to Rob Michaels, then that would mean Jack only won by one vote. And that one vote could have been Linda's. And what if *she* had changed her mind and voted for Rob. Then it would have been a tie..."

"Wait a minute," Maggie cut in, jumping to her feet, her green eyes flashing and her shoulders stiffening defiantly. "You've got no idea who Linda did or didn't vote for. This changing votes after the election has taken place isn't right. We can't justify fixing the ballots."

"For Pete's sake, Maggie," Judy snapped back. "Do you have to always act like such a goody-two-shoes? We're not electing a student council president. It's only a popularity contest. Do you honestly think a guy like Jack Brannigan deserves to be treated like a king for getting Gina pregnant?"

"I bet now that she's p.g. she won't be able to attend any of the Snow Daze activities," Sheila chimed in. "I mean, she's not going to be able to go skiing if she's pregnant, is she? And what about the tobogganing party Friday night?"

"She'll be stuck at home while Jack's out having fun, that's what," Judy said disapprovingly. "We're the three people from the coronation committee who are in charge here. I think we ought to take a vote. I say we tell Miss Boogstrom Rob Michaels won. You two can either agree or disagree. Majority will rule."

There were several moments of uncomfortable silence as Maggie waited for her friend's answer. But Sheila was avoiding all eye contact with her, so Maggie knew what her best friend was going to say long before she spoke.

"I'm with you, Judy."

"Then I guess it doesn't matter what I say, does it?" Maggie contended angrily.

"It matters to us—especially if you're not going to abide by the coronation committee rules that say all election results must remain confidential." Judy's tone was cautious. "Boogie told us we weren't supposed to tell anyone how many votes each person gets."

"Boogie doesn't know we're cheating!" Maggie laughed uneasily. "I can't believe you two don't see how wrong this is!"

"Maybe you should save some of that righteousness for Gina. She's the one who's not going to be able to graduate in June," Judy reminded her. "Think about it, Maggie. While Gina's shuffled off to some unwed mothers' home, Jack will be cruising the halls of Jefferson High."

Again there was a silence, and seeing the indecision on Maggie's face, Judy pressed on. "What's one vote? We're doing this for Gina, and if you have any compassion for her, you'll promise not to say a word about this to anyone."

Maggie knew she was wrong to agree, but it did seem so unfair the way girls were punished for getting pregnant when the guys were practically absolved of any blame. And she did have compassion for Gina, more than Judy or Sheila would ever know. Gina's mother worked at her dad's hardware store, and Maggie knew that the Loring family was a troubled one. What Gina's pregnancy would mean to a family already torn apart...

"Well?" Judy and Sheila were looking at her expectantly.

"All right. I promise I won't say anything," she reluctantly conceded.

The next day, when Rob Michaels was crowned Snow King at the pep rally, Maggie's eyes weren't on the newly crowned royals, but Jack Brannigan. He didn't look disappointed at all. In fact, he looked a little distracted. As soon as the program was over, she saw the reason for his distraction. He quickly found Gina and led her out of the school auditorium, his head tucked close to hers and his arm curved around her shoulders protectively.

Maggie felt a tap on her back and turned around to face Sheila, who was looking as guilty as Maggie was feeling.

"Don't worry, Maggie, no one will ever know."

CHAPTER ONE

The Present

MAGGIE STEWART CIRCLED the block twice before stopping at the big white house on the hill. Her indecisiveness was due to the reason for her visit: she had offered to help with the planning of her twenty-year high-school reunion and was now having second thoughts as to the wisdom of her decision. There were several words Dr. Walker had advised she eliminate from her vocabulary this summer—work and stress were two of them.

"Maggie, I want you to promise me that the only thing you'll work at this summer is getting completely rested and having fun. I want absolutely no stress in your life," he had told her in his deep, resonant voice, the one that reminded her of Vincent Price warning of some dark evil.

What stress could there possibly be in serving on the reunion committee? she asked herself as she parked her mother's station wagon under the shade of an elm tree. It wasn't as though she would be responsible for a large portion of the work. She had simply agreed to help Sheila with a few of the tedious details. Dr. Walker surely couldn't find fault with stuffing envelopes and licking stamps.

Besides, she needed something to occupy her time. She had only been in Duluth a week and already she was growing restless. She missed the excitement of Washington, D.C. Taking a leave of absence from her job as a government trade negotiator was something she never would have done had it not been for her health. She couldn't even remember the last time she had taken a vacation, and because of all the time owed her, she had been able to take three months off without losing any compensation.

Maggie didn't mind having some time away from her job, but she would have preferred to remain in Washington. Unfortunately Dr. Walker had known that she wouldn't have much of a vacation in the capital. She had never been very good at separating business from pleasure; as long as there were lobbyists around, she could find a cause to champion. A change of scenery as well as a change of pace had been prescribed if she was truly going to regain her strength. So she had packed her bags and moved back home to the quiet seaport on Lake Superior.

"It is quiet," Maggie murmured to herself, smoothing the wrinkles from the skirt of her two-piece linen outfit as she climbed out of the car. She was glad Sheila had suggested she come early so that the two of them could talk before the rest of their classmates arrived. It had been more than a year since she had last seen her friend, and the thought was accompanied by a twinge of guilt as she recalled the stack of letters that still sat unanswered on her desk in Washington.

Maggie pushed open the white gate and followed the cement walk around to the side of the house, and for just a moment she felt as though she were sixteen again and picking Sheila up on her way to school. She found herself glancing over her shoulder to the house next door as though expecting to see Steve Goodman sneaking peeks at her while he practiced shooting baskets at the garage hoop. Instead she saw a tricycle and a skateboard, and she knew that the Goodmans had long since moved away, like so many of her classmates had. Sheila and her husband had bought the place from her parents.

"Anybody home?" Maggie called out through the screen door and was immediately greeted with a squeal of delight.

"Maggie, is that you?" Sheila's still petite, but slightly heavier, figure came into view. She opened the screen door and ushered her friend in with an effusive hug. "Welcome home, stranger! Let me look at you." She pushed Maggie back an arm's length. "You look terrific!"

"I look anemic and you know it," Maggie returned with a gentle squeeze of appreciation.

"Just the fact that you don't need to lose twenty-five pounds in two months makes you look terrific to me," she admitted, a twinkle in her eye as she led Maggie into the kitchen.

"Have a chair while I put the finishing touches on this fruit salad."

Maggie smiled as she passed the refrigerator and saw two photographs taped to the door. One was yellowed and a bit curled around the edges—a picture of Sheila in a blue satin formal, taken the night of the senior prom. The second was Sheila the housewife and mother wearing an aerobics leotard. Maggie guessed it was quite recent.

"What's this supposed to mean?" she asked, pointing a polished fingernail at the prom photo. "Do you really want to look like Gidget again?"

"No, but I don't want to look like a walrus, either." She pulled two long-stemmed glasses from the cupboard. "What can I get you to drink? Are you on any medication that would make alcoholic beverages a no-no?''

Maggie shook her head. "Not anymore. Dr. Walker claims that three meals a day, a good night's sleep and fresh air are the only medicine I need.''

"Then you've come to the right place. There's not much else to do but eat, sleep and breathe in Duluth.'' She pulled a bottle of sparkling wine from the refrigerator. "What do you think?'' She held up the bottle for Maggie's inspection.

"It's my favorite—as if you didn't know.'' She couldn't help but smile at her friend's thoughtfulness.

Sheila shrugged. "That's what friends are for.''

"I'm sorry this friend was such a miserable correspondent this past year. I appreciated your letters.''

"You don't need to apologize to me, Maggie. Distance may separate us physically, but you know as well as I do that we will always be close in spirit.'' She filled their glasses, popping a strawberry into Maggie's before handing it to her. "I'm so glad you're going to be home for the summer.''

"Me, too,'' Maggie said, sitting down and sipping the wine appreciatively. "You're one of the reasons I decided to recuperate here rather than in Washington. It's going to be wonderful not to have to cram all of our catching up into one visit.''

Sheila sat down across from her and turned her attention to the fresh pineapple she had been cutting into small chunks. "So tell me how you're feeling—and I want an honest answer.''

"I feel fine,'' Maggie told her, then seeing Sheila's skeptical look added, "Honest. I have a tendency to get a little weak at the knees every now and then and I tire awfully easy, but I'm getting stronger every day.''

"You're too thin," Sheila said, the mild reproach dissolving into a giggle as she added, "Stick around me and I guarantee that won't be your problem for long." She shoved a candy dish filled with truffles in her direction. "Here. Have a chocolate."

Maggie chose a confection from the crystal dish and popped it into her mouth. "Umm. I'll take fat, single and happy over skinny, married and miserable any day."

Sheila's face grew sober. "I'm sorry about the divorce, Maggie. I wanted to call you, but I wasn't sure if it was a good idea for you to be talking about it."

"My divorce wasn't the cause of my illness, Sheila," Maggie assured her. "I know a lot people probably think that I fell apart because Brian left, but the truth is I brought it all on myself. You know what a workaholic I can be. Well, this time I overdid it. Too much work, too little sleep, too much stress . . . it all took its toll and the result was exhaustion." Maggie took another sip of her wine. "But enough about me. Tell me what's been happening in your life. You look great—as though you could have graduated yesterday."

Sheila nearly choked on her wine. "You are a diplomat. No wonder the government snapped you up."

"I mean it. If anything, you look better than when you were in high school. You didn't have contact lenses back then—just those black plastic glasses with the pointy tips."

Sheila groaned. "Weren't they awful? And I never dared take them off for fear I'd bump into somebody. I hated wearing glasses and once I could afford contacts I swore I'd never own another pair."

Maggie chuckled. "You got rid of your glasses and I gained mine." She opened her purse and pulled out a pair of large, square rimmed glasses and put them on. "What do you think? They're my power glasses...I wear them for effect. Of course it helps if I have a suit on as well."

"Definitely high power!" Sheila remarked. "Now you're really going to wow the reunion committee members. When I told everyone that you were back you should have seen how excited they were—especially when they heard you were working in Washington. You're probably the most successful graduate of our class." There was more than a trace of envy in her voice. "You get to travel all over the world, meet all different kinds of people."

"It sounds much more glamorous than it really is, believe me," Maggie asserted with a grimace.

"I still think most of the women are going to be green with envy when they see you. Do you know how many of us got married, had kids and have been stuck here in Duluth ever since?"

Although the question was punctuated with a giggle, Maggie thought she detected a hint of restlessness in her girlfriend's voice.

"Sheila, you've got a beautiful home, three great kids and a wonderful husband. A lot of women would envy you," Maggie said sincerely.

"You're not going to try to tell me you'd love to trade places, are you?"

Maggie had the grace to blush.

"Still the same old Maggie," Sheila said wistfully with a toss of her dark curls. "I bet you're already going crazy being stuck here in Duluth, aren't you?"

"All right. I confess—" she held up her hands "—I do miss the excitement of Washington and I am wondering how I'm going to survive three months of doing nothing."

"Correction. Three months away from your job. Not three months of doing nothing." She waved her paring knife. "You're going to be helping me with our class reunion. And there's a lot to be done."

"I don't understand how you ended up being in charge of the entire event." Maggie reached across the table and snatched a fresh strawberry from the cutting board. "I thought the class president was supposed to be responsible for organizing these things."

Sheila made a disgruntled sound. "Our class president is now a hotshot lawyer living right across the harbor in Superior, Wisconsin, but who claims he was never our class president."

"What?" Maggie's eyebrows shot up.

"Danny—" she cleared her throat "—excuse me, *Daniel* Richards told me personally that I must have him confused with someone else. He was never class president."

"Did you tell him to look on page ninety-one of the yearbook?" Maggie asked dryly.

"I told him quite a few things, but I don't think he was impressed. I ended the conversation by telling him I was glad I had the opportunity to talk to him, because now if any of our classmates ask what's become of him I can tell them the truth—nothing."

"Sheila, you didn't!" Maggie gasped.

"Of course I did. I mean, he could have at least made up a good excuse as to why he couldn't accept the job," she reasoned with a slight frown.

"What about the vice president?"

"Allan Carter? He's living in California. Besides, he organized the ten-year reunion—which you would have remembered if you had come," she said, wagging an accusing finger at her friend.

Maggie shrugged apologetically. "You still haven't forgiven me for that, have you?"

"Not when I managed to attend eight months pregnant and feeling like a water balloon ready to burst." She dropped another strawberry in Maggie's glass and refilled it with wine. "Anyway, after contacting what seemed like half the class, I became chairperson by a unanimous decision—no one else would do it."

"You always were a great organizer," Maggie complimented her with a lift of her glass.

"With some things, maybe." She slipped a piece of plastic wrap over the fruit salad and slid it into the refrigerator. "There. I'm organized for lunch anyway. Let's take our wine and go outside. It's such a beautiful day and summers are much too short to spend indoors. Besides, I want to show you what we did to the backyard."

Maggie followed her out a sliding glass patio door. "Sheila, this is lovely," she said admiring the newly constructed cedar deck that extended the length of the house. "I always did love the view you have from here. You and Tom were lucky you were able to buy this house from your folks. Remember all those sleep-overs we had here?" There was a wistfulness in her voice. "Everyone used to think we were nuts because we would set your alarm so we could get up to see the mist hanging over the lake in the early morning."

"And we'd spend hours out here watching the ships sail in and out of the harbor, dreaming of how we'd someday be going to just as many faraway places," Sheila added. "Well, you did it, Maggie. You've been everywhere and me—I'm still living in the same house I grew up in as a child.''

Maggie sighed. "The grass always looks greener on the other side of the fence. I know you're going to find this hard to believe, but there have been times when I wished for a house like this," she said, eyeing the big white structure affectionately. "You wouldn't really want to move away from here, would you?''

Sheila leaned over the railing of the deck and stared out at Lake Superior where a Coast Guard ship was passing under the aerial lift bridge. "I honestly don't know," she admitted candidly, then chuckled. "In any case, I don't think I need to worry about the opportunity presenting itself. Tom loves his job and the kids love their school.''

"Well, I don't think you'd want to trade your life here for a career in Washington, D.C. A career, I might add, that may be exciting, but is far from glamorous...unless you call having no personal life glamorous.''

"Does that mean there isn't a man in your life?" Sheila threw her an interested glance.

Maggie shook her head. "Unfortunately there hasn't been time for one. That's one of the disadvantages of my job.''

"I thought you enjoyed being single.''

"I do, but I miss the intimacy of a personal relationship. You can be single and be intimate. You can also be married and be lonely.''

"Were you?" Sheila asked, a faint note of surprise in her tone.

"Most of the time. I never felt as though Brian and I were partners. We were more like competitors," she said, sadness in her voice.

"That wasn't your fault," Sheila assured her. "He wasn't secure enough to handle any woman's success, and especially not his own wife's. Tom sensed that the first time we met him."

"He did? That's funny," she mused aloud. "I didn't realize it until I started making more money than he did."

"I hope that doesn't mean he took you to the cleaners in divorce court," Sheila said, concern in her voice. "I've heard all about these men who are suing their wives for alimony."

Maggie chuckled. "You can relax. He didn't contest the divorce settlement presented by my attorney. What's mine is still mine. But listen, I don't want to waste any more time talking about Brian. Tell me what you've got planned for the reunion. And you'd better tell me what you've got planned for me. I'm almost afraid to ask."

"Nothing stressful—I promise." She raised her hand defensively. "Actually things are going more smoothly than I anticipated. What I'd like you to help me with is the reunion book."

"The reunion book?" Maggie shot her an inquisitive glance.

"Umm-hmm. We want to put together something that will resemble a miniversion of our yearbook, only it will have current information on each of the graduates—and no pictures. The problem is we haven't been able to find everyone. The search committee's done a pretty thorough job, but there are still about twenty-five students missing." She walked over to the round picnic table and started digging through a cardboard box.

"Andrea Thomas was in charge of this, but now that her mother's been taken ill, she's had to resign." Sheila pulled out a sheet of paper and handed it to Maggie.

"These are the ones who are still missing. Andrea's included her notes on the sources she's already contacted, plus some leads."

Maggie gave the list a quick once-over. "Some of these names I don't even recognize."

"Considering our class had over four hundred students, that doesn't surprise me."

"What are the stars for?" Maggie asked, noticing that several of the names had asterisks beside them.

"Those are the people Barb Milton wants to include in the program."

Maggie looked at the list again. There was one name her eyes kept returning to—Jack Brannigan. Neither she nor Sheila had ever mentioned his name since graduation. Now it stared at her like a guilty challenge.

"I'm surprised no one knows where Jack Brannigan is," she commented aloud, although she kept her eyes on the paper in her hand. "I thought he and Gina Loring might have gotten married, but I notice her name isn't on the missing list."

"Gina's married to a doctor and lives out East— Baltimore I think is where I heard she is now." Sheila didn't make eye contact with Maggie, either. "Apparently she hasn't seen Jack since we graduated. No one has. Someone said they heard that he was a corporate executive for some advertising firm."

"Jack Brannigan?" Maggie repeated, raising one eyebrow. "Somehow it's hard to picture him in a business suit. I have more of an image of an Air Force Pilot, you know, Tom Cruise ten years down the road. He always wore that leather aviator jacket in high school."

"That's because his father was in the Air Force. Andrea tried to tell me she thought Jack had become a priest."

That brought an eruption of laughter from Maggie. "A priest!" she repeated in disbelief.

"Stranger things have been known to happen," Sheila told her. "Have you heard what Carl Langston is doing?"

"I suppose you're going to tell me he didn't become a professional singer as everyone expected he would." Her eyebrows arched delicately.

Sheila shook her head and began to giggle. "He sells lingerie at home parties!"

"You're not serious!" Maggie's mouth flew open.

"Oh, yes, I am! Talk about a waste of talent. Remember how we'd all go starry-eyed when the choir teacher would have Carl sing solo in class? Maybe he sings to the women as he's holding up the silk teddies."

Maggie could only shake her head, an action that caused the sun to highlight the red streaks in her chin-length auburn hair. "Well, I guess I find it easier to believe that Carl's a lingerie party host than to believe that Jack Brannigan has become a priest, although I suppose the corporate executive is possible. He was as sharp as a tack only he never applied himself. What do you want him to do at the reunion?"

"*I* don't want him to do anything," Sheila quickly denied, averting her eyes, which only made Maggie suspect that her best friend hadn't forgotten how they had fixed the Snow King contest in high school. "The evening program is Barb's territory, not mine. Speaking of planning, do you realize that all of the work for this reunion is being done by women? I'd like to know what happened to the men in our class."

"We'll find out soon enough," Maggie replied, her thoughts on one man in particular—Jack Brannigan.

The rest of the afternoon passed quickly. They were joined by seven of their classmates, and talk centered around the plans for the reunion. Maggie was impressed by how well everything was organized. She found herself truly enjoying reminiscing with her old friends, and was sorry to see their meeting come to an end. Just before she was about to leave, Barb Milton asked her about her missing persons' search.

"You know, Maggie, I'm really grateful that you agreed to help us find some of these people. It's going to make such a difference to the program."

"Sheila was telling me you're particularly interested in the starred names," she responded, trying to project polite interest. "What's the program going to involve, anyway?"

"It's supposed to be a surprise, but since you're going to be trying to find some of these people for us, I guess I can tell you a little bit about it." She laughed nervously. "We're going to have several presentations, including slides and a video that will revolve around our theme, a trip down memory lane. For example, one of the stops will be Snow Daze. We'll flash slides of the students involved in the celebration, and have the royal court come to the stage."

At the mention of Snow Daze and the royal court, Maggie glanced over at Sheila, but she was involved in another conversation and hadn't heard Barb's comments.

"The royal court?" Maggie repeated, ignoring the wave of guilt that rippled through her as memories she had since forgotten flashed before her eyes in startling clarity.

"Yes. We've managed to find all ten of them with the exception of Jack Brannigan. Of course, the important

two are the king and queen, and they've already said
they're coming. But it would make it especially nice to
have an even number so that everyone has an escort,
don't you agree?''

As though twenty years hadn't passed, all the guilt
came rushing back and Maggie felt an irresistible urge
to clap her hands and say, ''Attention! Attention,
everybody! Remember the Snow King coronation
twenty years ago? Rob Michaels didn't win. Jack
Brannigan did. I'm sorry. It was a mistake, but that's
the way it is.'' Instead she found herself nodding in
agreement. ''Yes, it would be nice.''

Barb continued to explain a few of the other memory lane stops, but Maggie found herself having trouble concentrating on the details. All she could think of
was how three senior girls had conspired to keep Jack
Brannigan from taking his rightful place as king of
Snow Daze. And now Jack Brannigan was among the
missing persons she was supposed to find. The question was: did she really want him to be found?

It was a question that nagged her all the way home.
She knew it was silly for her to worry about something
that happened over twenty years ago—especially
something as trivial as a Snow King contest. It was unlikely that very many people would even remember who
had worn the crown. Of course she remembered—she
knew it was the wrong guy. But would anyone else even
care? She wished that she had told Barb Milton the trip
down memory lane was a lousy idea.

When she arrived home, she was surprised to find her
parents seated at the kitchen table. It was obvious from
their expressions that they had been arguing before she
had walked in.

"Hi. You two are home early," Maggie commented cheerfully, giving them both a warm smile.

"Your father told me he wanted to take me out to dinner," Delores Stewart said in an accusing tone Maggie knew was directed at her father.

"I never said that. You're putting words in my mouth again," Herb Stewart snapped irritably. "I told you I wanted to work on the books this evening. That's what I do every Thursday evening—why would it be any different tonight?" He sat as straight and as tall as Maggie guessed he had when he was in the military service, and she marveled at what a healthy picture he presented. With only a touch of gray at his temples, he could have easily passed for a man in his late forties or early fifties rather than a sixty-four-year-old.

"Maybe I could take a look at the books, Pop. I'm pretty good with figures," she offered, trying to ease the tension between her parents.

Herb's response was inaudible, and before she could ask him to repeat what he had said, he had stormed out of the room.

"Mom, what's wrong?" Maggie asked, puzzled by both of her parents' behavior. "And don't tell me nothing. I've only been back a week, but I haven't been able to help noticing that you and Pop are having problems. It's not like the two of you to be arguing over every little thing."

Delores waved her hands helplessly, then clasped them together in her lap, her eyes downcast. "I wish I knew, Maggie. I'm afraid your father's lost interest in me," she whispered, choking back a sob.

"Mom, no!" Maggie insisted, dropping down to put her arm around her mother's shoulders. "You and Pop have always had such a solid marriage...one made in heaven was what you used to tell me and Karen. Partners at home and at the store.''

"Things have changed since you've been gone, Maggie.'' She shook her head disconsolately. "Your father's just not interested in me anymore. For a while I thought it was just a stage he was going through, but now I'm not so sure. He never listens to me.''

Maggie saw lines on her mother's face that she hadn't noticed the last time she had been home and there was more gray than brown in her gently waving curls. "Mom, I can't believe you're telling me this.''

"There's no point in trying to hide it, is there? You're living here with us and you've heard the things he says to me.''

"Are you sure you're not feeling a little sensitive right now? You and Dad have always worked so well together.''

She sighed. "Not anymore. When I ask him to do something at the store, he tells me he's going to do it, then he goes ahead and does something else.''

"Do you think that maybe Pop wants to retire?'' she asked, grasping for some explanation.

"Him? He's a workaholic—just like you,'' she said accusingly, unable to hide her irritation.

Maggie knew her mother was right. "Maybe he needs a vacation. When's the last time the two of you got away from the store?''

Some of Maggie's anxiety must have shown on her face, for suddenly her mother changed her tone. "Maybe we do need a break. I'll tell you what. I'll talk to your father about it tomorrow.'' She patted Maggie's hand. "Don't worry, love. We'll be fine.''

"I know you will, Mom,'' she said, kissing her mother's cheek.

But later that evening as Maggie prepared for bed and she could hear her parents quarreling once again, she couldn't help but worry. If her mom and dad's marriage didn't make it, no one's could. It was a sobering thought.

But concern for her parents' troubled marriage wasn't the only thing keeping her awake that night. Before she could fall asleep, she knew there was one thing she had to do. She crept downstairs to the den and rummaged through the stack of books in the closet until she found what she was looking for—her high school yearbook. Clutching it close to her chest, she raced back up the steps and fell across her bed. She flipped through the glossy pages until she found the section she was looking for.

Two complete pages had been devoted to Snow Daze and photos of the king, queen and their royal court. Her eyes focused not on the king and queen seated in the cardboard sleigh, but on the dark-haired prince sitting on the edge of the auditorium stage, which was covered with fake snow. The prince who should have been king—Jack Brannigan.

It was no wonder all the girls had been crazy for him, Maggie thought. He was by far the best looking guy in the photo. On the opposite page were several snapshots from Snow Daze activities, including a picture of the Snow Queen pulling Jack Brannigan on a toboggan up a steep hill.

Maggie turned to the index to look up the rest of Jack's pictures and was surprised to see that he hadn't been a part of any sports team or club. Most of the popular guys at school had been either jocks or club leaders, but Jack had been neither. The only other place he appeared in the activities section was in the group photo of the National Honor Society where he was seated directly behind Maggie and wearing a suit and tie.

She had been president of the National Honor Society yet she couldn't remember him being a member. It certainly didn't go along with the bad boy image he had cultivated while at Jefferson High. Rumors of his prowess with the female sex had only heightened his appeal to the girls at Jefferson. But even now, Maggie had to admit he was one nice looking guy.

What had become of him? Why hadn't anyone known of his whereabouts? Could he be a business executive? Maybe she did want to know the answers. Well, tomorrow she'd make a start on her search. If Jack was alive, she'd find him.

CHAPTER TWO

ALTHOUGH MAGGIE was able to locate nine of the twenty-five missing persons before the next reunion committee meeting, Jack Brannigan was not one of the nine. After countless hours on the telephone, she decided to place an advertisement in the local newspaper. Under boldface print that read Where Are They Now? she listed the names of the sixteen students still missing with the hope that someone somewhere would have information as to their whereabouts.

Besides putting her in touch with three more graduates, the advertisement produced a wide variety of calls, including one from a Mr. Brillman, a social studies teacher who now taught at another high school but had been at Jefferson High twenty years ago.

It was from Mr. Brillman that Maggie learned Jack Brannigan was neither a priest nor a pilot, but a successful businessman, just as Sheila had heard. According to the social studies teacher, Jack had been featured in an article in the *Wall Street Journal* several years ago—an article Mr. Brillman had clipped from the paper and added to his collection of news concerning former students. If Maggie was interested in seeing the story, she could stop by his office at school and take a look at his collection. She went that afternoon.

Mr. Brillman had taught social studies for almost forty years, and took great pride in what had become of his former students. He saved every magazine and newspaper article he could find concerning them. Together, he and Maggie sifted through the scraps of paper, Maggie listening patiently while Mr. Brillman stopped to relate anecdotes about his former students. Although she found it all interesting, there was only one person she wanted to read about, and she breathed a sigh of relief when Mr. Brillman finally handed her the yellowed newspaper clipping about Jack.

It only took her a couple of minutes to read the profile on the man the author had called the ''Mr. Fixit'' of a prestigious advertising firm in New York. In the brief biography she learned that Jack had attended an East Coast university, earning a degree in English before landing the public relations position with one of the top advertising agencies in the country. There were also several quotes—all complimentary—from business professionals as to what made Jack such a success in the high-powered world of advertising. Maggie found it all fascinating, and was disappointed that there wasn't a picture included with the article.

No mention was made of his private life, although the final line of the story indicated that Jack was married and living in New York. Immediately Gina Loring came to mind, despite the fact that Sheila had told her Gina was now married to a doctor. For some reason Maggie pictured Jack's wife as a dainty blonde.

Before Maggie left the school, she made a copy of the article and thanked Mr. Brillman for his help. Then she returned home to see if she could track down Jack at the advertising agency in New York. She was surprised to learn, however, that he was no longer employed by the prestigious firm. She did her best to find out why he had left and where he was currently employed, but she learned little.

"You look perplexed."

Maggie looked up and saw that her father had wandered into the kitchen and was pouring himself a cup of coffee.

"Still trying to locate your classmates?" Herb asked as he sat down across from her at the table.

Maggie sighed, then pushed her arms over her head in a catlike stretch. "Part of the problem is that the students whose parents were in the Air Force had no other ties to this area. Once they were reassigned, we lost track of them."

"Maybe you could track them down through the government?" He dropped a sugar cube into his cup and stirred it thoughtfully.

"We really don't have enough time to do that. Besides, I think that after twenty years, many of those parents would be retired by now."

Her father turned her yellow pad of paper around and read the name she had been doodling. "Jack Brannigan? Is he one of the missing?"

"Umm-hmm," she replied absently, sipping her coffee.

Her father rubbed his chin thoughtfully. "That name sounds familiar. Is he an old beau of yours?"

She suppressed a smile. "Not quite, Pop. If you recall, I didn't have beaus when I was in high school."

Her father ignored the remark. "Jack Brannigan, eh?" He stared pensively into space for several moments then snapped his fingers. "Now I know why that name's familiar. There's a pro fisherman by that name." He reached for the phone. "I'll call Lenny. He'll know where you can find this guy."

"Pop, it's okay. I don't think it could possibly be the same man. The Jack Brannigan I graduated with is in advertising in New York."

Again he ignored her remark and proceeded to dial. "Lenny knows all of the professional fishing guides in this area."

Maggie shrugged and waited while her father made the phone call, listening to his end of the conversation. As soon as he hung up, he gave her a thumbs-up gesture.

"Bingo! It's just as I thought. Jack Brannigan operates a launch out of Garrison on Lake Mille Lacs." He sat forward, resting his elbows on the table. "Lenny's not a hundred per cent certain, but he thinks he could be from Duluth. I bet that's him. I bet that's the Jack Brannigan you're looking for." His eyes twinkled at the thought. "Lenny says he's the one who invented that new lure everyone's talking about—the Branny Bait."

"The Branny Bait?" Maggie repeated with a chuckle. She didn't want to dampen her father's enthusiasm, but she was certain that her father was on the wrong track. She handed him the copy of the *Wall Street Journal* article. "Why would he leave a job like this to work as a fishing guide?"

Herb's eyes scanned the article, then he shrugged. "Not everyone's happy with bright lights and a big city."

"That's true," Maggie acknowledged. "But to leave advertising for fishing?"

"Sounds like every man's dream to me—getting paid to fish."

There was a faraway look in her father's eyes and Maggie realized that he was serious.

"If I were you, I'd check it out," Herb advised in his best paternal tone. "Wouldn't it be something if that was the man you were looking for? Lenny says that as a fishing pro, Jack Brannigan ranks right up there with the best." There was almost a reverence in his tone.

Maggie could see how exciting the possibility was to her father, and she smiled. "I suppose it wouldn't hurt to look into it. You did say Garrison, didn't you?"

"Lenny says you can probably find him at a restaurant called the Blue Goose. A couple of the launches operate out of there."

Maggie twiddled her pencil thoughtfully. "I'm going to have to drive over to Brainerd anyway. One of my classmates runs a print shop there and has agreed to do the reunion book for us at cost. As long as I'm going to be so close, I could swing by Garrison on the way." "I wouldn't be surprised if it was him," her father advised her.

"Maybe, but I have to tell you, Pop, I really don't think the Jack Brannigan I went to school with is a professional fisherman."

"Is he one of your old beaus, Maggie?" Herb asked for the second time.

"No, Pop, he isn't," she repeated, a tad exasperated.

He shook his head in regret. "That's too bad. I wouldn't mind meeting this Jack Brannigan. I could use a few tips on fishing."

"Maybe you want to ride with me?" she suggested.

"When are you going?" he asked, leaning forward eagerly.

"Tomorrow morning."

He sagged back in his chair with a sigh. "Can't. I have to be at the store tomorrow. We already have two gone on vacation plus your mother's got an appointment with the dentist."

He had removed his glasses to clean them with his handkerchief and Maggie noticed the dark circles normally covered by the lenses. "Pop, you work too hard," she told him, a comment he brushed aside with a wave of his hand.

"Hard work is the reason I'm as healthy as I am." He returned the glasses to the bridge of his nose and fixed Maggie with a stare. "Maybe you can take Sheila with you to Garrison?"

"Maybe."

Her father got up to leave, pausing on his way out to say, "If it is the same Jack Brannigan, tell him your father's got a nice muskie he might be interested in seeing."

"Sure, Pop," Maggie replied, returning his wink with one of her own.

As it turned out, Sheila did agree to accompany her on her search mission, but had to cancel at the last minute when her youngest child woke up with the flu. Maggie ended up making the trip alone, stopping first in Brainerd to make the necessary arrangements for the reunion books before heading toward Lake Mille Lacs in search of Jack.

It was nearly noon by the time she arrived in Garrison and the small resort town was buzzing with activity; a steady stream of fishermen wandered in and out of the bait shops and cafés. The Blue Goose restaurant was located on the shore of Lake Mille Lacs with only a ribbon of highway and a narrow strip of grassy land separating the restaurant from the water. There was no goose in sight but the restaurant was painted a bright periwinkle blue. Maggie parked the station wagon between a pickup and a white Corvette, noting that there were at least a half-dozen motorcycles lined up along the curb.

As she climbed out of the car she glanced at the vast expanse of blue water and saw a launch unloading passengers at the end of a long pier. Directly across the street at the end of the pier hung a large metal blue sign with the words, Launches Daily printed in white.

The aroma of beef grilling greeted her as she pulled open the door to the Blue Goose. She paused in the entryway, unsure whether she should take a left into the bar or a right into the restaurant. Shoving her sunglasses into her purse, she opted for the bar.

There were several unoccupied tables in front of the large plate-glass windows overlooking the lake, but Maggie chose one of the leather stools at the bar.

"Hi! I'm Joni. What'll you have?" asked the female bartender, a young blond woman with a bushy ponytail poking up from the side of her head. She was dressed in a short jean skirt that revealed plenty of thigh and a blue T-shirt that looked as though it was two sizes too small. Judging, however, by the way the male patrons were glancing at her, Maggie would have wagered that the men in the bar thought it was a perfect fit.

Maggie met the younger woman's curious gaze with a smile. "A cola, please."

"Diet?"

"No, regular is fine."

A tall slender glass was placed on a tiny square napkin in front of Maggie. "Is that it?"

Maggie placed a couple of bills on the counter and smiled her thanks. "Joni, could you tell me who I would talk to about one of the launches?"

"You want to go fishing?" Eyes outlined in blue regarded Maggie's white jumpsuit skeptically.

"Not exactly," Maggie answered with a twitch of her lips. "I'm looking for one of the fishing guides—a Jack Brannigan."

"Oh, you're looking for Jack." The warm, friendly tone took on a distinctive chill as she picked up the bills and plopped several coins down in exchange.

"Uh-huh. I heard that he operates a launch from here. He is a professional fisherman, isn't he?"

"Yeah—Jack's one of the best." There was a hint of pride in her voice that had Maggie wondering exactly what sort of relationship Joni had with the fisherman.

"Is he around right now? I saw a boat unloading when I pulled into the parking lot." Maggie spun around on the swivel seat and glanced out the windows to the lake.

"That would be the *Shady Lady*," Joni replied, following the direction of her customer's gaze. "She pulled in about fifteen minutes ago. But that's not Jack. He runs the *Wave Walker*."

"Do you know when he will be in?" Maggie turned back to face the bartender again.

Joni shrugged, and turned her attention to putting glasses away behind the bar. "If you came to see him, you're going to have to wait. Sometimes private charters stay out until late at night." She looked up at Maggie with what looked to be a challenge in her eye. "You want to wait around that long?"

"I'm not even sure he's the Jack Brannigan I'm looking for," Maggie confessed with a faint smile.

"Are you a friend of his?" The dark-rooted blonde couldn't hide her curiosity.

Maggie sipped the cola through the straw. "Not exactly. The reason I'm here is that our high school is having a class reunion and I'm trying to locate the Jack Brannigan who was one of our graduates. The man I'm looking for would be about six feet tall, dark brown hair, late thirties."

"That could describe a whole lot of men around here," Joni said with a toss of her ponytail. "Maybe you should take a look on that wall over there." She gestured to Maggie's right. "Jack's picture is probably over there somewhere. Whenever someone catches a big fish we usually try to get a photo to stick up on the wall. It's good for business." She smiled, then slipped under the counter. Wiping her hands on her apron, she led Maggie over to the wall covered with snapshots. Within a couple of minutes, she was pointing a finger at a photo of three men.

Maggie's eyes squinted as she focused on the photo beside the finger with the short unpainted nail. At first Maggie couldn't imagine which of the three could possibly be Jack. One was bald and her father's age, another was Asian and the third looked like a prophet. It was the prophet Joni zeroed in on.

"There. That's him, although this picture must have been taken last summer," Joni said thoughtfully as her fingernail tapped at the feet of the man with shoulder-length hair and a full beard. "Is he the guy you're looking for?"

Maggie pulled her glasses from her purse and took another look. Because the photo was slightly blurred and taken from a distance, it was difficult to distinguish the man's features. "It's hard to tell from this photo. If it is him, he's changed quite a bit since high school. Are there any other pictures of him?"

Joni quickly scanned the wall and shook her head. "Usually there are quite a few up here, but that's the only one I see at the moment." One of the men sitting at the bar whistled for her to get him another beer and Joni quickly scooted back behind the counter.

"You don't think he'll be back before this evening?" Maggie asked, following her back to the bar.

"I doubt it. If you want to leave him a message, I'll see that he gets it," Joni told her over her shoulder as she drew another mug of beer from the tap.

Maggie took a sip of her cola, then pulled a pen and notepad from her purse and scribbled a short note. As soon as Joni had finished waiting on her customers, Maggie handed her the folded piece of paper.

"Can I get you another cola?" Joni asked, tucking the note into the back pocket of her jean skirt.

"No, thank you." She left a generous tip on the counter, then took one more look at the picture on the wall, wondering if it could possibly be the heartbreaker from Jefferson High. There was something disturbingly familiar about his eyes, yet she couldn't believe this could be the man the *Wall Street Journal* had called the Mr. Fixit of the advertising world. She shrugged, and walked out into the bright sunshine.

Before starting up her car, she stared out at what appeared to be an endless expanse of blue water dotted with an occasional boat. Somewhere out there was Jack Brannigan. The question was, was it her Jack Brannigan?

"WHAT ARE YOU DOING BACK SO SOON?" a raspy voice called out as the skipper of the *Wave Walker* tossed a rope to the gray-haired man waiting on the dock.

"Caught the limit, Bud," came Jack's answer as he maneuvered the launch into the L-shaped alcove at the end of the pier while several fishermen stood on the deck anxiously waiting to show off their catch.

Bud secured the thick heavy rope then jumped on board, giving Jack a victory sign upon seeing the fish. "I thought maybe you got wind of that sassy looking redhead who was here looking for you," he said in an aside meant only for Jack's ears before disappearing to make his routine check of the engine.

Jack would have followed him and asked him what he was talking about, but the triumphant fishermen were gratefully pumping his hand and saying their good-byes. It was only after the last of the chartered guests had departed that he got his answer.

"Joni says there was a girl here looking for you earlier this afternoon—a real looker according to the guys in the bar." Bud gave him a crafty grin as he wiggled his eyebrows. "You've been holding out on me, Jack? You got a girl, after all?"

"Hardly." Jack chuckled mirthlessly. "Are you sure she didn't want one of the other guides?"

"Uh-uh." Bud shook his head adamantly. "She left a note. I've got it here somewhere," he said, shoving his weathered fingers into just about every pocket on his shirt and trousers in search of the piece of paper. He muttered a mild expletive. "Don't tell me I lost the damn thing."

"It's all right, Bud." Jack made a dismissive motion with his fingers. "It probably wasn't important."

"Not important?" he repeated in disbelief. "I don't understand you, Jack." He threw up his hands as if in defeat. "If I were your age and a beautiful woman came looking for me I certainly wouldn't dismiss it as not important. I'm trying to help you out here, not sic some she-devil on you."

Jack couldn't help but smile at the older man's earnestness. "I don't have any lady friends with red hair, Bud. But if it makes you feel any better, I'll talk to Joni about her, all right?"

"You better do it right away. She's getting ready to quit for the day." He nudged him toward the dock. "I'll finish up here for you."

Jack would rather have helped with the boat than go inquire about some female who had turned a few heads in the Blue Goose. He figured it was probably someone wanting to arrange a charter for her husband or her boyfriend. And that suited him just fine. He didn't want women contacting him for any other reason.

After Jill's death he had moved to Northern Minnesota for peace and solitude. All he wanted was to lead the quiet life of a fishing guide. Maybe Bud, having never lost a spouse, couldn't understand that. But then Bud hadn't known Jill.

Jack saw the kind of women who passed through the Blue Goose. Many were attractive. In fact, most of the guys he took out fishing commented on the number of beautiful women the place attracted. But he simply wasn't interested.

Unfortunately he never found out who the woman who had asked for him was. When he walked into the Blue Goose he learned that Joni had gone home early and wouldn't be back for a couple of weeks. Jack gave the patrons a cursory glance and left.

AFTER SEVERAL DAYS had passed and Maggie heard nothing from the professional fishing guide, she was convinced he had been the wrong Jack Brannigan.

Sheila, however, wasn't so sure, and did her best to convince Maggie she shouldn't be, either.

"If you thought there was something familiar about this guy, you were probably right," Sheila said, placing a plate of chocolate frosted brownies on her kitchen table. "I don't think you should be so quick to write him off as the wrong man." She handed Maggie a glass of iced tea.

"If you keep bringing out these wonderful chocolate things every time we work on this reunion book, I'm not going to be able to fit into any of my clothes when I return to Washington," Maggie complained as she reached for a brownie.

"You need the extra weight. I'm the one who has to get down to Gidget size, remember?" Sheila reminded her friend, taking one of the smaller brownies. "And don't change the subject. I bet this Jack in Garrison is our Jack."

"Do you honestly think that someone who had wowed Wall Street would now be a professional fisherman in Minnesota?" Maggie asked, licking the frosting from her fingers.

"Well, when you first told me what you had uncovered, I agreed with you. But when I happened to mention all of this to Tom, he said that if he had the opportunity to be a professional sportsman he'd do it in a minute." She wet her lips with her tongue, savoring every morsel of chocolate. "Maybe that's every man's fantasy—to be a professional sportsman."

"That's what my father said. Somehow I can't imagine the life of a professional fishing guide as being something one would envy." She dabbed at her mouth with her napkin. "If it had been our Jack, don't you think he would have at least acknowledged the message I left for him?''

"Maybe the little blond bartender didn't give him the message. You said she looked a little predatory.''

"Only until she learned the reason for my being there." Maggie sipped her iced tea. "There is the possibility that it is our Jack and he simply isn't interested in the reunion. Maybe he doesn't want anyone to know what's happened to him.''

"Oh, come on, Maggie," Sheila protested. "I can't believe that of our Jack. Why wouldn't he want us to know?''

"For one thing, he dropped out of a high paying, prestigious career to become a fisherman.''

"You think he's running away from something?'' Her eyes took on a mysterious glint.

"Not necessarily. All I'm saying is maybe he doesn't want to be found.''

"I don't know." Sheila paused, tugging on her lip with her teeth. "I'd rather believe he didn't get the message. Maybe we should go see for ourselves...talk to the man.''

"And how do you propose to do that? From the way Joni talked, I got the feeling this guy practically lives on the water.''

"Maybe we could hire him as a guide," Sheila suggested.

"And go fishing?'' Maggie wrinkled her nose.

"What's so bad about that? We used to go fishing all the time when we were kids," Sheila reminded her, putting her fists on her waist.

"Yes, and if I remember correctly, I was the one who always had to put the worm on your hook as well as take the fish off because you were too squeamish to touch them," Maggie told her with a sardonic grin.

"I still am, but that's why people go out on a launch. The fishing guide does all of that for you. Come on, Maggie," she begged with her most endearing smile, the one she had always used when they had been teenagers and she had needed to cajole her best friend into doing something. "Let's try it. I bet it'll be fun."

"You're serious, aren't you?" She stared at her friend in disbelief.

"Of course I am."

"But what about your kids?"

"They can spend the day with their grandmother."

"But we don't even know what time these boats go out or how much it costs..."

"I'll call and find out," Sheila interrupted, reaching for the cordless phone. "What did you say the name of Jack's boat was?" she asked as she raised the antenna.

"The *Wave Walker*," Maggie answered with a sigh of resignation. She watched as Sheila first called information to get the number for the Blue Goose restaurant, then made the phone call to Garrison.

"There are two spots on the one o'clock trip on Friday," she told Maggie, holding her palm over the phone. "It's sixteen bucks apiece." When Maggie groaned and made a face, Sheila said coaxingly, "Come on. It'll be fun. Please?"

Maggie threw up her arms in defeat. "All right...I guess," she mumbled as Sheila confirmed the arrangement over the phone, scribbling the information down on the notepad in front of her.

"There. We're all set," she announced, returning the phone to its base. "Friday at one. We're supposed to stop in at the Blue Goose and pay for our tickets about half an hour before it leaves. The *Wave Walker* will be docked at the pier across the street. We can either bring our own fishing rods or use the ones on the launch.''

''I suppose I could have my dad fix us up with a couple,'' Maggie offered reluctantly.

''That would be great!'' Sheila said cheerfully. ''Are you sure he won't mind?''

''I don't think it's any trouble. You should see his garage. It's full of fishing gear.''

''Smile, Maggie,'' Sheila urged her. ''If this is our Jack Brannigan, at least he won't be able to walk away from us until we've talked to him about the reunion.''

''And if it isn't *our* Jack?''

Sheila shrugged. ''It's going to be him, Maggie. I just know it.''

That's what I'm afraid of, she thought to herself, but only nodded in agreement.

WHEN MAGGIE CLIMBED into Sheila's mini van Friday morning clutching a windbreaker and her canvas tote in her hands, Sheila asked, ''What about the fishing rods?''

''Pop said he would get two of them ready for us and leave them on the porch, but he must have forgotten,'' Maggie told her, glancing once more at the house. ''I'm sorry.''

''It doesn't matter,'' Sheila assured her. ''We can use the ones on the boat.'' Seeing Maggie's unhappy face, she added, ''It's not the end of the world, Maggie Stewart.''

The once-familiar refrain now brought only a weak, nostalgic smile to Maggie's lips. ''No, it's not, but it seems that my father's having trouble remembering things. Now I know why my mother's been so frustrated lately. He's always telling people he'll do something, then he goes and forgets."

"He's probably been working too hard," Sheila said, shifting the van into gear and backing out of the driveway. "Whenever I stop in at the store he's always there."

"Now you know why I can't sit still. It's a hereditary weakness." She glanced at her friend's bare arms. "Didn't you bring a jacket?"

"It's in the back along with the cooler. I packed us a lunch and something cold to drink, too. I thought maybe we could picnic by the lake."

"What a great idea! Since you're driving and providing lunch, I'll treat for dinner—that is, if we survive this fishing expedition."

"Of course we're going to survive it," Sheila insisted. "Not only are we going to survive, we're going to have fun. Besides, it isn't often we get a whole day to ourselves without any kids tagging along. I'm going to make the most of the opportunity to spend a day with my very best friend from the sixth grade."

Maggie couldn't help but smile at Sheila's enthusiasm. "You're right. We will have fun. We always do."

And they did. The two-hour drive to Garrison was spent reminiscing and giggling, the two things they never seemed able to get enough of when they were in each other's company. They had allowed themselves enough time to stop at several antique shops along the way as well as an art barn where Maggie found a wildlife painting she couldn't resist buying for her father. After lunching at a picnic area on the northern shore of Lake Mille Lacs, they headed for the launch and the Blue Goose.

"It sure is hot," Maggie remarked, wiping the back of her hand across her brow as she stepped out into the bright sunshine. "I wonder if I shouldn't change into shorts before we get on the boat. I brought a pair in my bag."

Sheila glanced at her watch. "You have plenty of time. It's only noon. If I had thought it was going to be this warm I would have brought a pair myself." She had opened the back of the van and was reaching inside the cooler for a bottle of cold mineral water. "You can probably change in that rest room over there." She nodded in the direction of a small brick building across the street from the launch. "I think I'll go see if I can find us some more ice for the cooler."

Maggie grabbed her tote bag from the van and went to change in the women's rest room while Sheila headed for the closest gas station. When they met back at the van, Maggie was wearing a pair of baggy white shorts instead of her jeans.

"It looks as though some of the passengers are already getting onto the boat," she said, looking toward the launch. "Do you think we should be over there?"

From where they were parked they could see several men with fishing rods and tackle boxes walking out toward the large blue-and-white boat docked at the end of the long wooden pier.

"The woman who took our reservation said we didn't have to check in until twelve-thirty," Sheila answered, dumping a bag of ice cubes into the cooler.

Maggie shrugged. "Those are probably the eager beavers. It looks like it's going to be all men. I wonder if there will be any other women besides us?"

"Oh, sure. Look. There's one walking out onto the pier now." She shielded her eyes with one hand while pointing with the other.

"You mean that one with her arms wrapped around that guy in the green shirt?" Maggie stated dryly.

"All right, so she's with her boyfriend. At least it's another woman on the boat."

"Are you having second thoughts about going?" Maggie asked.

"No. Are you?"

"Somehow I don't see us fitting in with the crowd that's been filing out onto that pier. They all look like they're going fishing. Do we?" She eyed Sheila skeptically.

"You worry too much, Maggie. Are we going to lug this cooler with us or do you think there'll be beverages on the boat?"

"What time do you have?" Maggie asked, ignoring the question.

"It's not quite twelve-thirty. Why?"

"Because I think that boat is leaving without us."

Sheila looked up from the cooler. "You're right. I'd better go inside the Blue Goose and find out what's going on. I'll be right back," she called out over her shoulder before she jogged across the street.

While she was gone, Maggie watched as the launch slowly moved out onto the lake. She wished she could feel sorry that they had missed the boat, but personally she was glad they didn't have to check out its skipper. When Sheila returned, she was about to suggest they go back to one of the antique stores they hadn't had time to stop at, but Sheila spoke first.

"It's all right. We didn't miss the launch." She paused momentarily to catch her breath. "That blue-and-white boat wasn't the *Wave Walker*."

"It wasn't?" Maggie gave her a curious glance, waiting for her explanation.

"Uh-uh. See that other boat?" She put her hands on Maggie's shoulder and turned her slightly. "The small wooden one at the end of the dock?"

"That's not the *Wave Walker*?" Maggie's question sounded more like a whining plea.

"I'm afraid it is. And here's our passport to fun and excitement." She held up two red ticket stubs. "All thirty-two dollars worth."

"We spent sixteen dollars apiece to go out in the middle of the lake on that . . . that . . ."

"Launch," Sheila supplied. "It's called a launch. And don't forget, Jack Brannigan is why we're going out on that launch."

"I can't believe someone who's been as successful as he's been would leave New York city behind for that," Maggie said disdainfully. "Sheila, this can't be our Jack."

"Hey, if we don't check it out, how will we know?"

"But what if it isn't him and we end up spending four hours in the hot sun on that?" She gestured toward the wooden launch.

"Listen, we'll check it out first. We'll walk out to the end of the pier, talk to this Jack Brannigan, and if it isn't our Jack, we'll chuck the thirty-two dollars and go shop some more. Come on, Maggie. We at least have to go see if it's him."

Maggie eyed her skeptically. "I suppose you're right." She straightened her sunglasses and reached inside the van for her purse. "Are you sure you're ready for this?"

"As ready as I'll ever be," Sheila said with her usual good nature. "The gal inside the Blue Goose said I could leave the van parked over here and it'd be all right."

"What about the cooler? Should we bring it along? I don't think the *Wave Walker* has a lounge," she said with a humorless laugh.

Sheila looked out across the lake, shading her eyes with her hands. "It looks like most of those people heading out to the end of the pier are carrying them. We'd better bring it."

They each took an end and together carried the cooler toward the pier. When they neared it, Sheila instructed Maggie to stop for a minute and wait for her while she ran back inside the Blue Goose. When she returned, she was carrying two bright blue baseball caps with Blue Goose printed in white across the front.

"Now you look like everyone else," Sheila proclaimed, setting one of the caps on Maggie's red head.

Maggie couldn't help but laugh at the comical picture Sheila made as she pushed her long dark hair up inside the cap.

They hadn't gone but twenty feet out onto the pier when a man's voice from behind them said, "You girls need some help with that thing?"

Maggie and Sheila both paused to look over their shoulders at the young man directly behind them. Dressed in a neon-green tank T-shirt and a pair of shorts with geometric designs, he looked to be in his late teens or early twenties. A Minnesota Twins baseball cap sat cocked at an angle on his head.

"Do you want to go around us? We're not moving very fast." Maggie gave him a friendly smile.

"If you want, I'll carry that cooler for you," he offered, and as he moved closer, Maggie caught the scent of coconut suntan lotion mixed with a spicy cologne.

Maggie looked at Sheila who smiled and lifted her eyebrows.

"That would be very nice." The two women willingly relinquished their hold on the cooler, stepping aside so he could take charge of the cumbersome chest. They followed his long steps to the very end of the pier where he easily stepped onto the launch and deposited the cooler on the wooden deck.

"Thank you...uh..." Sheila began, looking inquisitively up at him.

"Ned. Ned Parker and this is my brother Nathan," he said, gesturing to another muscular man who Maggie thought looked like a clone of the muscle-bound knight except instead of a lime-green tank T-shirt, his was orange. Nathan sat threading nylon line into a fishing reel, but stood when his brother introduced him.

"Ned and Nathan," Sheila repeated with a gamine grin. "How nice. Twins. I bet you're college students."

"Yup, we are. Mankato State," Ned boasted proudly. "We're staying with four other guys at the Picture Window resort. Nathan and I are the only two who decided to go out on the launch today, though. You girls should find a place to sit before all the seats are taken." He glanced around the deck that was starting to fill up.

"Do you know how long it's been since anyone's called me a girl?" Sheila whispered in an aside to Maggie, then asked Ned, "Where's the skipper of this boat?

I think we'd better talk to him first—you know, show him our tickets and stuff.''

"He's up front. You can't miss him. He's wearing a captain's hat and he's sitting at the controls.''

Both Maggie's and Sheila's heads turned eagerly toward the front of the boat, but they couldn't get a glimpse of the fishing pro, because a small group of men were gathered around him.

Just then a couple of teenagers jumped onto the boat and plopped their gear down on the blue swivel seats to Nathan's left. "See what I mean,'' Ned pointed out. "You'd better grab a couple of seats or you might get stuck over there.'' He pointed to two chairs next to the wooden cabin in the center of the launch.

"Let's go see the skipper first,'' Maggie said to Sheila in a low voice, grabbing her by her shirtsleeve. "We might not *need* seats.''

Sheila agreed and the two of them made their way up from the back of the boat to the front. Maggie noticed that other than an elderly woman in a straw hat, she and Sheila were the only women on the boat.

"Excuse me, but could I speak to the person in charge here?'' Sheila asked in a sugary sweet voice that had the small group of men surrounding Jack Brannigan dispersing like oil in water. Maggie saw a broad-shouldered man in a chambray shirt and a captain's hat turn away from the control console and give his full attention to Sheila.

"I'm Jack, your guide. What can I do for you?'' The voice that spoke the words was as smooth as the waves gently lapping at the side of the boat. Although the beard was gone, there was a soft shadow darkening the face bronzed by many hours in the sun. His eyes were hidden behind the dark lenses of his sunglasses, but

Maggie knew they were as blue as the summer sky. There was no longer any doubt in her mind that they had found the heartthrob of Jefferson High. Her stomach did a tiny, little flip-flop—the way it had always done whenever she had seen his face coming down the school corridor. And just as it had always been the case when she was a teenager, she found her voice had deserted her. Fortunately Sheila's hadn't.

"Uh...hi, Jack." Sheila gave him a shaky smile and held up her red ticket stub for his inspection. "Do we need to show you our tickets or anything?"

Hearing the word we, Jack glanced over to where Maggie stood a few feet behind her. Maggie knew he was summing her up with one sweeping glance that raked her from head to toe, and she wanted to whip the baseball cap from her head and powder her shiny nose.

"Nope." Jack shook his head, then pushed the brim of his hat back off his forehead. "Just find yourself a seat and I'll take care of everything else." His smile revealed even white teeth and this time Maggie's stomach did an even bigger flip-flop.

"We'll be pulling out as soon as everyone's on board." He reached for a small clipboard that had been shoved up into a corner of the control panel. "Let's see. We should have eighteen here." He stood to count the heads on the launch, and as he strolled to the back of the boat, Maggie could see that he was tall, lean and every bit as attractive as he had been in high school.

"It's him," Sheila whispered in Maggie's ear.

"Does this mean we're going fishing?" Maggie asked, annoyed with herself for the thrill of pleasure that had shot through her when Jack's gaze had lingered on her legs. She waited for an answer, but she might as well not have asked the question, for Sheila had already gone in search of a seat.

CHAPTER THREE

"MAGGIE! OVER HERE." Sheila was waving to her from one of the seats near the wooden cabin—the spot Ned had advised them to avoid if possible.

Maggie dropped onto the chair beside her and groaned. "Nothing like being stuck in a corner. We can't even see Jack from here."

"Don't worry. Once we get to the spot where we're going to be fishing, we'll be able to circulate," Sheila returned cheerfully.

"At least we're near the bathroom." Maggie eyed the door in the wooden cabin suspiciously. "There is a bathroom in there, isn't there?"

"Of course there's a bathroom. Probably a very primitive one, but it's in there." Sheila had pulled a bottle of suntan lotion from her purse and was spreading white liquid on her arms. "This isn't such a bad spot after all. We're nice and close to the life preserver, too." She nodded toward the white ring hanging next to the door.

Maggie's only answer was a wry glance.

"Do you want some of this?" Sheila offered her the bottle of lotion.

"I'd better use mine," she answered, reaching into her tote bag. "You tan, I burn and peel."

"I think we must be ready to leave. I just saw Jack untie the ropes and now he's walking back up to the front," Sheila reported, craning her neck to see around the obstruction.

"What's in there?" Maggie asked, pointing to a large wooden box in the center of the craft.

When Sheila shrugged, one of the twins, noticing Maggie's gesture, said, "That's the bait. You want to look?"

"Not right now, thanks," Maggie replied with a weak smile.

There were several cranking and creaking sounds before the engines finally sprang to life and the boat slowly began moving away from the pier.

Maggie gave Sheila an apprehensive look as she felt the flooring beneath her feet begin to shake. "Do you suppose it's going to vibrate like this the whole time?"

"It's probably because he's backing out," Sheila reasoned.

"Or maybe that's why no one took these two seats," Maggie said dryly.

"Maybe we're over the engine or something." Sheila said, glancing down at her feet. "Don't worry, Maggie. It's perfectly safe. Look." She pointed to a small piece of paper covered in plastic that was posted beside the life preserver. "The Coast Guard's inspected it."

"I'm sure it's safe. It's just . . ." She searched for the right word and finally said, "Old. And noisy."

"At least we won't have to worry about anyone overhearing our conversation," Sheila noted.

"I can't believe that it's Jack running this thing," she said, looking around the boat with a distasteful frown.

"It's not that bad," Sheila insisted. "I think it's got a certain charm to it."

"Charm as in odor?" Maggie inquired with a lift of one eyebrow.

"Come on, Maggie, lighten up," Sheila urged her with a playful punch to her shoulder. "This is the way a fishing launch should look...and smell. And the captain certainly fits the image of the rugged outdoorsy type, doesn't he? He's even better looking than he was in high school, although he really hasn't changed all that much. I'm surprised you didn't recognize him from his picture."

"I told you, the picture I saw was of a man with a full beard and hair down to here." She tapped a finger on her shoulder.

"Yeah, well, he does have rather long hair compared to most of the men our age...especially the guys in Duluth," Sheila remarked. "Do you think he recognized either of us? His eyes seemed to linger on you but I don't know if it was because he recognized you or if he was just getting a good look at your legs."

"Sheila!" Maggie retorted indignantly.

"Well, you do have great legs, Maggie, and every guy on this boat who's got blood in his veins has already noticed them, believe me. It's a good thing I didn't bring my shorts. Between the varicose veins and the cellulite, my legs are a dead giveaway of my age." She chuckled. "I can guarantee you, Ned wouldn't be calling me 'girl' if I were wearing shorts."

The seat next to Maggie was vacant, although the way several of the men were looking in her direction, she wasn't sure it would stay that way for long. Sheila's comments about her legs only made her wish she had kept her jeans on—heat or no heat.

Once the engines were opened up full throttle, conversation became nearly impossible even between adjacent passengers, so Maggie settled back and enjoyed the ride, watching the shoreline disappear as the boat moved farther and farther out into the middle of the lake. Occasionally a welcome splash of water would spray across her skin, countering the effects of the hot summer sun.

Except for a couple of seats near the skipper, all of the bolted down chairs were out in the open with full exposure to the sun, and Maggie was grateful that Sheila had bought the baseball caps. Following her friend's example, she tucked her hair up inside the cap so that the air was cool and refreshing on her neck.

Everyone on the boat was very friendly, and as Maggie suspected, a couple of the men were friendlier than the others, offering to share their refreshments with Maggie and Sheila. It took the boat about half an hour to reach the spot where Jack dropped the anchor and turned off the motor. They appeared to be in the middle of nowhere, with only a blurred shoreline visible in the far distance. While the rest of the passengers were engrossed with tying up fishing lines and digging in tackle boxes, Sheila and Maggie sat with their hands idle.

"Now what do you suppose we do?" Maggie asked her friend, glancing around at the anglers eager to get their lines wet.

Her question was answered by Jack's appearance. He stood in the center of the launch near the large wooden box and made an announcement.

"The leeches and night crawlers are in here." A well muscled, tanned arm gestured toward the live-well, and Maggie whispered to Sheila.

"Now I know why I didn't want to come. I might have put worms on your hook when we were kids, but there's no way I'm touching a leech." She held up her hands in protest.

As if Jack had overheard her comment, he continued, "If anyone needs help setting up a line, I'll be happy to see to it. It's about twenty-six feet deep here and my advice is to fish about a foot off the bottom." He proceeded to give a few fishing tips, but Maggie didn't hear, for her eyes were focused on his hands, which had reached inside the bait box and were now attaching a leech to a hook on the elderly woman's fishing line. Except for the older couple, everyone else baited their own hooks.

"What about you two?" Jack looked at Maggie and Sheila expectantly when he had finished with the older couple.

"We need poles...or rods...or whatever," Sheila answered, spreading her hands in a helpless gesture.

Jack stepped back under the canopy and pulled two rods from a rack housing half a dozen fishing rods. He propped one against the bait box while he worked at setting up the other. Maggie watched long, narrow fingers deftly attach a large silver weight to the end of the line. Next he walked over to the side of the boat where he lowered the weight into the water, reeling and jiggling the rod until he seemed satisfied. He grabbed the nylon line, fastening a slip bobber and a rubber band to it in a matter of seconds. Then he reeled in the remainder of the line and replaced the silver weight with a hook.

"Ever fished for walleye before?" he asked Sheila, reaching inside the bait box for another leech.

"Oh, sure, but my husband usually takes care of setting up my gear," Sheila told him with an engaging smile.

"You just let this go as far as it wants to," Jack instructed her, lowering the leech into the water. "I've placed a rubber band on the line so that the bobber will stop at the right depth. All you have to do is watch for it to go under." He handed the rod and reel to her. "Got it?"

"Got it." She gave him a military salute and a smile. "Thanks."

Maggie didn't say anything, but watched as Jack repeated the process with the other fishing rod. When he was about to reach into the bait box, however, she spoke up. "Would it be all right if I used a worm?" The thought of a big fat blood sucker swimming on the end of her hook was enough to make her skin crawl.

"You're more likely to get a walleye if you're using a leech," Jack told her, a smile curving his lips.

"I know, but it doesn't really matter what I catch," she answered, then immediately felt a bit foolish. She had paid to come out on the launch to fish. The least she could do was make the most of it.

Jack shrugged and threaded a large night crawler onto her hook, the sight of which turned out to make Maggie just as squeamish as the sight of the leech writhing on Sheila's hook. When he gave her the same instructions and handed over the rod, she responded with an appreciative thank-you.

She had just sat down next to Sheila when she heard Jack saying, "It looks like you've got something there, Sheila."

"Oh, my goodness! I think I do and I think it's a big one!" Sheila exclaimed, jumping to her feet as she tried to reel in the line. "I don't know if I can get it in!"

"Sure you can." Jack moved closer to Sheila and Maggie noticed that he had a large net in his hand. "Don't try to rush it. Let him play with it a bit. Just take it easy."

"Ohh," Sheila whined. "I don't want to lose him."

"You're not going to lose him," Jack assured her. "Easy does it."

Maggie listened to Jack's soothing voice and watched as he coaxed Sheila in the art of landing a fish, and she soon saw why her friend was having such difficulty winding the reel. Jack skillfully netted the large fish as it broke the surface of the water.

"Oh, my goodness! It *is* big!" Sheila cried upon seeing the size of the fish she had caught. Jack deftly removed the hook and held the fish up for everyone's inspection.

"My guess is it's about eight pounds," he estimated.

There were several murmurs of appreciation from the other passengers at the announcement, then Jack stepped under the canopy where he inserted a fish scale into the walleye's mouth. "Yup. Eight pounds four ounces," he confirmed before placing the fish on top of the bait box where Maggie noticed for the first time the measuring markers painted along the edge.

"You've caught your limit of big ones," Jack said to Sheila as he checked the length of the walleye.

"You mean I can't fish anymore?" Sheila's face fell in disappointment.

Jack chuckled. "You can fish all right, but if you go catching any more over twenty inches long, we're going to have to throw them back. State law. But I don't think we need to worry. It's pretty unusual for someone to even catch one this size." His gaze moved from Sheila to Maggie. "I don't suppose you've got a stringer?"

Sheila shook her head. "We didn't bring any gear."

Jack went back under the canopy and rummaged through his tackle box, pulling out a wire rope, which he proceeded to thread through the walleye's mouth.

Then he moved over to where Maggie sat watching her bobber and carefully lowered the fish back into the water, attaching the rope to the side of the boat.

"If you hand me your rod, I'll get you another leech," he told Sheila, waiting for her to pass him the fishing rod propped against the side of the boat.

"Isn't this fun, Maggie?" Sheila exclaimed, swiveling back and forth on the chair as she waited for Jack to bait her hook.

"Hey! You'd better watch your bobber," Ned cautioned Maggie as he dropped onto the vacant seat beside her. "It looks as though you might have a strike, too."

Startled, Maggie shot forward. "Oh! I think I do have one," she declared, watching the top of her pole bend close to the water.

"Quick, Jack! Maggie's got one, too!" Sheila called out, jumping to her feet again.

Within seconds Maggie had an audience. Not only was Jack beside her, but several of the others were peering over her shoulder, watching as she carefully worked at reeling in her catch. At the first flash of fish, murmurs of anticipation rose around her. Just as he had done with Sheila, Jack coaxed her into taking her time to bring in her catch.

Maggie tried to concentrate on the fish, but Jack's presence beside her was a definite distraction. He was leaning over the side of the boat, his net in hand as he waited for the fish to surface, and she could see the powerful muscles of his arms straining beneath the cotton fabric.

"There it is!" Sheila announced as Jack's net swallowed the fish. "I think it's even bigger than mine!"

"Hey! What did you put on their hooks, Jack?" someone called out in good humor.

Jack simply smiled and said, "Yup. Looks like this one might be bigger than the other." He skillfully removed the hook, then held the fish up for everyone's appraisal. "This one might go nine pounds."

"Can you believe this, Maggie?" Sheila grinned widely at her friend.

"Nice catch, Maggie," Jack drawled, staring at her as though he were suddenly seeing her for the first time. After what seemed like an eternity but what Maggie knew had only been a couple of seconds, he turned away from her and went to measure the fish on the bait box lid. After weighing it, he looked at her again and said, "Nine pounds seven ounces. You've got your limit, as well. You want this on Sheila's stringer?"

"That'll be fine," Maggie said, unable to resist watching him as he pulled the stringer from the water and added her fish to the metal rope. He was handsome—so handsome it took her breath away and she felt her body tingle in unexpected pleasure. It had been a long time since she had had such a physical reaction to a man, and the thought was disturbing.

"You want to go with another night crawler?" he asked, his fingers brushing hers as he took Maggie's rod from her hands.

Maggie shrugged and gave him what she was certain had to be a bashful smile. "I guess so." She watched as he lifted the bait-box lid and bent over to reach inside for a worm, admiring the way the denim hugged his lean frame. When he had finished baiting the hook, he looked up—just as she was looking down his athletic body appreciatively. He passed her the rod and seemed about to say something when another one of the anglers demanded his attention.

Maggie was grateful for the sunglasses and the cool breeze whipping across her cheeks. She returned to her seat feeling a bit embarrassed at having been caught eyeing his rear end.

"What was he saying to you?" Sheila asked, watching her bobber dip and sway on the water. "Does he know who we are?"

"There was something in the way he said my name," Maggie replied as evenly as she could. "I think we'd better tell him why we're really here. Otherwise we're going to feel rather foolish."

"I would have told him right away, but you saw what happened. I barely had my line in the water and I caught a fish!" She waited for Jack to look in their direction again, then waved him over.

When he came with the net, Sheila giggled and said, "I don't have another one. We just wanted to ask you something." Her gesture encompassed Maggie.

The minute Jack had seen the two of them step onto his boat he had known they hadn't come to fish. But just why they were on his launch was a mystery to him. They weren't exactly sunworshipers nor did they appear to be on a manhunt. He had seen how they had ignored several blatant passes.

Both women looked familiar, although he knew he hadn't seen them on his boat before. He had been racking his brain trying to place them. Maybe if he asked the redhead to take off her baseball cap and sunglasses he'd remember where it was he had seen her before. With legs that could stop traffic, she wasn't the kind of woman a man would easily forget, which made his inability to place her all the more frustrating.

Jack propped one hand against the side of the wooden cabin and placed the other at his hip. "Ask away."

It was Sheila who plunged right in. "Did you graduate from Duluth Jefferson High?"

Jack's laconic grin slowly faded as he focused on Maggie. That was it. Maggie Stewart from high school. The brilliant but cool redhead whom everyone had labeled the goody-two-shoes of the class. Funny, but he didn't remember her having such a full, sensuous mouth or such great legs.

"You're Maggie Stewart," he stared in an almost accusing manner as he wondered if she could be the redhead Bud had said was looking for him last week.

"Yes. It's good to see you again, Jack." She stood, setting her rod down so that she could extend a hand to him.

Jack rubbed his hand on the leg of his jeans before offering it to her. Her skin was warm and smooth in his rough and callused palm. He would have prolonged the contact, but Sheila was introducing herself as well, and he had no choice but to accept her handshake.

"And I'm Sheila Wilson—at least I was the last time you saw me. Now I'm Sheila Campbell. I'm married, she's single," she said with an engaging smile.

"Sheila and Maggie." His grin reflected his recognition as well as his surprise at seeing the two of them on his boat. "It's been a long time, hasn't it."

"Twenty years," Sheila supplied. "Which is the real reason why we're here. We were hoping that you were the Jack Brannigan from our class so that we could tell you about our high school's twenty-year reunion."

"You two are planning a reunion?"

Sheila nodded eagerly. "It's going to be a wonderful party. We've reserved the ballroom of the Winston Hotel for dinner with dancing to follow. Actually there's a whole committee of us planning the event," she added with a modest grin. "Maggie and I are only the search committee. We've been playing detective trying to find the missing graduates from our class for about a month now."

"I'm surprised you found me," he said, trying not to sound annoyed that they had.

"Maggie deserves all the credit for that," Sheila told him, which had Jack closely scrutinizing his former classmate with the red hair.

"I did leave a message for you at the Blue Goose," Maggie said, a hint of censure in her voice.

So it was her, Jack silently mused. No wonder Bud had been so worked up over losing the message. Maggie's presence in the Blue Goose must have turned quite a few heads—especially if she'd had on a pair of shorts. Once more his eyes drifted over her shapely legs.

"You did get my message, didn't you?" Maggie asked, as though suddenly not sure that he had.

"Not exactly." His reply was vague and accompanied by what Maggie thought was a falsely sweet grin.

She waited for him to elaborate further, but he didn't. No explanation, no excuse as to why he didn't respond. "Not exactly?" Maggie repeated with a hint of irritation.

As if sensing Maggie's mood, Sheila interjected, "It doesn't matter. We've found you now and if you'll give us your address, we can mail you all the details."

Just as Maggie expected, Jack gave an evasive shrug that was softened by his apologetic tone. "I doubt that

I'd be able to attend. Summer is my busy season and it's almost impossible for me to get away."

Maggie continued to stare at him. He didn't want to come. She knew it and he knew that she knew it and he didn't care.

"Oh, what a shame!" Sheila went on. "We're planning this wonderful program and it's not going to be the same if you're not there, Jack."

He shoved his fingers into tight jean pockets. "I'm sure it's going to be a great party, but there's not much I can do about it. I'm sorry."

Just then someone had a fish on the line commanding Jack's attention, and with a polite nod, he excused himself.

"Sorry my eyebrow," Maggie murmured at his retreating figure. "Didn't I tell you he might not want to come?"

"What a shame." Sheila clicked her tongue. "He is one great-looking guy. I wonder if he's married. There was no ring on his finger."

"According to the article in the *Wall Street Journal* he is—unless he's divorced," Maggie said pensively.

"I can't imagine any woman divorcing that." She looked over to where Jack stood laughing with another passenger. "He is really gorgeous." Again she sighed. "Oh, well. I guess we'll just have to catch some more fish. Then we'll have an excuse to talk to him and we'll work on convincing him that he should attend." She swiveled around in her chair and dropped her line back into the water.

But most of the fish caught the rest of the afternoon were by the others on the boat, keeping Jack busy and leaving Maggie and Sheila cooking in the hot sun. When they did manage to hook a few more, Jack's manner toward them was as impersonal as it was toward the rest of the passengers. As the afternoon wore on, Maggie had the distinct impression that Jack was avoiding them, for even when he wasn't netting a fish or baiting a hook, he chose to stay on the opposite side of the launch and talk with several men.

"Fishing cool off?" One of the passengers asked as he came to stand beside Maggie.

"I think our beginner's luck is gone," Maggie said with a smile.

"You want to trade chairs? My buddy and I've got a little shade on our side of the boat."

Maggie glanced across to where the man had been sitting and nodded in agreement. "You don't mind?"

"Heck, no. Actually you'd be doing us a favor. You two have the hot chairs."

"In more ways than one," Maggie pointed out. "What do you think, Sheila?"

"I'm out of here," Sheila agreed, jumping to her feet. "Give me shade any day."

But despite sitting in the shade, Maggie was still warm, and although she and Sheila were the envy of nearly every other passenger on the boat, she wished they could return to shore. Jack's attitude toward them had changed since he had discovered why they were on the launch. And despite numerous attempts to talk to him, they had little opportunity to say much to him. Maggie thought it was probably for the best. Her heart skipped like a schoolgirl's every time she caught a glimpse of his tanned body. What she didn't need was to act like an infatuated teenager—especially over a married man.

When the boat returned to the pier in front of the Blue Goose, Maggie and Sheila had a stringer of fish worthy of a photograph, which is what the waitress filling in for Joni insisted they pose for when she saw them. Actually she took three Polaroid pictures—one for Sheila, one for Maggie and one to hang on the wall in the Blue Goose. Maggie carefully tucked the photo into her address book in her purse. Sheila tossed hers into the glove compartment. Neither one saw Jack walk into the Blue Goose and pull the third photo off the wall.

CHAPTER FOUR

"WELL?"

"Well what?" Maggie asked, looking over at Sheila who still had the Blue Goose baseball cap cocked to one side of her head even though they were back in the van heading toward Duluth.

"What did you think?"

"I think we were pretty lucky to catch so many fish. It must have been beginner's luck." Maggie had whipped off her cap and was threading her fingers through the thick red hair that had been bunched beneath it.

"I'm not talking about the fish and you know it," Sheila snapped a bit impatiently. "I mean what did you think of Jack?"

"I can see why he's got such a good reputation as a professional fisherman. He certainly knows what he's doing."

"Maggie Stewart!" Sheila said in exasperation. "I'm talking about how he looks, not how he catches fish!"

"He doesn't look much different than he did in high school, except I don't remember him being so tall and he's filled out a bit," Maggie said in a nonchalant tone.

"A little taller and he's filled out a bit," Sheila echoed sarcastically. "The man's grown six inches and there's not an ounce of flab anywhere on him. Jack is what we would have referred to in our younger days as a dreamboat.''

"We never called guys dreamboats when we were in high school," Maggie scoffed. "And if you sigh like that every time you mention Jack's name I'm going to think you are sixteen again."

"Come on, Maggie, you're not going to deny that you felt like sixteen when he looked at you with that lazy grin of his, are you? Don't forget you're talking to the girl who sat up with you until four in the morning while you swooned from the sheer thrill of being his square-dance partner in gym class."

As if it were only yesterday, the memory of alle-mande left and do-si-do flashed before Maggie's eyes. She might have been his partner, but he had looked right through her as though she hadn't even existed. It was a painful reminder of why he hadn't recognized her today. It did, however, give her a tiny twinge of plea-sure to remember the way his eyes had looked her over with an appreciative glance when they were on the boat. She may not have captured his attention when she had been a gangly teenager, but as a thirty-seven-year-old woman, she had been worthy of a brief ogle.

Determinedly, she pushed such thoughts aside. "The point is I'm not sixteen and neither is Jack," she told Sheila in a no-nonsense tone.

"No, you're two adults who both happen to be single."

"How do you know he's single?" Maggie demanded, unable to mask her interest.

"While you were in the ladies' room, I was grilling the bartender." She raised her eyebrows mischievously.

"He must be divorced," Maggie surmised.

"No, widowed."

"Widowed?" Maggie repeated, her voice revealing her surprise.

"Interested, are you?" Sheila asked with a coy tinkle in her tone.

"Only because I didn't expect anyone our age to be a widower," she answered grimly.

"Apparently his wife was killed in an automobile accident," Sheila told her, all traces of mischievousness gone. "Do you suppose that could be the reason he left his job in New York?"

Maggie's face was pensive as she absently stared at the passing scenery. "It's probably something we'll never know. I doubt he'll send back the alumni questionnaire we left with him."

"You're just going to have to think of a way to get him to the reunion," she stated matter-of-factly.

"Me?" Maggie protested. "I've done my job. I found him and gave him the information. I can't drag him to the reunion if he doesn't want to come."

"I hardly think you'd have to drag him," Sheila responded dryly. "The way he was looking at you I'd say he was more than a little interested in finding out more about you."

Maggie blushed like a schoolgirl, remembering how Jack's eyes had lingered on her bare legs when he had first noticed her presence on the boat. "I think the sun has fried a few of your brain cells. The only way Jack was looking at me was like a bothersome passenger who didn't know much about fishing."

"You can fool some of the people some of the time," Sheila retorted in a singsong voice, "but your best friend—never. I happened to see the way he was looking at you." She threw her a brief, curious glance.

"Admit it. Didn't your heart do a little flip when it saw him? After all, you did have a pretty big crush on him at one time if I remember correctly." Again the mischievous glint was back in her eyes.

Maggie had hoped Sheila would have forgotten about her teenage infatuation with Jefferson High's heartbreaker. She decided to treat the subject lightly. "And you, my very best of best friends, promised never to tell a soul," she said sweetly.

"And I didn't."

"Good. Then no one need ever know."

"Jack might be flattered if he knew—especially considering the way you look now."

"Sheila, don't you dare say a word," Maggie warned, the lightness quickly fading from her tone.

"You ought to know by now that I wouldn't do such a thing," she chastised her friend with a chuckle. "I've always been able to keep a secret—as you should know."

It was her last statement that caused an awkward silence to settle between them, and Maggie finally asked, "Are you thinking what I'm thinking?"

Sheila shot her a sideways glance. "About the Snow King contest?"

"You haven't forgotten, either, have you?" It was more of a statement than a question.

"I thought I had, until today when I saw Jack again after all these years. Maggie, haven't you ever wondered if we might have been wrong about him?"

"Haven't *I* wondered?" She had trouble keeping the irritation from her tone. "I was the one who was against changing the ballots in the first place. I never approved of any of it." Even after twenty years, the memory of her part in the affair stirred feelings of self-recrimination.

"I know, but we thought we were doing it for the right reasons." Sheila took the defensive. "And it was really at Judy's instigation. She played on our emotions."

"Maybe she did, but that doesn't absolve us from our part in it," Maggie said solemnly.

"At the time we were all so sure that Jack was responsible for Gina's pregnancy. What if we were wrong?"

"Then we were wrong," Maggie said exasperatedly, creating another silence in the van until finally she asked, "Why haven't we ever talked about this before now?"

Sheila's eyes were on the highway; she avoided even glancing in Maggie's direction. "I guess I've always been a little embarrassed by what we did, especially because I knew you disapproved and I felt as though I had let you down, siding with Judy the way I did. It was easier to sweep the whole thing under the rug rather than allow it to be a sore spot in our friendship."

"I know what you're saying. I never wanted to mention it to you, either." Maggie sighed and leaned her head back against the seat. "Besides, I really didn't think it was something we needed to do penance for for the rest of our lives. But every time Barb Milton brings up the subject of that stupid trip down memory lane and the royal court, I can't help but feel like a kid worried about getting caught with her hand in the cookie jar."

"Me, too," Sheila admitted in a low voice.

"Then shouldn't we feel relieved that Jack doesn't want to come? It will be a lot easier for us if he's not there."

"I suppose you're right," Sheila agreed. "On the other hand, if he did come, we could do something special for him at the reunion—like give him an award or something."

"I suppose we could give him one of those paper crowns from Burger King and a sash that says, The Man Who Should Have Been King," she said with a sardonic chuckle.

"Don't laugh. I'm serious," Sheila insisted, shooting a wounded look in her direction. "There must be something he's done we could acknowledge. We're going to be giving out awards for all those silly things like traveling the farthest and having the smoothest head."

"We're twenty years too late, Sheila," Maggie pointed out gently but firmly. "I think we ought to just forget about it. It's obvious Jack doesn't want to come to the reunion and there's really nothing for us to worry about."

"As usual, you're probably right," Sheila said with a sigh. "It might be better if he didn't show up at all, although if I were you, I certainly wouldn't pass up an opportunity to get to know him better."

Maggie shifted, crossing her arms across her chest. "I think that's one can of worms better left unopened."

Sheila groaned as if in pain. "I'm telling you, Maggie, the guy had the hots for you, but if you're not interested . . ." She trailed off with a helpless shrug.

Maggie dismissed her statement with a stifled yawn. "As I said earlier, the sun's affected your brain."

Sheila pretended not to hear. "You've got the perfect excuse if you do want to see him again," she said with a playful grin.

"What's that?" Maggie found herself asking.

"We've got his stringer."

IT WAS NEARLY DUSK by the time they pulled into the Stewart driveway. Herb, who had been gently rocking in the lawn swing, rose to his feet and came walking toward them, and Maggie guessed that he had been waiting for her return.

"I've got some fish for you to clean, Pop," she announced as she climbed out of the van.

Herb followed her to the back of the mini van where Sheila was shifting its contents in search of the stringer of fish.

"Holy smoke. Did you girls catch those?" he asked as Sheila and Maggie proudly displayed the metal wire with the fish suspended between them.

"Two of them are Sheila's and three of them are mine," Maggie replied, then gave her friend a quizzical look. "Do you know which ones are yours and which ones are mine?"

"The biggest one is yours and the rest..." Sheila shrugged carelessly, then giggled. "Your guess is as good as mine."

"The first thing we'd better do is take some pictures," Herb suggested, then shouted for Delores to bring him the camera.

When Maggie's mother appeared with the camera in hand, Sheila and Maggie posed in several comical positions and Herb finally managed to snap a few photos. As soon as he had separated the fish, he wrapped Sheila's in newspaper and put them back in the van.

After saying goodbye to her friend, Maggie followed her father over to the old picnic table behind the garage, the spot that had served as the designated fish cleaning area as far back as Maggie could remember.

"I better get my knife and a bucket of water," Herb said, letting the fish drop onto the grass.

"I'll get us some more newspaper and a pan for the fillets," Maggie told him.

"And tell your mother to turn on the yard light," he called over his shoulder before disappearing into the garage.

When Maggie returned, she spread the newspaper out across the table, then sat down on one of the weathered benches.

"Are you going to watch?" Herb asked, hearing the bench creak beneath her weight. "You used to be squeamish about this stuff."

"It's not so bad if they look dead." She glanced at the inert fish lying in the grass. "I never liked to see them flipping around right before you slice them open."

"These three won't be doing any dances," Herb assured her, bending over to grab a walleye by its eyes. "What's this one weight? It's almost a trophy size."

"Someone on the boat thought I should have it stuffed," Maggie told him, the thought causing her to shudder briefly. "It's over nine pounds."

Herb dangled it in front of him in admiration. "I'd be tempted if it were mine. Lenny would know the name of a good taxidermist, but what would you do with a stuffed fish?"

Maggie shrugged. "It wouldn't exactly fit into the decor of my apartment, would it?"

"It's a nice fish," he said with admiration, then picked up his fillet knife. "Last chance. You want a trophy or you want me to carve it up for dinner tomorrow night? There's enough here that we could invite Karen and her crew over as well. We could have an old-fashioned fish fry."

"Carve away, Pop," Maggie instructed. "I don't need a stuffed fish on a wooden board. Besides, I have the pictures." And she wasn't only thinking about the photos her father had taken.

"I wish I had caught this one," her father said with envy as he made a shallow slit from top to bottom in back of the gill. "I haven't even been out fishing yet this season."

"Didn't you go with Lenny on opening weekend this year?" she asked, surprised that her father would have given up his annual fishing trip with his friend.

"Naw," he drawled. "I haven't been able to take time off to go with Lenny for years." He skillfully carved away until he could lift two large pieces from the walleye. "Your mother's going to appreciate these fillets. We haven't had fresh walleye for quite some time now."

Maggie frowned. "Pop, Mom fried up some walleyes the first night I was home," she reminded him.

"Stuff from the freezer," he told her. "Hand me that shovel of water."

Shovel? Maggie nearly repeated the word aloud, but managed to pass the bucket of water to her father without drawing any attention to his misuse of the word. This wasn't the first time she had heard him incorrectly identify an object. She sat quietly watching him work, but a tiny frown marred her normally serene face.

"You never did tell me if that was the fellow you were looking for," he said when he had finished and they were rolling up the newspaper with the remains of the fish inside.

"Oh, it was," Maggie commented casually, watching her father toss the refuse into the garbage can.

"I knew it! Didn't I tell you it was?" Herb said with a self-satisfied sigh. "Is he coming to your reunion?"

Maggie shook her head. "He says he has to work, but personally, I don't think he's interested."

"Can't say I blame him. If I had the chance to spend a Saturday night out on Lake Mille Lacs fishing I'd hardly want to climb into a suit and tie...especially not in August."

"I know, but he can fish anytime. Our twenty-year reunion only happens once."

"I suppose." He handed her the pan of fish fillets. "Take this in to your mother. I'm going to put this stuff back in the garage," he said, gesturing to his fillet knife and honing stone.

When Maggie went inside, she found her mother in the kitchen whipping cream. "All finished?" Delores asked glancing over her shoulder.

"Umm-hmm. Dad suggested we invite Karen and the children over for a fish fry tomorrow night," she said, rinsing the fish under a cold stream of running water before putting them in the refrigerator.

"That sounds like a good idea. You haven't had much time to see them since you've been back."

Maggie wiped her hands on a paper towel, then asked, "What are you making?"

"I thought you and your father might like some strawberry shortcake before you go to bed. I found the most beautiful berries at the farmers' market this morning." She held up a small bowl of the red fruit for Maggie's inspection.

"Sounds scrumptious." She snaked a hand around her mother's shoulder and slid a finger along the rim of the bowl, scooping up a swirl of whipped cream.

Delores clicked her tongue and faked a hand slap.

"Umm-mm. It's been a long time since I've had real whipped cream." Maggie perched herself on the step stool beside the counter. "Mom, when did Dad stop going on his fishing weekends with Lenny?"

"He hasn't. What makes you think he has?" she asked, reaching into the cupboard for three plates.

"Just now when we were outside cleaning the fish he told me he hasn't gone in years."

Her mother set the plates on the counter then put her hands on her hips. "See what I mean about his fibbing? He's getting worse every day. Pretty soon he's going to tell you he's not married to me." Her tone was indignant.

"Mom, it's nothing to get upset about. Maybe I misunderstood him," Maggie tried to soothe her mother's ruffled feelings. "He probably said he doesn't get to go fishing as often as he liked to. Please don't be angry with him."

Just then Herb came waltzing through the back door, humming to himself as he drifted through the kitchen. "Got to wash my hands, then I'll be ready for my treat," he announced, giving Delores a pat on the behind before he disappeared again.

"Really, Mom, I think I probably did misunderstand him. Let's just forget it, okay?" Maggie pleaded.

Delores did manage to forget it, but only because when Herb returned he planted a kiss on her cheek and told her she made the best strawberry shortcake in the state of Minnesota. Both Herb and Delores listened with interest to Maggie's tales of her adventures aboard the

Wave Walker, and by the time Maggie said good-night, all thoughts of any problems between her two parents were forgotten.

The next morning, however, she awoke once more to the sounds of quarreling, and Maggie decided she would have a serious talk with her sister when she came to dinner that evening.

Five years separated Maggie and Karen, as well as quite a few other things, leaving more than miles between the two sisters. Maggie had always blamed their troubles on normal sibling rivalry. Being older and so much more like her father, she was closer to him than she was to her mother, which seemed to be a constant source of irritation to Karen. It mattered not that Delores favored Karen over Maggie, because it was Herb's favor she wanted.

Once Maggie went away to college and subsequently took a job out of state, the rivalry appeared to diminish, although she suspected that Karen never really overcame the problem of living in her shadow. Maggie was valedictorian of her class, the high achiever, the career woman, just as Herb had expected her to be. Karen, on the other hand, although bright and successful, was not the achiever Maggie was. Nor did Herb expect her to be, but that still didn't make Karen happy with not being Maggie.

Although at first Maggie had felt isolated living away from her family, she had taken heart in the fact that her relationship with her sister had improved with her absence. Although it still wasn't the close bond she had always hoped to someday have with a sister, Maggie was grateful that at least they had a relationship. She didn't realize, however, how tenuous that relationship was until she brought up the subject of their father.

They had just finished eating and were doing the dinner dishes while Karen's two daughters, Erin and Nicole, played croquet with their grandparents in the backyard. Sounds of the little girls' tinkling laughter drifted through the screen door, punctuated by an occasional deep guffaw from Herb.

"I'm glad you brought the girls over today, Karen," Maggie said, as she wiped off the kitchen table with the wet dishrag. "It's good to hear Pop's laughter. There hasn't been much of that lately."

"He's probably got a lot on his mind. He works six days a week at the store," Karen answered, standing on tiptoe to put a large platter on the top shelf of the cupboard.

"That's something I don't understand." Maggie was straightening the chairs as she spoke. "Why is he pushing himself at his age?"

"Pop's always pushed himself. You ought to know that. You're just like him."

"Yes, well look where it got me." She shook her head in self-recrimination. "I'm worried Pop's going to end up exhausted like I did. When's the last time the folks had a vacation?"

"They went to Hawaii for a week last February."

"That was almost six months ago. And he deserves more than a week off once a year."

"Yes, well try telling him that." Karen frowned as she sorted knives, forks and spoons into the proper grooves in the silverware chest. "He hates taking time off in the summer because that's when business is best. It's always been that way. You ought to know that. We never got to take summer vacations, remember?"

Maggie turned her attention to the stove, scrubbing between each of the burners as she spoke. "Well, I think a vacation is exactly what they need. They seem to be getting on each other's nerves. Until I came home, I never realized how much they argue.''

"They've been married for almost forty years. People married that long do argue, Maggie.'' Her tone was almost condescending, and Maggie felt slightly annoyed.

"Maybe, but I can't help but worry about them. Pop seems to be getting so forgetful. It's as though he's gotten old all of a sudden.'' She stopped her scrubbing and inclined her head pensively.

"Yes, well I guess when you don't come home but once a year, you do notice things like that,'' Karen said sourly.

Maggie bit her lip to keep from snapping a curt reply. Of utmost importance right now was her parents' happiness. She didn't need to be barking at her sister over petty jealousies. She finished wiping off the stove, then rinsed out her dishrag.

"You're right. I haven't been home so changes probably do seem more drastic to me than they do to you. But I can't help but notice how forgetful Pop's become and sometimes he doesn't make sense when he talks. Surely you must have seen changes in his behavior?''

"No, I haven't.'' Karen faced her with arms folded across her chest. "Why do you keep coming back to Pop?''

"Because I think there's something definitely wrong in our parents' marriage, and from what I can see, the something wrong is Pop. Mom has been suffering—''

"Mom's been suffering?'' Karen cut in, looking at her sister disbelievingly. Any attempts she might have been making to control her temper vanished. Two red stains colored her cheeks as she faced Maggie with fire in her eyes. "You haven't lived at home in twenty years, and now, after only being here for two weeks, you're telling me that Mom is suffering and Pop's the problem?"

There was a bitterness in Karen's tone that went far beyond the subject of her parents' troubles. Maggie had to grasp the edge of the counter to still the trembling inside of her.

"Why are you reacting so defensively?" she asked quietly, holding her sister's gaze. "All I'm saying is I think our father may have a problem and I'm concerned about him."

Karen's laugh held no humor. "If Pop has a problem it's because Mom works him to death at the store."

"Mom?" Maggie gave her a puzzled look. "Since when are you the one to be defending Pop's actions?"

"Someone has to. You want to blame everything that goes wrong on Pop. He's forgetful, he's argumentative, he's not making sense when he talks." She threw her hands up in the air. "Well, if you had the responsibilities he's had at the store, you'd be doing the same things. As far as I can see, it's Mom's fault. She's pushing him so he'll retire early."

For a moment, Maggie was stunned. Karen had always championed her mother. "I can't believe you're talking like this! Ever since I've been home, Pop's been irritable, tense, and downright difficult to be around. And from what I can see, Mom's not to blame for any of it. You don't live here, Karen. You don't see what goes on."

"I don't live here?" Karen repeated with heavy sarcasm. "I'm the one who's been here for them for the past twenty years. I'm the one who works in the store with them. Or doesn't that qualify me to make any judgments?"

"I'm sorry. That didn't come out right," Maggie apologized, feeling suddenly drained of her strength. She leaned against the sink and pushed the hair back from her forehead. "I don't want to argue with you, Karen. I'm just concerned about the folks."

"Well, you don't need to be." Karen's tone was hostile, causing Maggie to wince inwardly. "Your life may be coming unglued, but we're all fine here." With those words, she grabbed her purse from the cupboard and marched outside, letting the screen door slam shut behind her.

Maggie felt her legs buckle and a weakness threaten to overcome her. She sank onto a kitchen chair and dropped her head into her hands until her breathing became steady once again. This was just what Dr. Walker had advised her against—getting worked up emotionally. It was obvious that she and Karen were still on opposite sides after all these years. She was going to have to tread very carefully if she wasn't going to step on her sister's toes.

She closed her eyes briefly and exhaled a long, pent-up sigh. Why was it she could negotiate the most difficult trade agreements between countries miles apart in their attitudes, yet with her own sister she always seemed to fail miserably? Somehow, some way, she was going to work out an agreeable solution. It was going to be a long, long summer if she didn't.

CHAPTER FIVE

MAGGIE MANAGED to mend fences with her sister the next day, but peace came with a cost attached: the price was deferring to her sister's judgment for the sake of family unity.

Maggie could see that there was a certain amount of truth in Karen's assertion that her father's problems were a result of overworking, but she honestly didn't see her mother as the slave driver Karen had portrayed her to be. When Maggie attempted to talk to Herb about slowing down and taking things easier, he became defensive and irritable, which made her realize that if she were going to get through to him, it would have to be in a subtle way.

It was one of two problems troubling her during the next few days, the other being her ambivalence toward Jack Brannigan. As much as she hated to admit it, like Sheila, she was wishing there was something she could do to atone for the Snow King fiasco. But then she remembered his reaction to learning her identity and she was glad she wouldn't have to see him again.

She thought she had found the answers to both problems in the Sunday paper and made sure she had the opportunity to talk to her father the first thing Monday morning.

"Good morning, Pop," Maggie greeted him cheerfully as she wandered into the kitchen and found him seated at the breakfast table with a stack of pancakes in front of him.

"What are you doing up so early? I thought the doctor said plenty of rest," Herb said in a paternal tone Maggie recognized from years gone by.

She helped herself to a cup of coffee, then took her usual place at the table. "You know me. I can only sit for so long, then I have to get busy. Sheila and I are going to work on the reunion book today, but before I go over there I wanted to walk down to the harbor."

"You should have come down ten minutes sooner. You could have had some of this." He poked his fork in the stack of pancakes on his plate. "Your mother just left."

"Where's she off to so early?" Maggie asked over the rim of her cup.

"Karen's baby-sitter called in sick so she's going to sit with the kids this morning."

"Who's going to take Mom's place at the store?"

"We can get by without her," Herb stated confidently, adding more syrup to his pancakes.

Maggie's brow wrinkled. "Why didn't Karen call me? I could have stayed with the girls today."

"You just said you're meeting Sheila."

"Yes, but it's nothing that couldn't be put off until tomorrow." She sipped her coffee slowly. "I don't understand why Karen couldn't have at least asked me."

"She probably knew you were busy." When Maggie didn't comment, he advised, "Don't go borrowing trouble where there isn't any."

Maggie held her tongue, despite the overwhelming urge to tell her father she didn't need to borrow trouble when it came to her relationship with her sister. It was there without the asking. She took another sip of coffee then said, "Look. I found this in yesterday's paper." She shoved the newspaper advertisement highlighted in red marker toward her father's plate.

"Thirty-second annual walleye fishing contest—Lake Mille Lacs," Herb read aloud, lifting his chin as he read to get the benefit of his bifocals. "What? You think you're ready for the big time now that you caught that trophy fish?" He gave her a lopsided, teasing smile.

"It's not the big time and you know it." Maggie grinned right back. "It's an amateur contest and I wasn't thinking of me entering, but you."

"Me?" He looked surprised by her statement.

"Sure. You and Lenny used to enter all sorts of fishing tournaments. Remember the time you caught that big muskie and won a tent? All of us were so excited we made you take us camping along the North Shore."

"Yeah. It was the only time we ever used it. You and Karen cried the whole time we were gone just because a few bugs found their way inside the canvas." His lips quirked in remembrance.

"They were big, creepy crawly bugs," she said, her nose wrinkling in distaste. "Look what the prize is for this one—a travel trailer. I bet you don't need to worry about creepy crawlies when you've got a nice home on wheels to camp in."

Herb picked up the newspaper and looked more closely at it. "I haven't entered a fishing contest in years."

"Then why not try this one?" she urged him. "Even if you don't win the trailer, you'll probably get some nice fish. And they do taste good the way Mom fixes them."

Herb's eyes scanned the article, then he shook his head. "It's next weekend. Lenny's going to Grand Marais to see his new grandson."

"Then I guess you'll have to settle for me," Maggie said, pleased as punch that Lenny's grandson had chosen to make his arrival at this time. "I don't have any plans for Saturday."

"It's been a while since the two of us have gone fishing, hasn't it?" he reflected with a wistful smile.

"Too long, Pop," she agreed. "Should we give it a try?" She tilted her head in appeal.

"It's tempting," Herb said, his eyes brightening at the idea. "The trouble is we've got a sale starting tomorrow that runs through Saturday at the store."

"Uh-uh. You can't use work as an excuse," Maggie told him, shaking her head. "I've already discussed this with Karen and she assures me she can manage just fine, and that if it's necessary, she'll get extra help."

"And what do you propose we fish in? That old fishing boat of mine hasn't been out of the garage in years. The motor needs a tune-up." He made a disgruntled sound, waving his fork in the air. "Ha! It probably needs a complete overhaul."

"Maybe we could rent a boat or go out on one of the launch services," she suggested, undaunted by his skepticism.

"If there's a contest going on this weekend, you can bet the launches are going to be booked and every rental boat on the lake will already be reserved," he told her with an authoritative air.

"What if I can find us a couple of seats on a launch. Would you go?" She leaned forward, a hint of a challenge in her eyes.

"Are you thinking of calling that ex-beau of yours and getting on his launch?" One thick dark eyebrow lifted a fraction.

"He's not my ex-beau, Pop," Maggie said a little impatiently, recalling how disinterested Jack had been in her presence on the launch.

Herb took one last bite of pancake, then wiped his lips with his napkin. "That's too bad. It's probably the only way we would have been able to get a seat on his boat."

"Do you really think it'll be a problem?" she asked as he stood and carried his plate over to the sink.

"Maggie, if you can figure out a way to get us on the lake, I'll go."

She rose to her feet and gave her father a kiss on the cheek. "Great. It's a date then. This Saturday. Just you and me." She grabbed the newspaper from the table and started toward the stairs. "I'm going to go upstairs and make the arrangements right now. I'll stop by the store and let you know what I find out, okay?" And with a wink she was gone.

Maggie spent the better part of the morning calling various resorts and fishing services in the Mille Lacs area without finding a rental or launch available. She was hesitant to call the Blue Goose and request a seat on the *Wave Walker*, but after repeatedly hearing the same answer—"I'm sorry, we're full"—she finally decided that she had no other choice.

As her father predicted, the *Wave Walker* was booked, and not even Maggie's persuasive tactics could buy them a seat. She did, however, manage to get Jack's home phone number. For several minutes she debated about calling him, her glance volleying between the phone number written on the notepad in her hand and the Polaroid snapshot taped to the corner of the mirror. If only he had shown a little bit more interest in her. And if only she didn't have this crazy desire to see him again and at the same time the hope that she wouldn't see him again.

After several minutes of mental deliberation, she finally made the call. It rang at least eight times and she was about to hang up when she heard his voice.

"Jack, it's Maggie Stewart—from high school. I was on the launch last week," she reminded him.

"How could I forget? Everyone around Garrison's been talking about your nine-pound walleye." His voice sounded as though he were smiling. "What happened? Did you eat it or stuff it?"

She took a deep breath and willed her stomach to be still. "We ate it, and it was delicious." Her own smile made her voice light. "Jack, the reason I'm calling is that I want to bring my father fishing on Saturday, but I'm having trouble finding a boat. I called the Blue Goose and they told me your launch is booked, but I thought you might know of another service we could try."

"With the fishing contest being held this weekend, I'm afraid you're not going to have much luck," he said knowingly.

She exhaled a tiny moan of disappointment. "I was afraid that's what you were going to tell me."

"Do you really want to go fishing?" A thread of disbelief laced his words and Maggie felt her face warm at the reminder of her fishing trip with Sheila.

"Yes, I do," she said sincerely. "My father used to be an avid fisherman, but it's been a while since he's been able to get away from work. Actually I was hoping this could be a little therapeutic recreation."

She heard him sigh, then there was a short silence before he finally said, "If you promise not to try to persuade me to come to the class reunion, the two of you can come out on the *Wave Walker* with me," he suggested.

"But I thought you were full?"

"A private party has chartered the launch for the entire weekend, but from what I understand, there are only about ten people involved. You're welcome to come as my guests."

"Are you sure they won't mind?"

"Maggie, it is my boat." His voice was low with just a hint of amusement in it.

Again she felt herself blush. "In that case, I'd like to accept your offer."

"There is a problem, however." His voice changed, and Maggie wondered if he wasn't having second thoughts about his invitation. "We're scheduled to leave quite early in the morning on Saturday."

She was not about to allow Jack's less than enthusiastic offer prevent her from spending some time with her father. "That's not a problem," she assured him. "You just tell me what time you want us to be there and we'll be there."

After she had hung up the phone, she scrambled off the bed and pulled the Polaroid snapshot from its perch in the corner of her dresser mirror. As she studied the photo, Sheila's words echoed in her mind. Jack *was* a dreamboat. And if she was honest with herself, she'd admit that the fishing contest's appeal had had quite a lot to do with wanting to see him again. Ever since that day on the boat, she had felt like a teenager infatuated with the high-school heartthrob. Maybe it was time she found out just who the real Jack Brannigan was. Then she'd be able to put to rest all those schoolgirl feelings that had her gazing at his photo like a lovestruck teen.

Both Delores and Karen approved of the proposed fishing trip, and Maggie was optimistic that taking her father away from the hardware store for the day would be a start in getting him to relax and take life a little easier. She was also looking forward to spending some time alone with him and she hoped that he'd feel comfortable enough to talk about his work and not feel threatened.

Without nagging him, Maggie was careful to remind Herb to bring all of the necessary fishing equipment, and after he went to bed Friday night, she double-checked to make sure he had put it in the car. Because of the early departure, they were forced to get up before the sun had even risen. Maggie had packed a thermos of hot coffee and doughnuts for them to snack on while they drove the hundred miles to Garrison.

The sun was just peeking over the horizon when they reached the northern end of the lake, and the breath-taking effect of its ascent on the water gave Maggie goose bumps. Already there were legions of boats out, and Maggie was surprised by the number of vehicles parked alongside the road. Even the roadside park she and Sheila had picnicked in was jammed full of campers with boat trailers and motorhomes and tents lining the shore of the lake.

"Still think we've got a good shot at winning a prize?" her father asked, quirking his eyebrow.

"I can't believe the number of people!" Maggie said in amazement. "Where did they all come from?"

"Now you know why you couldn't reserve a boat. They don't call this the walleye factory for nothing," he reminded her. "Where should we park?"

"Anywhere along the highway is fine. Jack said we could pick up our contest entry forms at the bait shop next to the Blue Goose."

As soon as the Oldsmobile had been maneuvered into a small roadside space, Maggie and Herb walked the short distance to Pete's Bait and Tackle. While her father stepped up to the counter to get the necessary contest forms, Maggie waited beside the rectangular white case that at first glance appeared to be an ice-cream freezer but was in reality a cooler for leeches and night crawlers. A strong odor of fish permeated the air, and she watched as a couple of young boys peered into a bubbling tank of minnows. Her eyes sought her father and she saw him pointing to one of the hundreds of different types of tackle that were hanging on the pegboard behind the counter.

After paying for the fishing lure, Herb returned to her side and gave her a piece of paper. "Here. You have to fill this out and I have to give it back to the gentleman behind the counter." He nodded toward a man in a navy-blue smock and a baseball cap turned backward. "I figured you might as well enter, too."

"There's no place to write," Maggie said, looking around the crowded store.

"Use the top of the cooler."

Maggie grimaced as she set the paper on the transparent lid, trying not to notice the dark leeches swirling beneath her fingers. She quickly scribbled the information, then gave the form back to her father.

"Do we need anything else?" Herb asked, gesturing to the bubbling tanks of minnows.

"No. The launch service provides the bait."

"Great. Let's go." Herb started toward the door.

"Pop, you have to turn in the contest forms," Maggie reminded him, grabbing him by the arm.

Herb looked down at his hands quizzically. For a moment, Maggie wondered if he even knew what he held in his hands.

"I thought you said the gentleman behind the counter wanted the forms," she repeated.

Without another word, Herb returned to the counter and gave the man the papers.

"Should I get us a couple of sodas to bring along?" Maggie asked as she followed him out the door.

"I could do with some more coffee." He looked across the street to the Jolly Viking Café. "Do I have time to get the thermos filled?"

Maggie glanced at her watch. "We've got about fifteen minutes. See that wooden boat at the end of the pier?" Herb's gaze followed the direction of her arm. "That's the *Wave Walker*. Why don't I take our fishing rods and meet you there? While you get the coffee, I'm going to stop in that gift shop across the street to see if they have any sunscreen. I forgot to bring mine."

"Fifteen minutes?" He looked to her for confirmation.

"Fifteen minutes," she repeated, experiencing a tiny flutter in her stomach at the thought that in fifteen minutes she was going to see Jack again.

After purchasing a bottle of sunscreen lotion and a couple of rolls of Life Savers at the small general store, Maggie returned to the car to get the two fishing rods and the tackle box her father had stored in the trunk.

There was no activity on the long pier leading to the *Wave Walker*, and when Maggie reached the boat, she wondered if she hadn't made a mistake about the time because Jack was the only person on board. He looked up from the fuel gauge he had been fiddling with when he heard her approaching.

"Good morning. Are we too early?" She smiled shyly, and wondered what it was about him that made her feel like a schoolgirl.

"Nope. Everyone else is late." He moved over to the side of the boat and offered to take the fishing gear from her. "Come on aboard."

"Where is everybody?" she asked, glancing curiously around the empty launch as she stepped on board.

"I think this private group likes to party more than fish. When I dropped them off at midnight last night most of them went straight to the lounge in the Blue Goose. Judging by how much alcohol they consumed on the boat, I'm not sure any of them are going to be up to fishing this morning."

Worried, she said, "Does that mean you won't be going out?"

"It simply means they paid for me to take *you* fishing if no one else shows up." He looked past her shoulder to the shore. "By the way, where's your father?"

"Oh, he's coming. He stopped to get some coffee at one of the cafés." She tried not to stare at the way the washed-out denim of his jeans clung to his thighs, or the way his hair curled around the turned-up collar of his lightweight jacket. But unless she wanted to gaze at the water or the boat, she had no choice but to look at him. He wasn't wearing his sunglasses this morning and her own eyes were drawn to his, which were bluer than the water beneath them.

"Why don't you take these two seats near the front?" He gestured to the chairs directly across from where he sat. "These guys like to hang out the back, anyway."

Maggie set her pouchlike carryall down on one of the vinyl swivel seats. "I want to thank you, Jack, for taking us along on such short notice. Are you sure we're not going to be in anyone's way?"

He folded his arms across his chest and leaned back against the control panel. "As you can see, there's plenty of room even if all ten of them show up—which I sincerely doubt will happen."

His eyes were appraising her, causing Maggie to feel a bit self-conscious, and she eagerly looked away from their relentless probing. "I like your new look," she told him, giving the boat a thorough appraisal.

"You mean the paint job." Jack was pleased that she had noticed his attempts at refurbishing the boat, and smiled at the compliment. "It's amazing what a little paint can do, isn't it? The thing practically looks brand-new."

Maggie smiled in agreement and Jack felt his insides react to the warmth the smile brought to her face.

"How long have you been doing this?" she asked.

"You mean acting as a guide?" When she nodded, he said, "I guess it's been just a little over a year now. I only bought the boat this past April. Last summer I worked on another launch called the *Shady Lady*."

"And what happens to a professional fisherman when summer's over?"

Jack searched her features for some sign of mockery in her question, but there was none. Eyes as green as the Norway pines gazed at him with sincere interest.

"I go on the road, hitting some of the tournaments in different parts of the country where it's still warm. Then, as soon as the lakes freeze over here in Minnesota, I come back and move the ice houses out. I have twelve I rent out every winter for ice fishing."

"Then you really are a professional fisherman year-round?"

"Summer, fall, winter, spring—I fish or else I help other people fish." He looked past her and said, "I think I see a couple of them who are in need of a little guidance now." He nodded toward the pier where two men in jeans and plaid flannel shirts were carefully walking along the wooden boards. "They're not moving very fast, are they?"

Maggie smiled at the sight of the two men who appeared to be almost tiptoeing as they slowly made their way across the pier. As they approached the boat, she could see the reason why. Judging by their expressions, neither one was feeling well. Both men looked as though they might have slept in their clothes and neither appeared to have shaved for a couple of days.

"Morning," Jack called out, a greeting that was feebly returned, causing Maggie to suppress a smile. "Where's the rest of your group?"

One man laughed sarcastically. "I think this is it. The others decided to wait until you go out this afternoon."

Jack shrugged and raised an eyebrow. "*If* I go out this afternoon. The sky was pink this morning."

"You think it's going to rain?"

"Rain won't stop us, but thunder and lightning will." He looked at the two of them. "You want to go check and see if anyone wants to change his mind about going out this morning?"

"Anyone who goes back into that cabin this morning risks getting mortally wounded," one commented dryly, exchanging a wry look with his roommate. "I think we're it for this morning." He gestured at the two of them.

"I'm ready whenever you are," Jack told them, then glanced to where Maggie sat nervously looking for Herb.

"I wonder what's happened to my father." She glanced at her watch, then raised a hand to her forehead to shield her eyes from the sun.

"Is he wearing a green jacket and a tan cap?" Jack asked.

"Yes. Do you see him?" She stood and looked in the direction of his gaze.

"Could that be him over there?" Jack pointed to the wooden pier that ran parallel to theirs a couple of hundred feet away. "Here." He handed her a pair of binoculars.

Maggie knew without the power of magnification that it was her father. Through the field glasses, she could see his face clearly and he looked as though he had no idea that he was on the wrong dock.

"That's him," she confirmed, lowering the binoculars. "Do you think he would be able to hear me if I yelled at him?"

"Probably not."

She groaned. "I'd better go get him," she said, giving the binoculars back to Jack. "I'm really sorry about this."

Sensing her anxiety, Jack said, "It's all right, Maggie. We're not on any rigid schedule. We should probably wait a few extra minutes anyway to make sure no one else is going to show up."

Maggie sincerely doubted whether Jack would have waited for anyone else. She quickly jogged back to shore and rescued her father, whose reaction was to blame Maggie for directing him to the wrong dock.

Rather than argue with him, she let his accusations slide and led him over to the *Wave Walker*.

Herb's annoyance dissolved as soon as they boarded the boat and he was introduced to Jack. Any apprehension Maggie might have had over the wisdom of the fishing trip disappeared when she saw her father laughing and comparing fish stories with not only Jack, but the other two passengers as well.

Using a compass and binoculars, Jack took the boat far out into the vast center of the lake, just as he had the previous time. Whether or not they went to the same spot, Maggie didn't know. Once again they had picked up several smaller boats along the way, which her father explained were following the *Wave Walker* with the hopes of finding the fishing hot spot.

With only two other passengers on the boat, Maggie and her father had Jack's near-undivided attention as they fished under a sky scattered with puffy white clouds. As before, Jack saw to it that Maggie's line was set at the right depth and he baited her hook for her while her father listened eagerly to Jack's instructions and made the necessary adjustments to his own rod and reel. This time, however, Maggie didn't catch anything except a small perch, which she promptly removed from the hook and threw back into the lake, drawing a glance of admiration from Jack for her efforts.

"Not so squeamish after all," he commented, coming to lean against the side of the boat.

"Only when it comes to leeches. Pop always made me bait my own hook and take off whatever I caught," Maggie told him, glancing at her father who had shuffled over to the back of the boat to fish alongside the other two passengers. "If there was one thing he taught me, it was to be independent."

"So tell me about the independent Maggie. I have to admit, I'm a bit surprised that you're still single and living in Duluth."

"Actually my single status is relatively recent. I'm divorced." Before he could comment, she rushed on. "And I haven't lived in Duluth since we graduated. I'm only here for the summer."

"Then where is home?"

"Washington, D.C."

"I don't suppose there's much opportunity for fishing in D.C.?" he said with a grin.

"No, not exactly," she returned.

"So did you come home simply to plan the reunion?"

"Sometimes I think Sheila believes I did," Maggie said with a wry smile. "I really came home for rest. Like my father, I have a tendency to become much too preoccupied with work. This summer, however, I decided to treat myself to the kind of vacation we had when we were kids. Three months off with nothing to do but have fun. Only I have to confess, for a workaholic like myself, it's not easy."

"So you're still the high achiever you were in high school?"

"You thought I was a high achiever?" she asked, surprised that he had even noticed her in high school.

"President of the National Honor Society and voted by the teachers as outstanding senior girl in practically every activity the school offered." He rattled off her achievements with a note of admiration in his tone. "I'd say that would definitely classify you as a high achiever."

Maggie felt a ridiculous thrill at his knowing her high-school accomplishments. "I didn't think you noticed who I was in high school."

"Oh, I noticed you, Maggie Stewart." Suddenly his voice was serious, and the look in his eyes had her forgetting about her line dangling in the water and why she was standing beside him on the *Wave Walker*.

For just a few moments she was the teenaged Maggie waiting for him to ask her to dance at the sock hop. Only her father's voice jolted her back to the present as he called out to Jack to bring the net.

Maggie followed Jack to the back of the boat where her father was reeling in his line. "I think I've got a beauty," he said, his voice brimming with anticipation.

Jack quickly moved in beside him, ready to net the fish as soon as he brought it close to the surface. Just as Herb exclaimed, "I got it!" Maggie saw the tip of his rod spring back and her father uttered an expletive. "What were you doing? You lost it!" he hollered at Jack, startling Maggie with his outburst.

"I'm sorry, Herb. The timing was just a split second off," Jack apologized.

The exchange that followed between her father and Jack was enough to bring a rush of color to Maggie's cheeks. She couldn't believe that her mild-mannered father was behaving in such a manner.

"Pop, it's only a fish," Maggie interrupted, no longer able to witness the scene he was making.

With an uncustomary show of anger, Herb tossed his fishing rod on the floor of the boat and shrugged off her consoling hand. Then he disappeared into the rest room.

"I'm sorry—I don't know what came over him," Maggie said quietly.

"It's all right, Maggie," Jack answered. "It was my fault. I don't lose many like that."

"It doesn't matter whose fault it was, Jack. I can't believe my father reacted that way."

"It's nothing I haven't seen before," he assured her.

"But it's so unlike him. The reason I brought him out today was so he could relax and have a good time. Not so he could lose his temper and make a fool of himself."

"He didn't make a fool of himself," Jack said reassuringly. "Let's just forget about it, okay?"

"All right, but—"

"Look. Your bobber's under," Jack cut in.

Maggie was relieved when after reeling in the line she discovered a fish barely bigger than a minnow. Somehow her line had become tangled, which was what Jack was working at when Herb finally came out of the rest room. Much to Maggie's relief, her father apologized to Jack, then returned to his spot at the front of the boat.

The rest of the morning passed without incident, and Maggie couldn't help but admire Jack's easygoing personality. After the way her father had treated him, she wouldn't have blamed him had he been distant for the remainder of the trip. But he accepted her father's apology and went about his business as though nothing had happened, getting along well with the other men on the boat, too. Maggie was reminded of what a charismatic man her father could be. By the time the boat returned to the pier at Garrison, no one had caught any prize-winning fish, but it was obvious that her father had enjoyed himself. Before they left for home, he made certain his picture was taken with the fishing pro, along with the stringer of keepers they had caught.

All the way home Herb talked about what he was going to tell Lenny about his fishing trip with Jack Brannigan, the best walleye fisherman in the state. Maggie sat quietly and listened to her father ramble on about anything and everything he must have heard Jack say that day. But there was only one line running through Maggie's head.

"Oh, I noticed you, Maggie Stewart."

CHAPTER SIX

"I CAN'T BELIEVE Pop went into the store today," Maggie told her mother as they sipped iced tea in the shade of the umbrella shielding the round patio table from the sun. "You always told us that Sunday was a family day."

"Times have changed," Delores said sadly. "Customers want the store open on Sundays and you know your father's motto...give the customer what he wants." There was a hint of bitterness in her tone.

"I can understand having the store open, but I don't see why Pop has to be there. He has plenty of employees who can manage without one of you being there." She absently brushed away a fly that was buzzing around their empty plates. "Don't Karen and the children usually come visit on Sunday afternoons?"

"They'll be over even if your father's not here."

"But the point is he should be here, Mom."

Delores sighed. "To tell you the truth, Maggie, considering the mood he's been in lately it's probably better that he isn't here. He's been so irritable it's actually a relief when he's gone." As though suddenly embarrassed by her admission, she looked across the patio and exclaimed, "Oh, look! There's a hummingbird at the feeder."

"That's something I wanted to talk to you about," Maggie said gently.

"Hummingbirds?" Delores prompted.

"No, Mom. Pop's irritability. I'm concerned about his health."

"His health?" She gave Maggie a puzzled look. "Your father's as healthy as an ox. I can't even remember the last time he had a cold. Do you know he's never missed a day of work because of illness?"

"That may be true, but that's not going to be the case if he keeps working at the pace he is now. He's sixty-four years old. He doesn't need to work six days a week. He's earned the right to take things a little easier."

Delores's chuckle was sarcastic. "You'll never be able to convince him of that. If anything, he seems to feel he has to prove that he can run things better than ever."

"Maybe it would help if I had a talk with him?" Maggie suggested.

She shook her head firmly. "He hasn't listened to me or Karen. We've both tried to get him to ease up a bit, but you see the way he works."

"Is something troubling him?"

Delores stood and began clearing their lunch dishes from the table. "Maggie, I'd really rather not talk about your father if you don't mind."

"I'm sorry, Mom. I don't mean to pry, but I'm worried about him." She held the back door open while Delores carried the dishes inside. "Yesterday when I took him fishing I noticed he's getting more than a little forgetful. If I didn't know better I'd say he was almost acting a little senile."

"Senile?" Delores gave her a startled look, then quickly asserted, "Everyone's memory gets a little cloudy with age—your father's included."

"I don't think his is a little cloudy, Mom." She leaned one hip against the counter and watched her mother put away the leftovers. "Haven't you noticed how every once in a while he has difficulty finding the correct word to use? Yesterday he stuttered over the word car and finally he ended up pounding his fist on the Oldsmobile."

"He's overworked," Delores stated emphatically, as if that explained his behavior. "You know it and I know it, but the problem is he doesn't know it. If he'd take some time off he might be able to relax and maybe then he'd be his old self again."

"When was the last time he had his hearing checked?" Maggie asked thoughtfully.

Delores lifted her shoulders. "It was probably years ago." She paused to give her daughter an inquisitive look. "Is that what you think is wrong with him? He's hard of hearing?"

"It would explain why we have to repeat so many things we say to him. It might also explain his irritability. Maybe he's embarrassed that he doesn't hear so well anymore."

Delores stilled her busy hands and clamped them together in front of her. "It's not easy for a man like your father to grow old. Maybe it's tougher for him than it is for others—I don't know." She shrugged and looked down at her hands. "I just wish he would talk to me about it."

Maggie felt a rush of sympathy for her mother. "You and Pop have always been able to discuss everything. That's why you're still together after all these years and it's one of the things I've always admired about your marriage. There must be some way you can get him to talk about whatever it is that's bothering him?"

Eyes seeking understanding gazed into Maggie's. "Believe me, I've tried. But he gets so excited and irritable whenever I question him, we end up fighting and it's just not worth the hassle.''

"Mom, I think it's important that you ask him about his hearing," Maggie told her. "I know you want to avoid a confrontation, but if his hearing is at the root of his problems, think how much better it will be once the problem is corrected."

Delores stared at her daughter for several moments before finally agreeing. "All right. I'll talk to him about it."

A sudden thought occurred to Maggie. "You know what you could do? Take him to that health fair they're going to be having at the high school next week. That way you could get his hearing checked without having to drag him to the doctor."

Her mother pondered the idea, then said, "You know, that might be just the thing for him. He knows I've wanted to get my cholesterol level checked. I could ask him to take me and once we're there, I'll suggest he take advantage of the free checks as well." Her face brightened at the idea.

"And if for some reason he refuses to have the hearing test, at least then you'll know that his hearing is responsible for his erratic behavior."

"You're right. What a good idea." She smiled gratefully at her daughter and patted her hand. "Can you find out the times for me?"

"Sure, Mom. I'll call and get the information tomorrow."

The first thing Monday morning Maggie phoned the high school and learned that the health fair was indeed being held in the gymnasium on Tuesday and Thursday of the following week. When Delores managed to convince Herb to take her over to have her cholesterol level checked, Maggie decided she'd go along as well. To both Maggie and her mother's surprise, Herb willingly stopped at the various checkpoints at the health fair, including the hearing booth. The results of his tests were equally surprising. Herb was fine on all counts— blood pressure, cholesterol, hearing, vision and weight. Delores, however, was referred to her family doctor to have follow-up work done because of high blood pressure.

Herb's only comment at dinner that evening was, "I told you I'm as healthy as I was the day we were married."

Despite her father's assertion, Maggie wasn't convinced. In the short time she had been home, she had observed such radical changes in his behavior; now that she knew he was in good physical condition, she had to wonder about his mental state. She had also observed that her mother did her best to ignore the changes in her usually mild-mannered husband. Not that Maggie blamed her. It was easier to ignore some of the arguable points than to refute them. Even Maggie found herself tolerating behavior in him she never would have expected she would ignore. And like her mother, she discovered it was almost a relief when he wasn't at home.

Following her doctor's recommendations, she often slept late in the morning, which allowed her to catch up on much-needed rest as well as avoid seeing her father before he left for work. She had just finished having a late breakfast one morning when she heard a car in the driveway. Wondering if one of her parents had decided to come home for an early lunch, she peeked out the kitchen window and was surprised to see a Jeep Wagoneer in the driveway. The surprise turned to shock when she saw Jack Brannigan climbing out of the driver's side.

Maggie quickly let the curtain slip back into place and raced across the hallway into the bathroom to give herself a quick once-over in the mirror. An old sweatshirt and a pair of shorts was hardly the way she would have chosen to dress for seeing Jack again, but she only had time to drag a comb hurriedly through her hair before the doorbell rang. She gave herself one last glance, groaned, then went to answer the door.

"Jack . . . hi!" She opened the door wide for him to step inside.

"Hello, Maggie," he drawled. His voice sounded sexier every time she heard it. He was wearing another pair of washed-out jeans and a light blue knit shirt that made his eyes appear to be even bluer than she remembered.

"Since I had to come to Duluth to pick up a part for my boat I thought I'd drop this off in person." He handed her the reunion book questionnaire as he stepped past her.

"Oh, you filled it out. Great." She gave the paper a cursory glance and her face fell. "You didn't answer all the questions."

There was disappointment in her voice and Jack found himself wishing that he hadn't skipped over a few of the blanks. "I answered most of them," he said with a repentant grin.

"I'm sure there's enough information for the reunion book," she said with a diplomatic grin. "Can you stay for a while? I just made some fresh coffee." He looked as though he were debating whether he should or not and she added, "Or do you have an appointment to keep?"

Jack looked at the face scrubbed clean of any make-up and felt something stir deep inside of him. He could have easily mailed the questionnaire to her, which is what he was wishing now that he had done. She aroused feelings in him he wasn't sure he wanted stirred . . . feelings that clashed with his devotion to Jill. In the year and a half since his wife's death he had managed to keep away from anyone who could possibly be a threat to the privacy he now so richly cherished. That was one of the reasons he had moved to northern Minnesota. Except for the seasonal visitors and the fishermen, he had little contact with people—which was how he liked it.

He glanced at his watch, an appropriate excuse forming in his mind. But then he looked into her green eyes and instead of saying he had an appointment at the marina, he found himself admitting, "A cup of coffee would be nice." She looked surprised by his answer and he immediately tacked on, "But I don't want to interrupt your plans."

Self-consciously her eyes moved to her clothes. "Oh, you're not. I was trying to work up the energy to tackle the weeds in my mother's flower garden out back. Gardening is supposed to be therapeutic."

"You don't strike me as a woman who needs therapy." His blue eyes seemed able to see right into her soul, and Maggie felt a little nervous.

"Actually I need something to keep me busy. I'm not used to vacations where I've nothing to do." She could have added that she wasn't used to vacations period, but she didn't want to admit that to him.

She could see his eyes scrutinizing the pictures lining the wall in the hallway and suddenly she felt a little embarrassed. Included in the array of photos was her high-school graduation picture, and several pictures from her childhood.

"The family tree," she explained with a careless shrug and a grin.

His glance stopped at the picture of her two nieces in a silver frame that had Grandma's Darlings etched in black. "Yours?" he asked with a lift of eyebrows.

She shook her head. "My sister's. I don't have any children."

"Me, neither," he said, meeting her inquisitive gaze. "Is this the home where you grew up?" he asked as she led him through the kitchen and out to the sun porch.

"Yes. I was literally born here. There was a blizzard and Mom couldn't get to the hospital so my father delivered me—with the help of the nurse who lived next door." She showed him into a screened sun room filled with hanging green plants and comfortable wicker furniture. The fragrance of summer roses wafted through the louvered windows, mingling with the scent of freshly mowed grass. "Why don't you take a seat here and I'll get the coffee?"

When she returned, he was flipping through a paperback copy of Harvey Mackay's *Swim With the Sharks Without Being Eaten Alive.*

"Is this yours or your father's?" he asked, raising the book in the air.

"Mine."

He set the book back down on the coffee table. "I thought so."

"Why is that?" She sat down beside him on the floral chintz cushions of the wicker sofa, setting the serving tray on the glass table in front of them.

He shrugged. "You never mentioned your occupation when you were on the boat, but I figured if you've been living in D.C. you're probably swimming with some pretty big fish." He watched as she filled two china cups from the silver coffee server. "Are you?"

She passed him one of the cups and met his gaze. "I'm on staff at the Office of the U.S. Trade Representative."

"You're a trade negotiator?" There was a curious gleam in his eye.

"Umm-hmm." She slowly sipped her coffee. "Does that surprise you?"

He studied her briefly. Each time he had seen her she had looked like any of the other females running around Northern Minnesota. After seeing her with a baseball cap covering her red hair and now dressed in a ragged sweatshirt, he was having trouble imagining her in a business suit. At the mention of her job in Washington, he was reminded of the fact that she was from a world very different from his—the business world. The thought brought a slight frown to his face, and he finally said, "No, I guess it doesn't."

"Have you read it?" She gestured to the book on the coffee table.

He shook his head. "I don't think it's about the kind of fish I encounter in my profession." A hint of a smile turned up the corners of his mouth.

"How did you end up a professional fishing guide? I think most of us in high school expected you to follow in your father's footsteps and join the Air Force."

"I did. Right after we graduated I enlisted, but a tour of duty in Vietnam cured me of any ideas I had that I might want a career in the Armed Forces."

"You went to Vietnam?" Her delicate brows drew together slightly. "I didn't know that." Her expression turned pensive. "There's a plaque in the high school with the names of all of our graduates who served in Vietnam and I don't think your name is on it.''

He shrugged. ''I lost touch with the people back here after I graduated from high school. My dad had been assigned to another base while I was in Nam so there really was no reason for me to return to Duluth when I left the Air Force. Home had moved on—as so often is the case when you're in an Air Force family.''

''We've had trouble finding all the people from Air Force families,'' Maggie commented. ''Where are your parents now?''

''My father's retired from the Air Force and they're living in Texas.''

''Was he disappointed you didn't make a career in the service?''

''Madder than a skunk would be a better way to describe it, but he got over it.'' He smiled in recollection. ''And fortunately for me my mother is quite skilled at soothing his ruffled feathers.''

''What does he think of your current success? From what my father tells me, you're quite the celebrity when it comes to the sport of fishing.''

He laughed and rubbed a hand nervously along the back of his neck. ''Hardly a celebrity. If my name is recognized it's only because that person has been reading *The In-Fisherman*.'' He took another sip of his coffee. ''You never did tell me how you and Sheila managed to track me down.''

''Actually it was my father who recognized your name. When he mentioned there was a famous fishing pro by the name of Jack Brannigan, I didn't think it could possibly be the same person who had graduated in my class.''

"Why is that? What did you expect to find me doing for a living?" He shot a curious glance in her direction. When she didn't immediately respond, he said, "You know about my job with Comcor, don't you?"

Maggie nearly blushed as she nodded in response. "I read the article in the *Wall Street Journal*."

"That was several years ago. Where would you have found a copy of that?" There was a curious glint in his eye.

"I am on the search committee, Jack," she reminded him. "Actually it was your social studies teacher, Mr. Brillman, who told me about it. He keeps track of what's happened to all his former students. You should see the box of newspaper clippings and magazine articles he's collected over the years."

"I suppose you're wondering what happened—whose decision it was that I left corporate America for the waters of Minnesota?" There was an edge to his voice, a defensiveness.

She took another sip and fixed him with a candid appraisal. "I wouldn't be honest if I said I'm not curious as to why someone who had been tagged a 'Mr. Fixit' and credited with the success of an advertising agency like Comcor would make such a choice."

"Do you enjoy your job with the government, Maggie?" he asked her, noticing for the first time the faint sprinkling of freckles across her delicate cheekbones.

"Yes, I do," she answered honestly. "It's demanding, time consuming and stressful, but I wouldn't be honest if I didn't say I found it exhilarating. The busier I am, the better I like it, which is why I'm having so much trouble adjusting to the slow pace here in Duluth."

"And wondering why I would choose such a simple life-style after living in the fast lane in New York, right?"

"Why did you, Jack?"

He shrugged. "Some people take a leave of absence to travel or study abroad. I decided to take a year off to go fishing. It was something I had always wanted to try—making a living as a professional fisherman. Ever since I was a small boy and I'd get to spend part of summer vacation at my uncle's cabin in Wisconsin, I've had this fantasy about being a pro. So when the opportunity arose for me to make that decision, I did it. The problem was, after a year away from the hectic New York pace, I didn't want to go back."

"So you stayed here instead of returning to your career."

"This is my career now." He glanced at his watch and made a face. "I should probably get over to the marina." He stood and jammed his hands into the pockets of his jeans, staring at the slender woman before him. He had accomplished what he had intended to. She had his reunion questionnaire in her hand. There was no reason for him to linger, yet he found himself saying, "Would you like to have dinner with me? I'm not exactly dressed for anyplace fancy, but we could get something at Zeb's Bar and Grill."

"I'd like that," she told him without hesitation.

"You don't have other plans?"

"You mean besides watching the grass grow?" she quipped.

He clicked his tongue in admonishment. "This may not be New York or the nation's capital, but there's something special here you won't find anywhere else."

He gave her a promising smile that had her heart aflutter.

She returned the smile. "I'll let you convince me over dinner."

"I'll tell you how I get along with the walleye and you can tell me how you manage to swim with the sharks," he told her on his way out.

Maggie spent the rest of the afternoon wondering if she would have had the same feelings of excitement about her date if she hadn't had a crush on Jack when she was sixteen. She knew it was pointless to deny her attraction to him. She wanted to go out with him, but whether it was because she would have practically killed to have a two-line conversation with him over twenty years ago or because he was about the sexiest man she had encountered as an adult, she wasn't sure. As she slipped into a one-piece emerald-green jumpsuit with a cinch belt that emphasized her tiny waist, she decided it probably was a combination of both. However, when Jack arrived at her house and she saw the look on his face as his eyes made a swift but thorough appraisal of the clinging fabric, she knew it was the latter.

On the way to Zeb's Bar and Grill, they had to drive past the high school, the sight of which had both of them remembering youthful experiences that lent a nostalgic tone to the conversation. As they drove to the north end of the city, they reminisced about their days as teenagers, filling each other in on what they knew about certain members of the class.

Most of dinner, however, was spent talking about Maggie's job with the government, and just as she had expected, Jack had an excellent business acumen. Several times during dinner she had to stop and remind herself that he was no longer a rising star at Comcor but a fisherman. She wished she could tell if he was really enjoying their conversation or if he was simply being polite. All too soon the waiter was asking them if they were interested in an after-dinner drink and Maggie realized that instead of her finding out more about him as she had planned, they had talked almost exclusively about government policy and import quotas.

It had been deceptive, his interest in her work. If she hadn't known that he was totally removed from the corporate world, she would have assumed after their dinner together that he was caught up in the same frantic pace and competitive business world as she was. In fact, it was only when another of the bar's patrons recognized Jack and stopped at their table to talk briefly about fishing that she saw that there was the same enthusiasm in Jack's eyes for the sport as there had been for business. It made her realize how much she had centered her life around her work.

She really didn't have anything else to turn to *besides* her work, which was one of the reasons why she was so bored in Duluth. With so little free time in Washington, she had excluded hobbies from her life. And sports. Even her regular workouts at the health club had become so sporadic that she couldn't even say she was actively working at keeping fit. At one time she had been an avid racquetball player and a frequent visitor to the health club. Now she couldn't even remember the last time she had picked up a racquet. Her social life centered around professional obligations and the thought was a sobering one.

"I'm sorry about that." Jack's voice interrupted her musings and Maggie realized that the visitor had left. "I hope we didn't bore you."

"No, not at all," she told him, putting her hand over her glass when he would have refilled it with wine.

He gave her a dubious look. "You looked as though you were a million miles away."

"I was enjoying the view," she told him, watching the waves on Lake Superior crash against the rugged shoreline. "And getting caught up in a little nostalgia. Seeing those teenagers playing volleyball on the beach made me wonder if the high school kids today haunt the same places we used to."

"Like Hidden Beach and Mickey's Malt Shop?"

"The malt shop is gone," Maggie told him. "I went to take my two nieces there for ice cream and I discovered it's now a dry cleaners."

He released a mournful sigh. "What about the beach?"

"Oh, it's still there, but it's no longer hidden. When old Mr. McPherson died, the new owners donated enough land to the county so a road could be put in along with a public access to the beach. I haven't been there, but my sister says it's quite nice."

"Want to make like a couple of teenagers and drive over there?"

Every time he gave her that wide grin revealing a tiny dimple in his left cheek, she felt like a teenager. She glanced wistfully out the window. "It is a beautiful evening."

"If we hurry we can catch the sun setting."

If he had asked her to Hidden Beach twenty years ago she would have been ecstatic. Every student at school knew that the swimming hole was known as the place to go for romance. She looked again into blue eyes that seemed to sparkle with invitation.

He put down his napkin and signaled for the waitress. "What do you say? Should we give it a try?" There was a hint of a challenge in the husky voice.

She gave him an impish grin. "Why not?"

Hidden Beach was located on a small lake just west of the city on property that had belonged to old Mr. McPherson. Framed by tall pines, the crystal-blue water reflected only a handful of cabins. Until Mr. McPherson had died, there had been no public access to the lake, despite the fact that a third of the lakeshore was public land. But most teenagers didn't mind hiking in from the highway through the woods; the secluded nature of the white sand beach was what attracted them.

Since there were no lifeguards on duty, most parents, however, made the beach off-limits, and the local police made periodic patrols in an effort to maintain safety. However, like forbidden fruit, the beach only became more attractive to the teens, and parties were common both during the day and at night. Although Maggie had been to the beach during the day, only the wildest of the wild kids went to the beach at night—or so she had thought at the time. She'd bet money that Jack had been to the beach at night.

"William T. McPherson Park," Maggie read the wooden sign as Jack turned off the highway onto the newly paved road. They passed a series of signs and she added, "It looks like they have picnic facilities and a boat rental."

"It doesn't even look like the same area, does it?" Jack remarked as he followed the twisting road into the pines.

"I wonder why they had to cut down so many trees?"

Suddenly the lake came into view and Jack said, "At least they've managed to preserve the solitude of this place." He parked the Jeep at the end of the parking lot closest to the beach. "It doesn't look like very many people have heard of this place yet."

Maggie looked out and saw that the natural beach hadn't been tampered with, except now the smooth white sand was dotted with lawn chairs and adults rather than beach blankets and teenagers. Despite the chill in the evening air, several swimmers were still in the water, although most of the visitors were gathering their belongings together and heading for home. A lifeguard wearing a sweatshirt and a pair of swim trunks sat atop a tall, square wooden tower, a radio softly playing beside him.

As they slowly wandered across the tarred road to the sandy beach, Maggie heard Jack sigh and knew that he was noting some changes that had taken place. Gone was the wooden raft that had been constructed from junkyard barrels and discarded lumber. What once had been an unrestricted swimming area was roped with buoys. The old rickety wooden shed that had served as a change room had been replaced by a small brick building housing public dressing rooms. Where there once had been a campfire pit there was now a small playground for preschoolers and Maggie's eyes immediately picked out the No Open Fires Allowed sign posted at the beach's entrance.

As the sun dropped lower into the west, the lifeguard made the announcement on his megaphone that the swimming area would be closing for the day.

"They look like they're freezing," Maggie commented as one by one the swimmers came shivering out of the water.

"The air temperature's probably lower than the water temperature by now," Jack said, kicking aside the white sand with the toe of his shoe. "That's why we would always build a fire."

Maggie gestured to the sign prohibiting fires. "Only in the good old days."

Jack looked around. "Do you suppose Half Moon is still here?"

"Half Moon?" She looked at him quizzically.

"Maggie Stewart, you don't mean to tell me you haven't been to Half Moon?"

She continued to look perplexed. "I think you're forgetting who you're talking to. Miss Goody-Two-Shoes," she reminded him. "I only came here once on a dare when I was sixteen."

"And you've never been here at night?"

She gave a mock look of horror. "And risk ruining my reputation?"

"Well, then come on." He took her hand in his and began walking toward the forest of trees to their left. "If you haven't seen a sunset from Half Moon, you haven't seen a sunset."

CHAPTER SEVEN

JACK'S HAND was comfortably warm compared to the chilly evening air that now felt damp against her skin.

"Are those shoes suitable for climbing?" he asked, pausing at the foot of the path leading into an area thick with trees.

Maggie glanced down at her sandals. "How much of a climb is it?"

"It's not bad, but the ground does become rather uneven the closer we get to Half Moon," he replied.

"Are you sure one doesn't have to be sixteen to be doing this?" She lifted one eyebrow skeptically.

"You can do it, Maggie." He gave her a look that had her heart reacting as though she had already climbed to the top of the hill.

When they reached the top of the hill, both were slightly winded, causing Jack to remark, "We used to run all the way up here when we were kids." He turned her around by the shoulders until she was facing west. "I think the climb was worth it, don't you?"

"Oh, Jack! It's beautiful!" she exclaimed in awe as the setting sun dissolved from a tangerine globe into a collage of pinks, oranges and golds streaking the sky and reflecting onto the mirror-smooth surface of the dark water. "This scene could be on a postcard."

There was a gentleness in his voice as he said, "I never get tired of watching the sun set on a lake." They stood in silence for several moments before he said, "This is why it's called Half Moon." He gestured to the rocky ledge that was arced in a semicircular bluff. "See that path?"

Maggie nodded, curious as to where the narrow strip of dirt could lead, for it appeared that the ground dropped straight away to the water.

"There's a ledge under this cliff." He answered her unspoken question.

Cautiously she peered over the edge, then stepped back. "And kids climbed down there?"

"That's why this was known as a hot spot for lovers. They'd steal a few kisses, then leave their mark on the rocks. They'd spray paint their initials on them." With his foot, he absently kicked at the loose gravel. "I'm surprised this hasn't been fenced off."

"I don't think many people know it's here."

"Only the Jefferson High Eagles, eh?" He gave her a knowing smile.

"The Jefferson High Eagles who defied authority," she amended.

"Do I detect a hint of reproach in that statement?"

She shook her head reflectively. "More like envy. Every kid in school wanted to come to Hidden Beach, but you know as well as I do, Jack, that a certain crowd hung out here, and unless you were a member of that crowd, you didn't come."

"Ah yes, that wonderful adolescent pecking order. Isn't that why we never knew each other in high school, Maggie? Because you were in one group and I was in another and never the twain shall meet?"

"Probably," she agreed, regret in her voice.

"I would have liked to have known the sixteen-year-old Maggie." There was a sincerity in his voice as he reached for her hand.

"I guess you'll have to settle for a thirty-something Maggie," she said lightly, then with a flirtatious lift of her eyebrows added, "I think this Maggie's more fun than the sixteen-year-old anyway."

"Yes, but right now if we were sixteen, we wouldn't be talking." His thumb was gently massaging the back of her hand.

"No, we wouldn't," she agreed, a mischievous light in her eyes. "But then if I were sixteen I probably wouldn't have been brave enough to do this, either." With her free hand she pulled his head close and pressed her mouth to his in a teasing, gentle kiss that was all pleasure and warmth.

Startled amusement sparkled in his eyes when she released him, as did another emotion, one which sent a flood of heat to Maggie's insides and caused her to say, "And I *know* I wouldn't have been brave enough to do this." She boldly pressed herself against him and this time when she kissed him, her tongue parted his lips, exploring and tasting him, while her fingers buried themselves in the silky thickness of his hair. As the kiss deepened, Maggie felt his arms tighten around her, and before she knew it, she was no longer the aggressive one.

At sixteen she had fantasized about Jack Brannigan, but nothing could have prepared her for the rush of feelings or the wild, primitive need his touch ignited within her. Instinctively she arched herself against him, inhaling the musky scent she had come to recognize as his.

When Jack lifted his head, her lips were quivering and her cheeks were flushing with desire. She could feel his breath, uneven and warm, as it mixed with the cool, crisp air to caress her face. Held tightly in his arms, she could feel the hardness of his body, and as if in answer to his unspoken message, Maggie felt a long forgotten ache stirring restlessly in the pit of her stomach.

Just when she thought he was about to cover her mouth again, she heard the sound of his palm making contact with flesh. "Now I remember why we never stayed up here very long past sunset," he said, swatting a mosquito on his forearm. "Mosquitoes love warm blood." He brushed her lips lightly, then reluctantly released her with a groan. "I think we'd better return to the Jeep. Now that the sun's disappearing, the temperature's going to be dropping, too."

Still reeling from the impact of his kiss, Maggie couldn't think of anything clever to say, but simply slipped her hand in his and followed him as they retraced their steps leading back to the beach. When they emerged from the woods onto the white sand, it was unusually quiet, with only the sounds of the loons and the crickets breaking the silence.

"I think this is the first time I've seen this place deserted at night," Jack reflected as they strolled hand in hand across the beach toward the parking lot.

"There may not be any parties or bonfires, but it's not exactly deserted. Look." She gestured toward the parking lot. When they had arrived, there had only been a couple of cars parked in the rectangular lot. Now there were all sorts of vehicles scattered around at what looked to be planned intervals, and Maggie knew the reason. Teenagers still regarded Hidden Beach as the place for romance.

"Maybe things haven't changed so much after all," Jack commented as he opened her door for her. When he was seated beside her, he placed his arm across the back of her seat and said, "As tempting as it is to pretend we're a couple of teenagers, I don't think there's enough room in here for any serious misbehaving."

Then, as if he couldn't resist, he stole a long, hard kiss, a low rumble coming from his throat. "I think we'd better leave before we steam up the windows like the rest of these kids." He removed his arm from the back of her seat and stuck the key into the ignition. "Besides, it looks like the curfew patrol has arrived."

As the Jeep made a hasty exit, Maggie looked back over her shoulder and caught a glimpse of a police car slowly cruising into the parking lot. "I think you're right. Things haven't changed so much after all."

There wasn't much conversation on the way back to the Stewart home, and Maggie was reluctant to analyze the reason why. At first she thought they were both caught up in the nostalgic memories their day together had triggered, and the silence was not uncomfortable. But when they pulled into the Stewart driveway, she couldn't help but feel that Jack had withdrawn a bit.

"I'd like to see you again, Maggie," he said quietly, surprising her.

"I'd like that, too," she told him, wondering why he was looking out the front window rather than at her. It was almost as though he didn't want to admit that he wanted to see her again. Once more, the silence returned, and finally Maggie said, "I guess I'd better go in." She was about to reach for the door handle when Jack's arm across her stomach stopped her.

When she felt his other arm go around her shoulders, she turned her face to his. The look she saw in his eyes before his mouth captured hers rekindled the ache she had felt on Half Moon, and she returned his kiss with an urgency she had never dreamed she was capable of. Locking her arms tightly around him, she wanted his kisses to go on forever, for never in her life had she felt such a rush of pleasure from a single kiss. When Jack's hand found the gentle swell of her breasts, she gasped, not because of the exquisite sensation his touch evoked, but because a bright beam of light had suddenly flooded the entire backyard and the driveway.

"This is worse than the cops." Maggie groaned as Jack reluctantly let her go. "I guess at my age, my father believes he's doing me a favor by turning on the yard light." She shrugged apologetically. "Would you like to come in for a nightcap?"

"Are you sure your father won't mind?" he teased with a grin.

"You'll probably get a warmer greeting than me," Maggie returned, then led him into the house.

If Maggie didn't know better, she would have thought her father was waiting up for her, but then she saw the bowl and spoon on the table and she knew that he was getting himself something to eat.

"Where have you been?" Herb demanded as soon as they stepped in the back door. "You missed dinner."

"Jack and I had dinner at Zeb's, Pop," Maggie replied smoothly. "I called Mom and told her I was eating out."

"Did you have a good time?" Herb asked, offering his hand to Jack.

"It was nice," Jack answered for both of them. "How are you, Herb?" He pumped the older man's hand, then shoved both of his hands into his pockets.

Herb nodded absently. "I'm just getting myself a snack before I turn in. I always sleep better if I have a bowl of cornflakes before I go to bed." He pulled a box of cereal from the cupboard, then asked for the second time, "Did you have fun?"

"Yeah, Pop. We had a great time," Maggie replied, watching him shake a small pile of cornflakes into the plastic bowl.

"That's good," Herb said with a satisfied smile, moving over to the refrigerator. "Caught any big ones lately?" he asked Jack as he reached inside for a pitcher of orange juice.

"Nothing that could match Maggie's," Jack answered. "Of course we're getting to that time of year when fishing slows down a bit."

"Yup. Too hot," Herb agreed, carrying the plastic juice pitcher over to the table. Maggie, noticing he didn't have a glass, took one from the cupboard and set it on the table next to his bowl. But instead of pouring the orange juice into the glass, Herb covered his cornflakes with it. "You let me know when they start biting again. I'd like to come out on the launch," he told Jack, seemingly unaware of his mistake.

"Sure thing, Herb," Jack responded as if nothing out of the ordinary had happened.

For a moment Maggie didn't know if she should comment on her father's mistake or pretend not to have noticed. She knew that there was no way Jack could not have seen Herb pouring orange juice on his cereal, yet she didn't want to risk upsetting her father, especially in Jack's company. "I invited Jack in so that we could have a nightcap," she announced uneasily.

"Well, I'll get out of your way here and take this into the den." He picked up his spoon and the orange-juice-drenched cereal.

Maggie's hand on his shoulder stopped him. "It's all right, Pop. You stay here. We'll go downstairs."

"Oh, sure. You go on. You know where everything is." He dismissed them with a wave, then sat down at the table. "It's good seeing you again, Jack," he said as Maggie took Jack's arm and directed him toward a flight of stairs leading to the game room in the basement.

"What would you like?" she asked him, motioning for him to take a seat at the bar while she went around the other side. She avoided his eyes by reading off the names of the different liquors on a shelf before finally adding, "There's also some beer in the refrigerator."

"What are you having?" he asked, perching himself on one of the backless stools.

"How about a brandy?"

"Sure." He reached across the bar to finger a wooden statue of a hobo whose knapsack had Herb's Place etched on its side.

"If I can just figure out where my father left the brandy decanter," she said, her eyes scanning the row of bottles. "He's moved things around since I was last home." She stooped to look in the cabinet where the glasses were shelved and when she stood back up, she held the bottle of brandy in one hand and two balloon-shaped glasses in the other. "Found it," she announced triumphantly.

"I like your dad, Maggie," Jack said sincerely, watching her fill the glasses.

She smiled. "I know the feeling's mutual."

"You seem to have a good relationship with him," Jack commented, accepting the snifter with a smile of thanks.

"We've always managed to remain close despite the distance between us. If I have any regrets about my job in Washington, it's being so far away from my family.

My visits home are too far apart." She took a sip of the brandy. "And now that my parents are getting older, I realize what a difference time can make. I can hardly believe how much my father has aged since the last time I was home."

"Not having met your father when he was younger, I can't comment on that. But I have to tell you, Maggie, that he looks in great shape. How old is he?"

"Sixty-four, and you're right." She stepped around to the front of the bar and climbed onto the stool next to Jack's. "He's in great physical condition. He has more stamina than some of his employees who aren't even half his age. And he does look a good ten years younger than he is, which is why it's difficult for me to admit that he's starting to behave like a senior citizen."

"What do you mean?"

"He's becoming rather forgetful, which is especially difficult for me to accept because he's always had such a sharp mind." She traced the rim of her glass with her fingertip. "If I didn't know better, I'd think he was suffering from a touch of premature senility. Occasionally he'll do things that remind me of my eighty-year-old grandfather."

"I take it he normally doesn't pour orange juice on his cornflakes?" His mouth curved up ever so slightly, ever so gently.

She shook her head in regret. "It's little things like that that have me wondering if he isn't pushing himself too hard at the store. I know better than anyone else the crazy things lack of sleep and too many hours on the job can do to a person."

"Is that the voice of experience talking?" He raised his eyebrows inquisitively.

Maggie sighed. "I'm afraid it is. When I said I was taking a summer vacation I didn't mention that it was an imposed vacation. If my doctor hadn't prescribed it, I wouldn't have come home."

His lips twitched at the corners. "So you really aren't back in Duluth to help Sheila with the reunion."

She managed a weak smile and shook her head. "Unfortunately I'm a lot like my father. I love to work. But all work and no play can lead to exhaustion, which is why I'm worried about my father."

"When's the last time he had a complete physical examination?" His eyes narrowed thoughtfully.

She lifted her shoulders. "Getting my father to admit he doesn't feel well is difficult, but getting him to a doctor is nearly impossible. The best we could do was take him to the health fair at the high school, and he passed all the tests he took with flying colors." Suddenly feeling as though she had already said more than she should regarding her father's health, Maggie deliberately changed the subject:

"Speaking of my father, I should show you that muskie he was bragging about when we were on the *Wave Walker*." She slid off the stool and beckoned for him to follow her. She flicked on a light switch that lit up the far end of the room where a pool table rested beneath a low-hanging oblong lamp. On the wall were numerous plaques and trophies, but it was the large fish mounted to a cedar board that drew Jack's attention.

"I can see why your dad's so proud of this," he said as he stood admiring the trophy-size fish. "It's a nice catch." He looked around the room until his eyes spotted a vacant wall. "You could have had that walleye of yours mounted and put on display over there."

She shook her head. "This room is reserved for Dad's triumphs," she said, her fingers toying with one of the numerous bowling trophies that lined the shelf that ran the perimeter of the room.

"And who's responsible for this?" Jack had moved over to examine more closely a mural on an adjacent wall.

"My sister, Karen. She did that while she was attending art school," Maggie told him, coming to stand beside him in front of the seascape her sister had painted on the wall.

"She's an artist?"

Maggie shook her head. "A bookkeeper. She gave up her dreams of becoming an artist to marry the boy next door, had two children and ended up working at my parents' hardware store."

"You sound as though you disapprove."

"Not really. I admire any woman who puts her husband and children first in her life. Unfortunately for my sister, her husband didn't deserve to be first. They were divorced shortly after the birth of my younger niece."

"One of the 'Grandma's Darlings' I saw upstairs?" he asked with a half grin.

Maggie smiled. "Both Erin and Nicole are a couple of darlings. If there's one thing I have enjoyed about coming home, it's being able to spoil them rotten. I love to take them shopping, buy them whatever they want and stuff them full of ice cream!" She chuckled gleefully. "It's probably a good thing I don't have kids of my own."

"Would you want to?" he asked softly.

For a moment she said nothing, wondering why she didn't have a ready answer. In the past she had always been able to answer that question without hesitation.

But that was because in the past she had been married to Brian, and there hadn't been a question of whether or not she *wanted* a child. Brian was sterile. But Brian was no longer a part of her life now, and no longer did she automatically have to rule out the possibility of maybe someday becoming a mother.

"Yes...someday," she answered, then felt a little foolish. For someone her age, someday couldn't be too far off. She raised her glass to her lips to avoid his eyes. "And only if they inherit their aunt's artistic talent," she said after taking a sip of the brandy.

"Are you saying you don't paint seascapes for a hobby?" he said teasingly, following her lead in lightening the mood.

"I don't think there's an artistic bone in this body," she admitted, taking a seat on the leather sofa, then inviting him to do the same. "I was lucky I could stay within the lines on those paint-by-number kits we had when we were kids, which is why they didn't put me on the decorations committee for the reunion. I'm much more comfortable searching for people than trying to match colors and designs."

"How is the search going?" he asked as he sat down beside her.

"Now that I've found you, there are only fourteen missing."

"Do you think most of the graduates will be coming to the reunion?"

"Sheila says about two-thirds of the registration forms have been returned."

He lifted his eyebrows. "That many?"

"Are you having second thoughts? There's still time to change your mind if you want to come." Maggie was thinking how much she wanted him to come and was hoping he'd say yes.

Instead he said, "That's what Barb Milton told me when she called."

"Barb called you?" A niggling pang of guilt made its presence known.

"Umm-hmm." He took a sip of brandy, then added, "She did her best to convince me I should attend. It seems she's got something planned having to do with the royal court from Snow Daze and she's determined to reunite all of us." He sounded as unenthusiastic about the idea as Maggie was.

"From what I've heard, Barb's got quite a program lined up, although she's being rather secretive about it," she managed to say in a casual tone despite the uneasiness broiling about inside her. "Some sort of trip down memory lane."

"Do you think people really want to be reminded of stuff that went on twenty years ago?"

"Well, of course they do." She giggled nervously. "That's why they're coming to the reunion...for all those memories. I really wish you could come, Jack. I think you'd have a good time."

He gave her a contemplative look. "Maybe I could find someone to take my place on the *Wave Walker* that weekend. But I'm not sure I want to be up on stage taking a trip down memory lane."

"It's only a small part of the program. Sheila told me Barb intends to get practically everyone in the class up on the stage at one time or another. If you really think you can make it, I'll add your name to the reservation list."

"I'd better check with a couple of people first," he told her, and Maggie wondered if that meant he might bring a date. The image of Joni at the Blue Goose immediately came to mind.

"You can let me know. We still have a couple of weeks before we have to turn in the final count to the hotel staff." Noticing that Jack had swallowed the final sip of his brandy, she asked, "Can I get you another?"

He shook his head as he handed her the empty glass. "I'd better get going. I've got a charter that leaves at six tomorrow morning." He stood and, reluctantly, Maggie rose, too.

"Thanks again for dinner, and for showing me Half Moon." She gave him a beguiling smile. "I had a wonderful time, Jack Brannigan."

He lightly brushed her lips with his. "You're welcome, Maggie Stewart." For several moments he stood gazing into her eyes, and Maggie wished she knew the reason for the wistfulness there.

"It was fun being a couple of teenagers again," she said to break the silence.

His knuckles gently grazed her cheek. "I know one thing. If we had to do it over again I wouldn't let adolescent peer pressure keep our paths from crossing."

"There were over four hundred kids in our class, Jack. It would have been impossible to know every one of them," she reasoned.

He sighed. "I suppose you're right, but I have to confess. Before I filled out that alumni questionnaire, I dug out my old yearbook. As I sat down and looked at all the pictures of our classmates, I was amazed at how many of them were strangers to me."

"I know. I felt the same way when I saw all those rows of pictures. Who knows why we chose the friends we did back then?'' She shrugged her shoulders help-lessly.

"Part of it had to do with proximity. If we had been biology lab partners things might have turned out a lot differently,'' he said with a grin. "I just never had the opportunity to get close to you.''

"What about gym class?'' she couldn't resist asking.

"Gym?'' he quirked an eyebrow. "If I remember correctly, we didn't have coed physical education back then.''

"No, but we did have the session on square dancing where the girls joined the boys in the gymnasium.''

"And you were in my session?'' His expression held disbelief.

"I was your partner!'' she said with mock indignation. "Or at least I was for one day. Mrs. Flynn, the gym teacher, put us together when your regular partner was out sick and mine had a sprained ankle.''

"You're kidding me, right?''

"Uh-uh. It's true. Unfortunately your partner returned the very next day and when Mrs. Flynn gave you the choice of me or sexy Suzie...''

"Sexy Suzie?'' he interrupted with a laugh.

"You don't remember her?'' When he shook his head, she said, "Then I don't feel so bad that you chose her over me.''

This time his sigh was almost one of agony. "I can't believe I'd pass you by, Maggie.''

She simply lifted her eyebrows and shook her head in feigned admonition. She didn't tell him that at the time, her heart had nearly broken in two and that it had taken her a week to get over the rejection. "'Tis true, Jack.''

"All I can say is I made some pretty foolish mistakes when I was in high school." Although his tone was light, there was a hint of gravity in it as well.

His words stayed with her long after he was gone. Once more she pulled out her yearbook, but this time her fingers sought Gina Loring's name in the index. Was she one of the foolish mistakes he was referring to? Until now, she had successfully pushed all of the old rumors concerning Jack Brannigan to the back of her mind. But now, she was beginning to wonder just what the teenage Jack had been like. The Jack she had spent the evening with couldn't have been the boy who had gotten a girl pregnant and then walked away from his responsibility.

People change, she told herself. Yet there was a strange feeling in the pit of her stomach at the knowledge that he *could* be the father of Gina's illegitimate child.

She snapped the book shut and closed her eyes.

CHAPTER EIGHT

DURING THE FOLLOWING WEEK Maggie often found her thoughts returning to Jack's relationship with Gina Loring, especially when she received Gina's questionnaire for the reunion book and saw what was written on line four—the space provided for listing the names and ages of the graduate's children. Gina listed three names, but it was the first one that captured Maggie's attention—nineteen-year-old Jack.

It was on that same day Jack phoned with the news that he had found someone to take his place on the *Wave Walker* and would be able to attend the reunion after all. Maggie couldn't help but wonder if he knew that Gina was flying home for the event. When he invited her out to dinner, she decided she would casually mention the names of some of their former classmates who had already registered and slip Gina's name into the conversation.

However, once she was actually seated across from him, she discovered it was easier said than done. Even though he appeared to be interested in hearing which of their classmates had registered for the reunion, Maggie found herself reluctant to mention Gina. As much as she wanted to observe Jack's reaction to the other woman's name, she wondered if maybe it wasn't better that she leave the subject alone. After all, Jack owed her no explanations about his past.

Yet she wanted explanations. Twenty years may have passed, but she wasn't any less curious as to what had happened between him and Gina during their senior year. It was obvious that Gina hadn't given her baby up for adoption as everyone in school had suspected would be the case. But then she hadn't married Jack, either, which was what the romantically idealistic Maggie had always hoped would be Gina's fate.

However, Gina had married and lived happily ever after, according to her own words on the questionnaire. It might not have been the storybook route, but she was still married to the same man, which was more than could be said for a lot of her classmates. As the reunion questionnaires continued to trickle in throughout the week, it came as no surprise to Maggie that divorce had been a part of many of their lives. It had been a part of hers.

One day, her thoughts turned to Brian. At the time of their wedding, everyone had thought they would have the perfect storybook marriage. They had been the talk of Washington—the handsome young congressional aide and his lovely bride. Maggie sighed wistfully at the memories of those early months of marital bliss. After all the pain the divorce had created, she often forgot that they had been happy in the beginning, that they had been in love at one time.

But it was easy to forget. Probably because it took more than love to make a marriage work. It took fidelity, respect, trust and a whole list of other things Maggie had always taken for granted as being components of love. Maybe that was why she was now having difficulty accepting that she and Brian had once been in love; in her book, love was synonymous with all those other things. She shook her head to clear away the unwanted thoughts that always managed to cloud any fond memories of her marriage. She tried instead to focus her attention on the statistics she was compiling for the reunion book.

Sadly, she realized that that was all her marriage was—a statistic in the wrong column. She decided to put aside her marital status calculations and move on to another category. She was in the process of figuring out what percentage of their class still lived within a twenty-five mile radius of the high school when Jack called to ask her for another date.

"Did I catch you at a bad time?" he asked in a voice Maggie was coming to recognize as deliciously seductive.

"No, I'm glad you called," she said warmly, a smile spreading across her face. "I need an excuse to take a break. Sheila practically has me doing a demographic study of the alumni."

"Are you going to be tied up this weekend or can I invite you to watch a sailing regatta on Mille Lacs?"

"A sailing regatta! Oh, Jack, that sounds like fun. When is it?"

"All day Sunday. A friend of mine who's racing has invited a few people over to watch from his place on the lake. Hopefully he'll win and it'll be a real celebration."

Maggie's heart was thumping madly in her chest. "You don't have to work?"

"Nope, I'm covered," he said, his voice sounding sexy and promising. "What about you? Are you free?"

"Yes, and I'd love to come. What time?" She hoped her voice didn't sound as anxious as her heart felt.

"I told John we'd be at his place around twelve-thirty."

"What should I bring?"

"If it's warm you'll probably want to have your swimsuit along. Last year it was quite hot and most of the guests made use of his pool."

"He lives on the lake and he has a pool?" A thread of disbelief edged her voice.

Jack chuckled. "John believes Mille Lacs has two purposes—fishing and sailing. Swimming he does in a pool where the water's warm and there aren't any leeches."

"Oh, that's right—leeches." She made a face. "I think I'm going to like your friend John."

"I'm sure the feeling will be mutual," Jack said, and felt a strange lump of annoyance. John Callen liked nearly every woman he set his eyes on and that thought didn't exactly sit well with Jack. He could just imagine the leering look in his friend's eyes when he showed up at the party with Maggie.

"Where should we meet?" Maggie wanted to know.

"How about at the big fish around noon?"

"Great. I'll see you then."

Maggie knew the spot he referred to. In the center of Garrison at a roadside rest stop stood a statue of a big walleye, designating Lake Mille Lacs as the walleye capital of the world. Tourists often stopped to admire the view of Lake Mille Lacs while children would pose for pictures beside the walleye.

Maggie thought the rest of the week couldn't pass quickly enough. She found herself anticipating her date with Jack as though she were a schoolgirl. At first she wasn't going to mention it to Sheila, but when her best friend suggested they get together on Sunday to work on the reunion book, Maggie told her about her plans to see him.

"Maggie Stewart, do I detect a hint of romance in the air?" Sheila asked as they sat opposite each other at the kitchen table folding flyers and stuffing them in envelopes.

"I'd be lying if I said I wasn't attracted to him, Sheila. The jury's still out on whether or not it can be called a romance."

"Maybe you'll be able to convince him to come to the reunion."

There was a small pause, then Maggie said, "He is coming."

"He is?" Sheila gave her a shrewd look as she stopped folding. "It must be because of you. I remember how opposed he was to the idea when we were on his boat."

"I doubt that the reason he changed his mind has anything to do with me," Maggie told her, although privately she was hoping it did. She shoved another stack of flyers in Sheila's direction. "Jack told me Barb got in touch with him about that stupid part in the program when she's going to have the Snow Daze royalty up onstage."

"You haven't told him about what we did, have you?" she asked anxiously.

"Of course not, but I have to tell you, Sheila, I feel a bit awkward every time the topic comes up."

"This probably sounds ridiculous, but I've got this awful feeling that somehow it's all going to come out during the reunion and we're going to end up looking like a couple of first-class idiots." Sheila leaned back in her chair. "I mean, can't you just see all the work we've been putting into this thing going up in smoke because of someone discovering what we did twenty years ago?"

"Relax, Sheila. If no one has suspected anything up to this point, I don't think you need to worry," Maggie wrapped a rubber band around a stack of envelopes all ready to be mailed.

"That's just the problem. I think someone does suspect."

That caught Maggie's attention. "Who?"

"Miss Boogstrom. She called me the other day to tell me she's coming to the reunion."

"She is? I thought she had retired and was living in that senior citizen apartment complex over in Superior."

"She is, but she wants to come to the reunion. And to make matters worse, Barb Milton has asked her to announce the names of the Snow Daze royalty during the program. I keep envisioning this horrible scene where Boogie is up at the lectern reading off the names and suddenly in the middle of the program she stops." Sheila jumped up and began gesturing dramatically with her arms.

"I can see it all now. Just when she's supposed to announce the names of the king and queen, the spotlight suddenly shifts to our table. And then Boogie jabs her skinny, wrinkled finger in our direction and hollers at us in that horrible nasal tone we always hated to hear when we were in school."

In a falsetto voice, Sheila exclaimed, "There they are! Sheila Wilson and Maggie Stewart. The two little girls who made a mockery of our Snow Daze by fixing the contest so that Rob Michaels wore the crown instead of Jack Brannigan. After all these years, they are finally going to pay!" Sheila's face contorted in horror before she collapsed in a heap on her chair, her cheeks crimson.

Maggie couldn't help but laugh at Sheila's impersonation of their former teacher. "You, my dear friend, are the one who has been working too hard. For one thing, even if Boogie does know the truth—which she doesn't—she certainly wouldn't choose the trip down memory lane program as the place to make the truth known. Think of how embarrassing it would be for Rob Michaels." She licked an envelope and pressed the flap shut.

Sheila brushed her hair from her forehead and sighed. "You're probably right. I guess I am overreacting a bit. But I can't help feeling a little guilty, especially since I've met Jack and seen what a great guy he is. Doesn't it bother you, Maggie?"

"Yes, it does," she admitted. "And several times I've been tempted to tell him the truth . . ."

"Oh, Maggie, you wouldn't really do it, would you?" Sheila interrupted, shooting forward to lean over the table in supplication.

"Maybe then we could quit worrying about it. It's hardly worthy of all the anxiety it's creating in us."

"Maybe it isn't, but I have spent the past six months getting ready for this reunion. You know how much hard work and effort has gone into making sure everything goes smoothly. We can't let anything spoil it." Her last statement carried a warning.

"Nothing's going to spoil it," Maggie assured her. "And despite the feelings of regret I have, I really don't see what good it would do to own up to something we did in high school."

Her words seemed to put Sheila at ease. "I think you're right. Besides, we need to consider how Rob Michaels would feel if we were to make such an announcement after all these years. And there isn't any point in bringing it up with Jack—not if this is just a summer fling."

Hearing Sheila refer to her relationship with Jack as a summer fling had Maggie questioning her feelings for him as she drove to Garrison Sunday morning. She had never been one for flings of any sort, not even when she was in college and the era of the flower child saw most of her friends flitting like butterflies from lover to lover. Unable to give away her emotions lightly, she had never been successful at cultivating casual relationships.

After her failed marriage with Brian, she had been reluctant to become involved with another man, and she could count on one hand the number of times she had gone out on what could be classified as dates. Now she found herself attracted to a man, and enjoying the sensation, especially since she hadn't thought she'd ever feel such pleasure again.

The closer she got to Garrison, the faster her heart began to beat. When she drove past the big fish and caught a glimpse of Jack in the midst of a group of people, butterflies began to flutter in her stomach as well.

Although a good crowd had gathered for the sailing event, there weren't as many cars as there had been fo the fishing tournament, and Maggie managed to find a spot not far from the concrete concourse sporting the giant fish. Before getting out of the station wagon, she checked her makeup and hair in the visor mirror.

Jack had been watching for her arrival, and separated himself from the men he had been talking to as soon as he saw the blue station wagon pull into the parking lot. As he crossed Highway 169 to greet her, Maggie saw that he was wearing white trousers and a nautical polo shirt. The wind was tugging at his hair, but it was obvious that he had been to a barber since the last time she had seen him. The dark brown hair still teased the collar of his shirt, but the top and sides had been cut shorter. His eyes were hidden by a pair of dark sunglasses.

"Am I late?" Maggie asked, noticing several colorful sails already adrift on the lake.

"Not at all. The competition's taking place in Wigwam Bay, which is just up the road from here. We can take my Jeep." He gently led her across the parking lot to where the Wagoneer sat outside the Blue Goose.

When they were seated inside, he leaned across the seat and gave her a kiss. "I'm glad you came, Maggie."

"Me, too," was all she seemed capable of responding, because her lips were still tingling from their brief but sensual encounter with his.

"It's going to be a beautiful day for sailing" he told her as he started the engine and pulled out onto the road. "There's just enough wind and plenty of sunshine. Did you bring your swimsuit?"

"It's in my bag." Automatically her hands shifted to the canvas tote bag on her lap.

Jack glanced at the canvas bag and immediately began to conjure up images of what her swimsuit would look like. She was wearing a large, baggy white top that hung low off her shoulders and despite fitting loosely, couldn't hide the voluptuous curves beneath it. When he had climbed in beside her he had caught the flowery fresh scent of her cologne, which even now, despite the windows being opened, filled the inside of the Jeep. She had pulled her red hair away from her face and secured it with a bright green scarf tied in a bow, the color of which matched her long, gauzy skirt. She looked simple, yet sexy, and he wished now more than ever that he hadn't told John he would be at the party.

Silently he berated himself for allowing John to talk him into viewing the race from his place. He should have taken Maggie out on the *Wave Walker* and watched the race from the water where they would have been alone. They could have brought their own food and drinks and spent time really getting to know each other. Now he was going to have to share her with a couple of dozen other people, and the thought brought him no joy. Especially when many of those people were single men who classified any single woman as fair game.

"Is anything wrong?" she asked, which made him realize that he had been frowning.

He quickly beamed a smile in her direction then said, "I was just thinking that John's probably invited quite a crowd of people and you're not going to know any of them. Maybe it would be better if we skipped the party."

"Oh, no," she insisted. "I want to go—really. In my line of work, I'm quite used to walking into a roomful of strangers. Often times they don't even speak the same language as I do. It'll be nice to be with Minnesotans again, and I'm looking forward to meeting your friends."

Jack suppressed a groan of disappointment and pulled the Jeep into a long, tree-lined gravel driveway that led to a large A-framed home on the northwest shore of the lake. Already, half a dozen cars were parked beside the tennis court located to the right side of the driveway. Noise could be heard coming from a fenced area to their left, and Maggie could only surmise that it was where the swimming pool was located.

"Sounds like the party's already started," she commented as they climbed out of the Jeep.

Immediately Jack came to her side and put a possessive hand in the middle of her back as they crossed the cement patio leading to the pool area. With his other hand, he pushed open the tall wooden gate and ushered Maggie inside. The first thing she noticed was a row of bikini-clad bodies stretched out on loungers trimming the edge of the pool. There were several people splashing around in the water, and from what Maggie could tell, they were all younger than she. Several round tables with umbrellas dotted the perimeter of the pool and Reggae music was piped through a speaker system.

One of the bikini-clad bodies rose from a lounge chair and started toward them. As she came closer Maggie recognized the blonde as Joni, the bartender from the Blue Goose. One look at her hot-pink neoprene swimsuit told Maggie that it wasn't only T-shirts that Joni wore too small. The two-piece swimsuit barely covered her generous curves, leaving one with the impression that certain parts of her were in danger of falling out, should she get excited.

It was obvious by the gleam in her eyes that Joni was excited to see Jack, and Maggie held her breath as the younger woman reached out and grabbed his arm.

"Jack! We were beginning to worry that you weren't coming," she cooed, batting false eyelashes heavy with mascara. Judging by the amount of makeup Joni wore and the jewelry flashing around her neck, wrists and ankles, the swimsuit's sole purpose was for fashion.

Jack discreetly disengaged his arm from Joni's hands and pulled Maggie close. "Joni, I'd like you to meet Maggie Stewart. Maggie, this is Joni."

"Joni and I have already met," Maggie said with a warm smile.

"Oh, that's right," Joni added, giving Maggie another cautious appraisal. "You came into the Blue Goose looking for Jack because you went to high school together." She had sidled up to Jack and was acting as though he were her date, not Maggie's.

"Where's John?" Jack asked, glancing around.

"He's already out on the lake. I'm supposed to see that everyone's taken care of until he gets back. Can I get you a drink?"

Jack glanced at his watch. "We'll get our own, thanks," he told her with a gentle wink. "Why don't you make sure everyone realizes that the race will be starting shortly."

"Oh, yeah. I'd better see that there are enough chairs out on the lawn." She wiggled the tips of two of her fingers in a goodbye gesture before disappearing around the side of the house.

As Maggie and Jack made their way to the portable bar beneath a lime-green striped awning, he introduced her to several of the guests and Maggie was surprised to learn that most of the people at the party were not local residents, but weekend visitors from the Twin Cities of Minneapolis and St. Paul.

John Callen, Maggie learned, was a general contractor who lived in Minneapolis but spent his weekends at the lake. She met a wide assortment of people, all of whom seemed to be quite interesting, including a sales representative for a textile manufacturer who found Maggie's position as a trade negotiator more entertaining than the sailing regatta, much to Jack's dismay.

Maggie fit in beautifully, and Jack saw firsthand how she had attained such success as a diplomat. Not only was she a good listener with a compassionate nature, but her knowledge of foreign economies and international trade drew respect and admiration from those listening. She managed to fit in to the eclectic crowd better than he did, looking perfectly at ease sitting on a canvas deck chair as she watched the multicolored sails glide past.

As it turned out, John's party did turn into a victory celebration, and as Jack expected, his good friend's eyes did bulge with interest when he was introduced to Maggie. It didn't take long before John had taken her under his wing and was steering her away from the small group of people surrounding Jack, a group consisting primarily of men interested in the subject dearest to Jack's heart—fishing.

Normally Jack would have been content to sit and talk fishing, but today he didn't want to be debating the pros and cons of the catch-and-release program or answering endless questions as to which lure worked best in which lake. Not while John was talking with Maggie. From the way she was smiling, it was apparent that she found whatever it was he was talking about amusing. When she disappeared into the house with him, Jack felt a flare of irritability, and it took all of his willpower not to follow them inside.

He tried to concentrate on what was being said around him, but his eyes kept returning to the glass patio doors where just minutes—but what now seemed like hours—earlier, John had disappeared with Maggie. It was only as he stood staring at the house waiting for them to reappear, that he admitted to himself the reason for his irritability. He was jealous. It was a sobering thought, for it meant that he cared for Maggie more than he was willing to admit. When she emerged through the patio door alone, her eyes sought his. As if by silent communication, they both started toward each other.

"That is quite a house," she said as he met her halfway across the thick green lawn.

"Did you get the grand tour?" he asked, trying not to visualize John's hand touching her as he guided her through the house.

"It's beautiful, but when you told me a friend of yours had a place on the lake, I was expecting something like that." She pointed to a cozy little log cabin barely visible through the row of pines on the edge of John's property.

"This is actually more of a year-round home than a cabin, as you probably gathered from seeing the inside. John's got all the conveniences of his home in the city."

"And a few more. I have to admit, I've never seen a bathtub with a permanent table fixed in the middle set with six drink glasses and plastic straws." She chuckled.

"John's bathroom is an entertainment center. Some people prefer formal dinner parties. John likes to invite a few close friends over for a soak."

"He's an informal sort of a guy," she remarked casually. "Judging by this party, you'd never guess that when he's not here, he's building skyscrapers."

"Unlike me, he drops out of the corporate world on weekends," he said, sounding as though he was trying to be sarcastic.

"Have you known him long?"

He gave her a curious glance and was about to answer when Joni called out to them.

"Come on, you two. Get your suits on. Water volleyball starts in fifteen minutes and we need two more bodies."

So much for my theory that the swimsuit hasn't seen any water, Maggie thought to herself as she watched Joni dart away without waiting for any answers.

"What do you think?" Jack was looking at her expectantly. "Are you up for volleyball? I should warn you. In John's water games, competition can get pretty fierce."

In more ways than one, Maggie thought to herself as a couple of bikini-clad women headed for the pool. "I'm not sure about playing water volleyball, but a swim would be nice."

"Maybe we ought to go someplace a little less crowded," Jack suggested, glancing around the concrete pool area. "I know of a lake that has no leeches lurking on its sandy beaches. And there's no chlorine—just clear, cool water."

Maggie looked at the sea of scantily clad bodies and felt a wave of relief at his suggestion. "Are you sure you don't mind leaving?"

In answer he led her over to the edge of the pool where John sat with his legs dangling in the water. Despite his friend's protest that the party was just beginning and they hadn't even eaten, they managed to say their goodbyes and take their leave without too much of a commotion. Maggie was grateful that Joni was nowhere in sight when they made their departure. Within a few minutes, they were back in the Jeep and driving along the highway bordering Lake Mille Lacs.

"Where are we going?" Maggie asked when he turned off the scenic route and began driving away from the resort area.

"Ever been to Lake Magda?" He answered her question with a question, closing the windows with a touch of his finger to keep the dust from coming inside the Jeep.

When she responded negatively, he added, "Ever *heard* of Lake Magda?"

Again she shook her head, saying no again and chuckling. The road grew narrower as the Jeep drove deeper into a grove of birch trees, and the sun became shadowed in the dense woods.

"Actually Magda's only one of its names. I think it's had at least half a dozen or so, including Long Lake and String Lake," Jack explained.

"String Lake?" Maggie raised an eyebrow quizzically.

"You'll see how inappropriate that name is in about two minutes. Magda was the wife of the man who originally owned the farm that encompasses seventy-five percent of the land surrounding the lake."

The road angled sharply, then suddenly came to an abrupt end. Lake Magda sat before them like an enormous blue gem surrounded by lush green farmland.

"See what I mean? It hardly looks like a piece of string, does it?"

Maggie smiled at the sight of the nearly perfectly round lake. Then Jack reversed gears and backed the Jeep into a driveway Maggie hadn't even noticed until now. Split cedar-rail fencing lined the driveway and she realized they weren't at a public beach but someone's home—a home, that although not quite as large as John's, was an architectural beauty. It looked like a miniature ski chalet set among the birch and pine trees.

As Maggie climbed out of the Jeep she noticed the wooden sign swinging from two cedar posts. It read, Brannigan's.

"Welcome to my world, Maggie," Jack said softly.

CHAPTER NINE

"IT DOESN'T have all the luxuries John's place has and it's small, but then I don't have to put up with the traffic and all the weekenders, either," Jack told Maggie when he had finished showing her around the chalet-styled home. "The only other residents live across the lake— a Finnish farmer named Henry Saarinen and his family."

"It's so quiet I feel as though I should be whispering," Maggie said softly as they stepped out onto the wooden deck at the front of the house. Two loons were playing in the water several hundred feet from the shore, their distinctive calls echoing in the silence. "This could have been the set for *On Golden Pond*."

Jack smiled appreciatively. "Come and I'll show you something Henry Fonda didn't have on his golden pond." He took her hand in his and led her around the side of the house and down the steps out to a fenced pasture behind the garage. When they reached the gate on the four-rail fence, he unhooked the latch and gestured for Maggie to precede him.

"I think Dixie's probably in the shade," he said, leading her across the pasture in the direction of a small wooden shed with a lean-to attached to its side. It was painted the same cocoa brown as his home, and even had a row of decorative gingerbread trim across its gable.

"Dixie?" Maggie raised her eyebrows inquisitively, but Jack's only answer was a mysterious grin. Expecting to see perhaps a pony, she was surprised to discover Dixie was a dark brown llama with a long, white graceful neck and doelike brown eyes. She had been lying down in the shade of the lean-to, but upon their arrival and the sound of Jack's voice, she had risen and had come over to greet them, sniffing Maggie.

"Mind your manners, Dixie," Jack warned, petting the animal's long slender neck.

"Can I pet her or does she need to get to know me first?" Maggie asked, instantly smitten by the affectionate animal.

"Go ahead," Jack urged. "She loves attention and she's as gentle as a lamb. If she blows in your face, it's only because she's trying to be friendly."

"Well, aren't you the loveliest creature I've ever seen!" Maggie gushed, brushing her hand over the thick woolly coat. "Is she the only llama you have?" she asked Jack, looking around.

"Yes, which is why she loves so much attention. Llamas are very social creatures, and she'd be much happier if I had a companion for her—preferably another llama but she'd settle for a sheep or a goat."

"Of course she would. No one likes to be alone, do they, Dixie?" Maggie cooed at the gentle creature, enchanted by her new friend. Jack watched as Dixie responded with her usual amiability to Maggie's attention. "Can I feed her an apple or something? What does she eat?"

"You mean besides tree bark, twigs and anything else in her path?" Jack answered wryly. "You can give her a handful of oats. There's some over there in that bin." He pointed to a wooden box in the lean-to.

Maggie walked over to the long narrow container and reached for a handful of the feed, only to discover that Dixie was right behind her, ready to stick her head in beside Maggie's hand.

"Oh, look . . . she's hungry," she marveled, allowing the llama to lick the oats out of her hand.

"She's going to be your friend for life. She didn't even have to do anything to earn that treat."

"Well, she deserves special treats," Maggie said, hugging the animal to her. "Just for being so sweet. How did you ever end up with such a wonderful creature?"

"She belonged to Jill," he said quietly, his grin fading.

"Your wife?" Maggie gently probed.

"Mmm-hmm. Shortly before her thirtieth birthday we were on our way to see some friends in North Dakota when we noticed a billboard advertisement for a llama farm near Fergus Falls. Jill was a great one for stopping at out-of-the-ordinary places and, as usual, she persuaded me to take a look. As soon as she set eyes on Dixie, she fell in love with her, and before I knew it, we were the proud owners of a three-hundred-pound llama." He shook his head reflectively. "It didn't matter that we didn't have a place to keep her or a trailer to transport her in."

"You didn't have all of this?" Maggie asked, waving her arm extensively to include the small shed and lean-to.

"We didn't even have the house. At the time I was still dividing my time between New York and Minneapolis. Officially my office was in New York, but Jill hated living there, so I tried to do most of my work out of the Minneapolis branch. That way we could keep an apartment in Minnesota, which is what she always wanted, since her family all lived in this area.''

"So what did you do with Dixie?''

"Henry Saarinen, the Finnish farmer I told you about, offered to board her for us. We had already purchased the land from Henry with the intention of building a summer home, but there never seemed to be enough time to have the plans drawn and get construction underway. It was because of Dixie that we finally made the time and got started. Before ground was even broken for the house, though, Jill insisted that the workmen build the shed and put up the fence.''

"Now that I've met Dixie, I guess I can understand her sentiment,'' Maggie said with an understanding nod.

"Unfortunately, work never did get started on the house. That summer Comcor pulled their branch office out of Minneapolis, sending me back to New York.''

"And Jill had to leave Dixie behind?''

"Since she had just signed a teaching contract for the next school year, she decided to stay in our apartment in Minneapolis while I commuted on weekends. I had an offer from an advertising agency in Minneapolis, but at the time I didn't think it would be wise for me to leave Comcor. I was too close to reaching all the goals I had set for myself.''

"Did you reach all your goals?''

"Professionally, yes.'' There was a faraway look on his solemn face as though he were remembering the personal goals he hadn't attained. "Unfortunately it didn't seem to matter after Jill died.''

"Is she the reason you dropped out of the corporate world, Jack?'' Maggie asked softly.

He sighed and averted his gaze. "It's true that her death caused me to do a lot of soul-searching. Ever since I can remember I had this idea in my head that I was going to work damn hard so that by the time I was forty, I wouldn't ever have to prove myself to anyone again. Well, I did work hard and I don't need to prove anything ever again."

"And you're happy living the life of a professional fisherman?" she probed in the direct manner he was coming to expect from her.

He shrugged. "It's been so long since I've been truly happy, Maggie, I'm not sure I'd recognize real happiness if it jumped up and bit me in the face. I can honestly say I don't miss spending every waking minute being obsessed with my work—which is what I was doing when I was in the corporate world."

Maggie had stopped stroking Dixie and the llama was moving back over to the shade, but neither Jack nor she seemed to notice.

"I think work's more likely to become an obsession if it's a job you truly enjoy." She gazed at him probingly.

He gave her a wry grin and said smugly, "I know what you're thinking, Maggie."

"You do?" she asked skeptically.

"Yeah, I can hear it in your tone of voice. You think the only reason I left advertising was that I lost my wife and I'm hiding away here in the wilderness. And I'd wager that you think I'd be happier back in the rat race in New York."

"You were good in New York, Jack," she told him, not bothering to deny his assumptions.

"I'm not doing so badly as a fishing pro, either," he reminded her. "You know, it's too hot to be arguing the merits of corporate America in this pasture. How about that swim I promised you?''

Maggie looked over to where the sparkling blue water glinted in the afternoon sun. ''You don't think the loons will mind if we join them?''

''They're used to my company,'' he told her as they started back toward the lake. ''You can use my room to change. Just come on down to the dock when you're ready.''

When Jack had shown her around the house, Maggie had only caught a glimpse of the bedroom. Now that she had a few minutes to herself, she studied the place curiously, admiring the wildlife art that adorned the walls. There was just a hint of Jack's musky scent lingering in the air, which made being in his room and seeing his personal things almost an intimate experience.

When she had changed into her one-piece turquoise swimsuit, her eyes automatically sought out the mirror on the dresser. Not only did she catch her own reflection, but she saw a portrait on the bedside table.

Maggie turned around and crossed the room to pick up the five-by-seven-inch photograph resting on the wooden nightstand. It was a picture of a lovely, youthful-looking woman with long blond hair, blue eyes and a dazzling smile. There was something familiar about the face, and it was only after she set the photo back down that she realized why. There had been an identical photograph on John Callen's fireplace mantel. Automatically Maggie's eyes searched the room for other photographs, but there were none. *It must be Jill,* she silently surmised, *Or is it?*

Suddenly it occurred to her that there could be other women in his life. After all, Jill had been gone for almost two years. Even though it was obvious that her death had changed his life dramatically, that didn't necessarily mean he was still grieving over her loss. Grabbing her towel, she ignored the temptation to look for any signs of a woman's presence in his life and headed toward the beach, thinking as she walked through the house furnished in earth tones that it looked as though a man had decorated the place.

When she reached the dock, she saw that Jack had shed his clothes for a pair of navy swim trunks. He stood with a towel draped around his shoulders, and Maggie could see that his entire body was a golden bronze.

"I thought you'd be in the water by now," she said, trying not to feel self-conscious while his eyes did a thorough study of her body.

"I thought it might be easier if we took the plunge together," he said, smiling at her with a tenderness that made her skin tingle.

"Are you trying to tell me the water's cold?"

"In May it's cold. In July it's refreshing."

Maggie slipped her thong off her left foot and dipped her toes in. "Brrr. Are you sure it's July?"

Jack dropped his towel on the wooden bench on the end of the dock and said, "What do you want to do? Wade in gradually from the shore or take the boat out to the raft? It's not deep enough to dive in from here."

"Take the boat."

Jack smiled and winked. "My kind of swimmer." He climbed inside the rowboat bobbing beside the dock, then offered her a hand. Putting her thong back on and taking the seat in the bow, she watched as Jack settled himself on the middle strip of wood and began rowing them out into the lake. It didn't take much effort for him to move the boat across the nearly placid water, yet with each stroke of the oars Maggie could see the muscles tighten in his arms. It was only a matter of minutes before they were at the swimming raft and Jack was securing the rowboat to its side.

"It's deep enough for diving from here, but if you swim in about ten feet you should be able to touch bottom," he told her as they stood side by side on the edge of the raft. "You ready?"

She kicked off her thongs again and let her towel fall in a heap beside them. "You're sure there are no leeches?" She gave him an apprehensive glance.

"Honest." He held his hand up as though he were taking an oath. "I've never even seen a teeny one in Lake Magda. Besides, even in Lake Mille Lacs they're not out in deep water but near the shore. They cling to rocks, and as you saw, I've got all sand on my shoreline—no rocks."

"Okay." She gave him a trusting smile then moved closer to the edge of the raft until she was standing beside him. "On the count of three. One...two..."

At three they simultaneously hit the water in nearly perfect synchronization, surfacing within a couple of feet of each other seconds later.

"Too cold?" Jack asked when she came up gasping for air.

"No, it feels wonderful!" She tipped her head back into the water so that her hair fell away from her face.

"Want to swim out to that island?" He gestured with his head toward a small outcrop of rocks.

Maggie squinted as the sun glared off the water. "How far is it?"

"Probably the equivalent of about ten laps in a pool."

"I should be able to make that." She started to swim back to the raft. "Let's dive from the raft first, though, okay?"

Jack followed her up the metal ladder, unable to resist staring at the dripping wet flesh on her thighs. It didn't help that her swimsuit had crept up, allowing him a tantalizing glimpse of a rounded cheek. When she turned around to speak to him, he knew he was going to have to avert his eyes, because the front of her swimsuit was clinging like a wet T-shirt, outlining her generous curves and emphasizing her nipples. Before his swimsuit revealed his reaction to hers, he quickly stepped over to the opposite side of the raft and looked out across the water. Shielding his eyes with his palm, he willed his body not to think about how delectably sensuous she looked.

First it had been her top that had tantalized him, looking as though it could easily fall off her shoulders. Now it was her swimsuit, rising in provocative distraction.

"We should jump from this side," he told her, keeping his eyes focused on the rocks a short distance away. "It isn't as far away as it seems. Once we've gone about three-quarters of the way, we'll reach the sandbar that surrounds the island. You can see the buoys marking its location." He didn't look at her again until they were both back in the water and swimming side by side, matching each other's strokes.

By the time they reached the island, which as Jack had said, consisted of several large rocks, Maggie knew that she had overestimated her strength. Exhausted, she climbed up onto one of the rocks and said breathlessly, "Now what do we do?"

"We make like a couple of seals and bask in the sun," he said with a chuckle, turning his front side up to the sun as he flattened himself against a rock.

"That sounds wonderful," she said, nearly collapsing onto a boulder. "I didn't realize how out of shape I was."

Suddenly realizing how worn out she really was, Jack said in a concerned voice, "I'm sorry, Maggie. I had forgotten that you're home this summer recuperating. When you're ready to go back, I'll swim ahead and get the boat."

"No, I'm fine, Jack. Honest." She held up her hand and gave him a big grin. "At least I will be once I've had a few minutes to catch my breath."

And she was right. Within a few minutes her breathing had returned to normal and she was able to climb up onto the largest rock. "This is really a beautiful lake. It was worth the swim out here just to be able to see nature at its best."

Jack could hardly believe that she had echoed his exact sentiments. He didn't want to stare at the voluptuous figure languidly resting just inches from him, but this time his eyes didn't listen to his brain. She was beautiful, she was intelligent and she was arousing feelings in him he didn't want to be aroused.

Fortunately Maggie didn't seem to notice the effect she was having on him, because her attention had been captured by a string of ducklings inching their way across the water. "Oh, look! Aren't they precious?" she crooned, carefully moving closer to the water to observe the parade of tiny fuzzy bodies trailing after their mother. "I wish we had something to feed them."

Seeing the expression of enchantment on Maggie's face, Jack would have gladly swum to shore and back for some bread crumbs if he thought the ducks would be there upon his return.

"It's peaceful out here," Maggie said when they had paddled out of sight and she was once more stretched out flat against a large rock. "Have you ever noticed how the sky can be so blue it almost looks white?"

Jack agreed, but again he found himself looking not at the sky but at Maggie. He would have been content to lie there the rest of the afternoon watching her, listening to her rediscover the beauty of nature, a beauty she probably had forgotten existed after living in the city for so long.

"Are those thunderheads over there?" she asked, sitting forward and pointing to the northwest where a dark band of clouds with fluffy white tops provided a sharp contrast to the canopy of blue sky overhead.

Jack, too, shot forward, his attention drawn to the sky. "Looks like it's raining north of here, but it should miss us. Although I suppose to be safe, we'd better head back," he said as he reluctantly rose to his feet. "Why don't you wait here and I'll go get the boat?"

Maggie was about to protest, but as she stood she felt the muscles in her legs weaken. Seeing her slight wobble, Jack insisted she wait for him to row the boat out to pick her up.

Touched by his concern, she watched as he quickly swam the distance back to the raft. Twenty years ago she never would have expected the heartthrob of Jefferson High to be so gallant. But then twenty years ago she hadn't known the real Jack Brannigan, only the image created by his classmates. Now she had to question whether Jack was as bad as his reputation had painted him to be, or whether time had simply worked its miracle, maturing a wild, reckless boy into a responsible, caring man.

At any rate, she decided it really didn't matter. She liked Jack Brannigan the man, she enjoyed his company, and she wanted to spend more time with him. Consequently, when he asked her to stay for dinner, she accepted without hesitation.

Using Jack's room to get dressed again, she couldn't keep her eyes from staring at the photo beside his bed. How many women had there been in his life in the past twenty years? She shook her head as though to shake away the thought. Giving herself one last cursory look in the mirror, she straightened her off-the-shoulder top and ran her fingers through her wet curls, then went to find Jack.

She found him in the living room, one arm propped against the window frame as he watched large raindrops splatter against the glass. "It wasn't as far north as I thought," he said, grinning as a loud clap of thunder split the air.

"Summer storms can creep up so fast," Maggie said, suddenly feeling self-conscious about her wet hair. She wished she would have taken the time to reapply her makeup, which by now was only a trace of what it had been earlier in the day. "Is this going to create a problem with dinner?"

He shook his head as he moved away from the window. "We can do the steaks indoors," he told her, motioning for her to follow him into the kitchen.

"What can I do?" she asked as he began pulling food from the refrigerator.

"Which do you prefer—salad or stir-fried vegetables?"

She thought a moment, then said, "Stir-fry."

He smiled. "Good choice. The wok's in the cabinet behind you. I'll pop the potatoes in the microwave and do the steaks."

Maggie didn't know if it was because they had made the dinner together or whether she was so hungry anything would have tasted heavenly, but she was convinced that steak and baked potatoes had never tasted so good as they did on Jack's deck. The summer shower had ended just as quickly as it had begun, allowing them to eat out on the wooden deck at the front of the house. It was a slow, leisurely dinner, filled with laughter and good conversation. The air was sweetened with the smell of summer rain and before they were finished eating, the sun even managed to reappear, creating what Maggie thought was the most beautiful rainbow she had ever seen.

"This really is a wonderful spot, Jack," she told him, her eyes scanning the panoramic view. It was such a romantic, idyllic setting, she found herself wondering if he had shared it with Jill. "Have you lived here long?"

"Not even a year yet." He set his wineglass down and made a mental survey of the place, Maggie's question reminding him of the difficult time he had had moving into the house. "It is a wonderful spot," he said, echoing her sentiments, and silently debated whether he should tell her the house had sat empty for six months before he had been able to face moving in without Jill.

"You're lucky to have so much privacy. So many of the lakes in this region have their shores lined with resorts and summer homes."

"I think Magda's name should be Lost Lake. For some reason, developers haven't discovered Henry's fertile fields. And Henry assures me that as long as there's a Saarinen breathing, there'll be a Saarinen farming his land.''

"How did you manage to convince him to sell you this piece?'' she asked, her wineglass poised halfway to her lips.

"I didn't.'' He leaned back in his chair and sighed.

"You didn't.''

"No, it was Jill. This was her dream—to have a summer home on the lake.''

Maggie noticed the shadows in his eyes, and she reached out to cover his hand with hers. "I'm sorry, Jack. It must have been very painful for you to lose her.''

He looked up from his hands and saw the compassion in her eyes. "I just wish she could have seen how it turned out. The last time she saw it there was sawdust on the floors and fiberglass insulation stuffed between the two-by-fours.''

"I'm sure she would have loved it,'' Maggie said softly.

"That's what John says. He's the one who got her so excited about the place.''

"John?''

"Yes. Jill was his sister. I'm not sure if that means we're still brothers-in-law.'' He shrugged effortlessly. "Not that it matters, for we've been friends since college. It was through John that I met Jill. I was his best man at his wedding.''

"I didn't realize John was married,'' Maggie said, a tiny crease in her brow.

"Divorced . . . twice.'' He held up two fingers. "He's a heck of a nice guy, but marriage material he's not. Jill was always making excuses for him and blaming his ex-wives, but some men are simply better off single. John's one of them."

"I don't think I'd argue with you about that," she murmured dryly.

"He made a pass at you, didn't he?" Before she could reply, he answered his own question. "I should have known he wouldn't be able to resist. Both of his wives have been redheads."

Maggie couldn't help but laugh. "Jack, he didn't make a pass at me, but if he had, I'm sure it wouldn't have been anything I couldn't handle. I'm thirty-seven years old and in my profession, I'm accustomed to dealing with advances. Some of the foreign men I meet at the negotiating table expect all American women to behave like the women on *Dallas*."

The idea of any man making a pass at Maggie was abhorrent to Jack, yet he forced a smile to his lips. "Well, my dear friend John is as smooth as some of those television characters."

Maggie hid her smile. "If anything, I'd say that John was acting protective toward you. This may sound funny, but I think he might have thought that I was the wrong kind of woman for you."

Jack held her gaze for several moments, studying her face. Somewhere deep inside himself he felt a surge of emotion for this woman seated across from him. Her hair had dried in untamed waves, giving her a provocative sophistication despite her casual appearance. How John could possibly think she wasn't the right kind of woman for any man baffled him. He stood and reached for her hands, gently pulling her to her feet.

Quietly he said, "You're the first woman I've taken over to John's house since Jill died."

"That was why you looked so uncomfortable when I was talking to him. You should have said something, Jack, I would have . . ."

He silenced her with a finger on her lips. "That's not the reason I was so uncomfortable." The look he gave her was long and searching; his finger gently nudged her lower lip in a sensuous caress.

"It wasn't?" she whispered, her lip quivering from the gentle touch of his fingertip.

"Uh-uh." His fingers slid over her silky smooth skin to trace the delicate curve of her jaw until his hands framed her face. "If you were going to be talking to anyone, I wanted it to be me," he said, feeling her warm breath mingling with his as his head bent closer to hers. "And if you were going to be laughing into anyone's eyes, I wanted it to be mine."

Maggie trembled and arched against him, irresistibly drawn by the power of his words. Shivers of awareness rippled through her and she felt the sensual awakening in him. She locked her arms around him, loving the strength and hardness of him. Slowly she lifted her head until her lips teasingly brushed his. Her actions drew a ragged breath from Jack.

"Taking you to that party today was difficult for me—not because I didn't want John to see me with you, but because I didn't want to share you with anyone," he whispered against her lips. "All I've wanted to do ever since I saw you step out of that car this afternoon is this."

As sudden as the summer storm that had swept across the lake a short time ago, desire struck with an emotion-shattering quickness. Jack's mouth captured hers in a possessive, hungry kiss that had her lips parting in response to the sweet pressure of his tongue. Like the soft summer rain, his lips dropped a stream of kisses across her cheek until his tongue found the delicate softness of her ear.

"Ah, Maggie," he said, his voice husky with pleasure. "Do you realize what you do to me?" He feathered a line of kisses down the smooth column of her throat until his lips reached the bare skin of her shoulder.

Maggie couldn't speak. She buried her fingers in his thick hair, anticipating the moment when his mouth would return to take possession of lips that were still quivering from his kiss. She knew exactly what she was doing to him, because he was doing the same thing to her, and she loved it. She wanted him to want her, to need her, as much as she ached for him. As if he heard her silent communication, his lips once more found hers while a hand slid inside the baggy white top to grasp a firm breast.

Unexpected sensations created havoc with her breathing as a gnawing sweetness begged for him to fill an emptiness created by lonely nights. As much as she wanted him to do just that, she knew that she wasn't prepared for the reality of loving Jack. Experience told her that if she didn't do something soon, the runaway emotions would have their way. Just as the most exquisite sensation threatened her rationality, she stiffened in his arms.

Instantly Jack sensed her withdrawal, although he wasn't able to release his hold on her until he looked in her eyes and saw the emotion there. She didn't need to tell him that she wanted him just as much as he wanted her—it was all there in her eyes. As was her uncertainty as to whether or not they should have stopped.

"I'm not ready—" she began only to have him cut her off with a finger across her lips.

"I know," he said softly, holding her gaze for what seemed to be an eternity. "You do something to me, Maggie, that no woman's ever been able to do." He sighed and rubbed a hand across the back of his neck. "God, I wish there wasn't a hundred miles separating us. And I hate the thought of you driving such a distance at night."

"Jack, I have to go back," she said as firmly as she could while every nerve in her body was screaming she should stay.

"I know." He took her hands and raised them to his lips. "When can I see you again?"

"Have you got plans for the Fourth of July? My family's having its traditional Independence Day picnic up at Gooseberry Falls. Lots of fried chicken, potato salad and cold beer...a little softball with my cousins and aunts and uncles." She looked up at him in a most appealing way.

"I'm scheduled for a charter, but I'll see if I can't get someone to cover for me. Do they still have the fireworks out on Minnesota Point?"

"Yes. We can see them from our backyard, but it'd be more fun to go down to the point. They're also having a street dance. Maybe we could brush up on some of those old rock tunes they're going to be playing at the reunion."

"Will you go with me, Maggie?" he asked, his eyes holding hers.

For an answer she reached up and kissed him, her lips still warm and slightly swollen, then gave him a husky yes.

CHAPTER TEN

AS IT TURNED OUT, Jack was unable to find anyone to take his charter on the Fourth of July, much to Maggie's dismay. However, by the end of the day her disappointment had changed to relief because the Stewart annual picnic had been anything but a celebration.

The day had started out sunny, but by noon the clouds had moved in along with unseasonably cool air and a steady drizzle that dampened everyone's spirits. Despite her mother's efforts to make the picnic festive, anything that could have gone wrong, did. The cooler with the liquid refreshments had been left at home, one of Maggie's nieces cut her hand on a piece of stray barbed wire, and instead of laughter and encouragement, sounds of anger and disappointment were heard throughout the day.

Even the normally good-natured family softball game became an arena for flaring tempers. At one point, Maggie heard her father yell, "What are you throwing the damn ball for?" in a voice that was strange and frightening to her as well as the younger children. Later, wet and barely speaking to one another, they had all packed up and gone home to dry out in front of the Stewart fireplace and hopefully mend a few fractured feelings.

Karen had taken her daughters home to change their clothes, and while Delores put away the picnic things in the kitchen, Maggie decided the time had come for her to have a serious talk with her father. She found him adding newspaper to a pile of kindling in the fireplace in the family room.

"Only in Duluth can you have a fire on the Fourth of July," she commented wryly, rubbing her hands up and down her arms to take away the chill.

"Get me the matches, will you, dear?" Herb instructed in a voice that reminded Maggie of the gentle father she had loved so dearly as a child.

She reached for the rectangular box on the mantel and handed it to him. "Are Uncle Bert and Aunt Lena coming over to watch the fireworks tonight?"

"Everyone's coming back. They just went home to get some dry clothes," he told her, adjusting the damper on the fireplace. "Hand me the matches, Maggie," he repeated, looking up at her.

"Pop, you've got them in your hand," she reminded him gently.

"What the—" He broke off, slightly confused, then pulled a match from the box and lit the kindling. Maggie took one of the wing chairs in front of the fireplace and watched as her father carefully tended the fire until it was burning evenly.

"There. That ought to do it," he claimed, closing the wire-mesh curtain.

"Come sit, Pop," Maggie urged, patting the leather armchair beside her. "You need to dry out, too."

Herb lowered his large frame into the chair with a slight moan of fatigue. As he stretched his legs out in front of him, he said, "Not the best of holidays, was it?"

"It's hard to pretend you're having fun when there's a cold rain intruding," Maggie offered as an explanation to their disastrous day.

"It's not the first time it's rained on our picnic." He sighed and rubbed a hand across the five-o'clock shadow on his jaw. "I don't know. It seemed as though everyone was snapping at each other."

"Bad weather has a way of bringing out the worst in people," she rationalized, even though she knew that some of the discord was directly attributable to her father.

"I'm sorry I barked at you today, Maggie," he apologized.

There was such a sadness in his face, Maggie had to swallow to relieve the lump in her throat. Touched by his apology, she reached over and squeezed his hand. "It's all right." There was so much compassion and understanding in his face, it gave her the courage to broach the subject of his health. "Pop, there's something I've been wanting to talk about with you." She didn't release his hand, but covered his long, slightly wrinkled fingers with hers.

"This got something to do with that fellow you've been seeing?" he asked with a half smile. His glasses had slipped down on his nose and he was looking at her over their rims.

Maggie couldn't prevent her grin. "Why would you think it has anything to do with Jack?"

"The last time we sat and had a father-daughter talk in front of this fireplace you had just graduated from college and you were telling me you had met this fellow and you hoped I was going to like him."

"Brian." Maggie shook her head reflectively. "Has it really been that long since we've sat in front of the fire and talked?"

"You don't come home as much as we'd like you to, Maggie. Now don't go getting defensive," he said when she opened her mouth to speak. He pulled his hand out from under hers and gently patted her knuckles. "Your mother and I know that you've got a lot of responsibilities with your job. And I, more than anyone else, understand your dedication to your work. You're a workaholic—just like me." There was pride in his voice and Maggie felt herself warming inside. "That doesn't mean I don't miss our talks in front of the fire or our walks along the harbor. Now what is it you want to talk about?"

For a minute Maggie had almost forgotten the reason for their conversation. Listening to her father's deep, soothing voice, she felt as if all of her adult years had slipped away and she was once again a young girl, asking her father's advice on what college to attend, what business program to study. He was her ultimate hero, her ultimate authority. Then she looked over to the fireplace and saw that the poker was not with the rest of the andirons, but stood sticking out of her mother's potted philodendron. Concern furrowed her brow.

"Pop, when's the last time you had a complete physical examination?" she asked.

"A physical? I'm as healthy as an ox." He snorted and made a dismissive gesture with his hand. "You saw what happened when your mother and I went to the health fair. She's the one with high blood pressure." A wry sound rumbled out of his throat.

Sensing his uneasiness with the subject, she chose her next words carefully. "The health fair was pretty basic. I thought it might not be a bad idea for both you and Mom to go in and have thorough checkups."

Herb rose and walked over to stoke the fire, only the poker wasn't with the andirons. Frustrated, he looked around until Maggie jumped up and retrieved it from the potted plant. When she handed it to him, his lips tightened and he quickly averted his eyes from hers.

"Pop, look at me," she demanded as he stood staring into the fire, poker at his side. After a long silence, Herb finally turned to face her.

Maggie's voice was gentle when she spoke. "Physically you may look and feel great, but I think we both know that something isn't right. Maybe it's simply a matter of working too hard—"

"You're just like your mother, aren't you?" he interrupted, shaking off the hand that she had rested on his forearm. The poker clanged as he slammed it back into the andiron stand. "The reason you want me to see a doctor is that you think he'll tell me that I'm getting too old to keep working. That's it, isn't it? You think I should retire." Hazel eyes glared at her in accusation.

"That's not true," Maggie denied, trying to keep her voice level and calm. "I know you love your work and I'd never ask you to give it up. But ever since I've come home I've been noticing that something's not right, Pop."

"What do you mean something's not right?" he said roughly. "I go to work every day, I do my job, I do the yard work, I play golf, I go fishing. I tell you, I feel fine."

"But you don't act fine. You're forgetful—you make silly little mistakes like pouring orange juice instead of milk on your cereal and you just put the fireplace poker in Mom's philodendron.'' She inhaled deeply to steady her voice. ''That's not the behavior of the man I know as my father.''

''So that's it? You don't like the way I'm behaving?'' He looked at her indignantly. ''Well, who are you to criticize me?'' he demanded angrily, his voice rising with each successive word. ''This is my house and anytime you don't like the way your father behaves in it, you can always pack up your things and leave!''

Unprepared to be the recipient of such hostility from her father, Maggie was too stunned to react. Never in her life had he spoken to her in such a manner. For several moments they stood staring at each other, suspicion in his eyes, disbelief in hers. She swallowed back the well of tears that was threatening to rob her of speech. ''I—'' she began, only to be stopped by her mother's appearance in the doorway.

''Maggie, there's someone here to see you. He says his name is Jack.''

Upon seeing Delores, Herb turned his back to Maggie and stared into the fire.

Maggie's lower lip was trembling and she stilled it with her teeth. ''Where is he?''

''In the kitchen,'' Delores answered, glancing from her daughter to her husband and back again.

Without another word to her father, Maggie rushed from the family room and out to the kitchen where Jack stood near the back door. He was dressed in a pair of jeans and a lemony cotton knit sweater that made his broad shoulders look even broader. If it weren't for her mother trailing behind her, Maggie thought she might have been tempted to fling herself against one of those shoulders and cry her eyes out.

Instead she managed a weak grin and said, "I thought you had to work."

Jack took one look at Maggie's pale face and knew something was amiss. "After all the rain this afternoon, the charter canceled. I'm sorry I missed your picnic."

"It wasn't much of a picnic in the rain. We all got wet." She gestured to her still-damp clothes, then, suddenly conscious of her mother lingering in the doorway, she said, "I'm sorry, Mom. I should have introduced you. This is Jack Brannigan. We went to school together at Jefferson High."

"It's all right, Maggie. Jack and I have already introduced ourselves, haven't we?" Delores said with a wink in Jack's direction. "Can I interest you in some coffee? I was just about to pour a cup for Maggie's father."

"No, thanks," Jack politely declined. "I was hoping I could talk Maggie into going down to Minnesota Point to watch the fireworks display with me. I think the rain's finally moved out and other than a little chill in the air, it should be a beautiful night."

"What a lovely idea," Delores crooned, pouring coffee into a heavy blue mug that said Herb's Cuppa on the side. Before taking it in to her husband, she turned to Maggie and said, "You'll want to change your clothes first. You don't want to catch a cold." Then she winked once more at Jack and disappeared through a doorway, calling out over her shoulder, "Have fun!"

"Once a mother always a mother," Maggie said, suddenly feeling inexplicably shy and self-conscious about her disheveled appearance.

Jack smiled in understanding. "What do you think? Do you want to go down to the point or did the Stewart family picnic take all the spunk out of you?"

She bit her lower lip and shook her head. "Let's just say I've already seen a few fireworks."

He took her hands in his and gently asked, "What's wrong, Maggie?"

Sounds of quarreling could be heard coming from the other room and Maggie's eyes met Jack's intensive ones. "I'll tell you about it later. I'm really happy you're here and I'd love to go watch the fireworks, but Mom's right." She looked down at her wrinkled slacks and said, "I'd better change first. Are you sure you don't want some coffee while you wait?"

"Would you mind if I left for a bit and came back?" he asked. "I've got something I should take care of and this way you could take your time and not be rushed."

"No, I don't mind at all," Maggie answered, feeling relieved that she would have time for a hot shower.

"Are you sure you're all right?" he asked, placing his fingertips against her cheek.

She simply nodded and smiled weakly.

He replaced his fingertips with his lips, then said, "I'll see you in about forty-five minutes, okay?" He studied her quietly for a moment, then closed his arms around her, unable to leave her without first holding her close to his heart. Despite her smile and the softness of her kiss, he knew that she was hurting inside, and the knowledge left him with a feeling of helplessness. It also made him realize that his feelings for her ran deeper than he had ever expected they would.

Later, as Maggie stood beneath the spray of hot water, she decided she didn't want to analyze her feelings for Jack, but she did want to simply take comfort in the fact that he was there for her at a time when she needed him. However, it wasn't Jack she was thinking about as she dressed for her date, but her father.

Never in her thirty-seven years had he spoken to her in such a scathing tone of voice. She tried to tell herself that it was only because he wasn't himself that he had been able to say such hurtful things to her, yet there was little comfort to be found in such a thought. She knew that before she left with Jack, she was going to have to speak to him. Not even as an emotional teenager had she ever left the house in anger. She quickly dressed and applied only the minimum of makeup, allowing herself enough time to make amends with him.

When she went downstairs, however, she discovered that Karen and her family had returned, as had Bert and Lena, and several cousins, and she was sorry she hadn't confronted her father before she had gone upstairs to shower. Taking a deep breath, she walked into the family room where everyone was gathered and made her way over to her father's side.

Despite her concerted efforts to get his attention, Maggie was unable to manage even a few minutes alone with him; he deliberately ignored her attempts to speak to him. She could hardly believe that he was behaving in such a manner. Never had she known her father to act childishly. Frustrated, she excused herself and went out to the kitchen where she found Karen getting a glass of soda.

"Mom says you and Pop had words this evening," Karen commented, giving Maggie a curious glance before screwing the cap back on the bottle of soda.

Dejectedly Maggie dropped her jacket on the back of one of the kitchen chairs. "All I said to him was I thought he should get a complete physical examination and he blew up. He ranted and raved like some sort of crazy person. Then he told me if I didn't like the way he behaved, I could leave.''

Karen slipped the plastic two-liter bottle back into the refrigerator. ''Why do you have to keep harping on Pop's health? Mom says you've been on her case about it ever since you came home.''

''I haven't been on her case,'' Maggie denied, cringing at her sister's accusing tone. ''And I'm not *harping* about anything. I'm concerned—which is what you should be. In case you haven't noticed, our father is not well. Or do you call drinking a beer for breakfast normal behavior?''

''Surely you're not suggesting he has a drinking problem?'' Karen gasped.

''I don't know what his problem is, but you're not going to stand there and tell me that that man in the other room is the same as he was the last time I came home.'' She was feeling shaky all over and slumped wearily onto the closest chair.

''Of course he's not the same. None of us are,'' Karen exclaimed, facing her squarely. ''You only come home once a year, Maggie. What makes you think that you're in any position to tell us what's normal and not normal behavior for Pop?''

Maggie wielded the blow with remarkable composure considering how weary she was feeling. She already had one member of her family not speaking to her; she wasn't about to let her sister be the second.

Suppressing the retort that was on the tip of her tongue, she calmly said, ''All I'm saying is that I think Pop should have a complete checkup. Whether or not you want to admit it, Karen, something isn't right with him.''

"You keep saying something isn't right with him," Karen exclaimed, throwing her hands up in a gesture of frustration.

"Because it isn't! How can you not see it? You work with him every day at the store." Maggie lifted her eyes in supplication. "You know he's irritable, he's forgetful, and sometimes he's downright silly. Look at how he was acting today. I think the girls were even a little frightened of him."

At the mention of her daughters, Karen appeared to take Maggie's words more seriously. Before she could respond, however, there was a knock at the back door.

"That'll be Jack," Maggie told her, grabbing her jacket from the back of the chair. Before leaving, she paused with her hand on the doorknob. "Look, I don't want to argue with you. Why don't I call you tomorrow and we can arrange to meet for lunch?"

Karen quietly agreed and Maggie hurried outside into Jack's waiting arms.

"Are you anxious to see me or did you just want to get out of there?" he asked as she nearly barreled into him in her hasty exit. He encircled her with one arm so that his face was only inches from hers.

She pulled him out of the stream of light shining through the kitchen door and into a dark corner on the porch where she kissed him. "I wouldn't have been able to greet you properly if you had come inside. Too many people hanging around," she told him a little breathlessly.

"Maybe we shouldn't go down to the point. There's going to be lots of people hanging around down there, too."

Her fingers were pressed up against his chest and she could feel his heart beating beneath them. "I'd say we could watch the fireworks from right here, but in about twenty minutes this backyard will be crawling with Stewarts.''

''And you promised to dance with me at the street dance,'' he reminded her.

''You're right. I did and I will. Dance with you, that is,'' she said, forcing a grin.

''First, I have to give you something.'' It was then that Maggie realized he had been keeping one arm behind his back. When that arm appeared, she saw there was a straggly assortment of red, white and blue carnations in his hand.

''A couple of waiflike kids on the corner were selling these. I know they're not exactly florist fresh, but they are real.''

Maggie moved back over to the stream of light shining through the glass on the kitchen door and held the flowers up for inspection. ''Ohh! They're beautiful,'' she told him in a voice that was close to a sob. After the argument with her father and his ensuing silent treatment, then the unpleasant scene with her sister, Maggie felt as though her emotions were right on top of her skin. ''Thank you,'' she managed to croak before she started to cry.

''Maggie, what is it? What's wrong?'' Jack asked, wrapping his arms around her and tucking her head against his shoulder.

''I'm all right, Jack,'' she mumbled into his sweater. She pushed herself away from him and wiped at her tears with the back of her hand. ''It's just been a long time since anyone's given me flowers plus it's been a long day and when I get tired I get sentimental.''

"There's nothing wrong with being sentimental," he told her, trying to pull her head back against his shoulder, but she resisted.

"I know, but I'm fine now." Seeing his skeptical look, she added, "Really."

"Look, maybe it wasn't such a great idea to go watch the fireworks. You're tired..." The tenderness and concern in his face tugged at her heartstrings.

"Jack, I want to be with you."

The look she gave him allowed his heart to rule his head. "You want to bring those with you?" he asked, pointing to the carnations.

"Yes—and not because I don't want to go back inside," she told him, cradling the flowers in her arm as though she were holding an infant. "I just want them with me." She held out her other hand to him. "Come on. Let's go celebrate the Fourth of July."

With a grin Jack slipped his hand in hers. By the time they reached the street dance, Maggie had forgotten about the turmoil that had spoiled her holiday. After a medley of rock and roll tunes that had them jumping and hopping like a couple of teenagers, they both agreed they should leave the fast numbers for the younger dancers in the crowd and only sway to the slow music.

Instead of watching the fireworks with the crowd of people spread out across an area the size of two city blocks, Jack suggested they do as many others had already done—spread a blanket on one of the grassy hills overlooking the harbor. Huddled closely together with Jack's blanket wrapped around their shoulders, they watched as the dazzling display lighting up the sky was reflected in the dark waters of the harbor, producing oohs and aahs from the crowd below.

After the final bang resounded and the crowd slowly began to disperse, Jack suggested they stop at a twenty-four-hour café where they warmed up with hot chocolate and hot apple pie with ice cream. Maggie's half-wilted carnations were sticking up out of a glass of water in the center of the table.

"So how does this compare to the way you usually spend your Fourth of July?" Jack asked, glancing around the half-empty café. A country and western tune could be heard in the background amid the low din of clanging dishes. "I would imagine that Independence Day in the nation's capital is quite an event."

"It depends on who's in office, but generally there's quite a bit of fanfare with the usual parades and appearances by politicians," Maggie told him, scooping up the last bit of ice cream with her fork. She savored the final piece of pie, then said, "Actually I prefer the small-town celebrations. There's more of a patriotic feeling to them."

After the waitress had refilled their cups, Jack asked, "Are you ready to talk about what was wrong back there at your parents' home?"

Maggie's glance had strayed to an old gentleman who sat by himself in a corner booth, his jacket frayed at the edges, his face lined with worry as well as age. Unbidden came the memory of her father the day he had put on an old paint-stained shirt to wear to church. She jerked her eyes from the old man and met Jack's inquisitive gaze. Within a matter of minutes, she had poured out all the unhappy details of the picnic, including her confrontations with both her father and her sister.

"I'm sorry, Jack. Now that I've said all of these things aloud I realize how trivial it must sound to another person." She shook her head apologetically. "You just drove a hundred miles to see me and I'm boring you with our family squabbles."

He reached across the table and took her hand in his. "I don't think you could ever bore me, Maggie. I'm glad you told me about your father. From what you've said and from what I saw of his behavior that day you came fishing, I think you're right to be concerned."

"Yes, well you're probably the only other person who feels that way. Ever since I've been home I've felt like I've been on the outside looking in when it comes to my family."

"Maybe that's because you are. You told me you haven't lived here for twenty years."

"But I've always come home at Christmas. And it's not like I don't call my parents and keep in touch. My family's important to me," she insisted, unable to keep from sounding defensive. "It always has been and it always will be, but that doesn't mean my job isn't important, too. It's unfortunate that my job keeps me from being here with my family, but that doesn't mean I don't love and care about them."

"Are you trying to convince me or yourself?" he asked gently.

She met his gaze and held it, not bothering to answer his question. It was a little unnerving to think that he might understand her better than she understood herself, yet it made her realize that her attraction to him was more than physical.

"Thomas Wolfe may have been right. Maybe you can't go home again," she said quietly.

"Do you really want to?"

"If you had asked me that six weeks ago I would have had a definitive answer. Now I'm not so sure anymore."

"Does that mean you're actually getting used to living in the slow lane?" he asked with a lift of his dark eyebrows.

"I still miss the fast lane, but I have to confess, this slower pace does sort of grow on you, doesn't it?" She sipped her hot chocolate thoughtfully. "This summer certainly has been full of surprises. I never expected to be sitting in Mildred's Café on the Fourth of July with the heartthrob of our senior class."

Jack laughed. "Heartthrob? Are you serious?"

"You must have known that practically every girl in school drooled when you walked by."

"You're joking, aren't you?"

"Come on, Jack. You don't need to be modest with me," she teased.

"*I* was a heartthrob?" he repeated in disbelief, then laughed sarcastically. "I wish I would have known. It would have made it a lot easier to ask girls for dates."

"Oh, you're not going to try to tell me you lacked for dates?" This time she was the one with the incredulous look on her face.

He grinned sheepishly. "I suppose I had my share, but there were a lot of girls at school I never would have asked out simply because I knew they only went for the jocks."

"But you were so popular!"

"Me? Popular was guys like Rob Michaels."

At the mention of the Snow King Maggie felt a pang of guilt.

"I would have gone out with you," she said earnestly.

"I wish I had known you then, Maggie. But listen, is it too late to ask you for that date now? What do you say we go to the reunion together?"

"I'd like that. And not because I want to see the look on everyone's face when Maggie the goody-two-shoes walks in with Jack the heartthrob."

"No? Then why?"

"Because I think I've fallen a little in love with Jack the professional fisherman."

CHAPTER ELEVEN

"I'M A LITTLE IN LOVE with you, too, Maggie," Jack said softly, leaning both elbows on the table between them so that his head was closer to hers. "So what are we doing in here?"

Maggie wasn't sure how she had expected him to react to a statement that surprised her as much as it did him. He dug deep into his pocket and threw a couple of bills on the table, then stood and grabbed her by the hand. She barely had time to snatch the wilted carnations from the glass of water before he was leading her outside to the Jeep where he held the door open until she had climbed inside. As soon as he was seated beside her he stuck the key into the ignition and started the engine. But before he pulled out into the street, he turned it off again and looked at her.

"I just realized that it's a hundred miles back to my place and you've got your folks living with you. So where do we go?"

They stared at each other and then, as if by silent communication, their eyes moved to the blue-and-white neon light blinking Vacancy on the rambling stucco building a short distance up the street. Maggie's eyes drifted back to Jack's.

"What do you think, Maggie? You don't need to go home and face your family tonight. You can spend the night with me."

Once more her eyes were on the Lakeside Motel and its flashing invitation. Right now more than anything in the world she wanted to be with Jack. In fact, she needed to be with him, and there was no reason for her to hesitate in telling him that. But before she could speak, her eyes caught sight of a familiar blue Oldsmobile cruising past the motel.

"Jack, I think that's my father," she said, her fingers tugging on his sleeve as she watched the car inch its way toward them, its driver obviously making a thorough search of both sides of the street. "It is him," she confirmed upon seeing the driver's face as the car crept closer. When it turned off the main boulevard and onto a side street, Maggie gasped. "Oh, my God! He's going the wrong way on a one-way street!"

In a flash, she was out of Jack's Jeep and running across the nearly deserted intersection. She managed to catch up with the slowly moving Oldsmobile before it had traveled more than a quarter of the way down the block.

"You're going the wrong way!" she hollered, running alongside the car and flailing her arms in order to get her father's attention.

When Herb saw her, he stopped and rolled down the window, a look of confusion on his face.

"You're going the wrong way on a one-way street," Maggie repeated, leaning up against the car, her breath coming in ragged intervals.

As though suddenly aware of his mistake, Herb anxiously looked around, then drove the car up over the curb, across the sidewalk and into a convenience-store parking lot. Maggie followed on foot, relieved that she had stopped him before an accident had occurred.

"Pop, what are you doing?" she demanded when he had opened the door and climbed out of the car.

"I was worried you weren't going to come home," he told her, resting his weight on the open door for support. "I didn't mean what I said, Maggie. I don't want you to leave."

Suddenly the image of the forlorn looking old man in the café flashed in her mind. She noticed that her father had misbuttoned his sweater and there was the same lost look on his face that had been on the face of the stranger in the café.

"Oh, Pop." She groaned, wrapped her arms around his slouching body and hugged him close to her while Jack stood across the street watching the scene.

"It's been our family home for thirty-nine years," he told her quietly. "It belongs to all of us—you, me, your mother, Karen, Erin and Nicole. You'll always have a place with us." For the first time in her life she thought she detected a break in the voice of the man who had always been the one to wipe away her tears.

"I know," she managed to say, despite the emotion tightening her throat. When he released her, she looked into his face and saw fatigue. "Why don't you get back into the car? I'm going to say goodbye to Jack and then I'll drive you home."

At the mention of Jack's name, Herb glanced across the street. "You don't need to drive me home. I'll be fine. You go with your fellow." He shuffled his feet and would have climbed back into the car, but Maggie stopped him.

"It's all right, Pop." She wished she could have listened to him and gone with Jack, but the image of him driving absently down the one-way street was too fresh in her mind. "Jack was just about to bring me home anyway." She ushered him around the front of the car and held open the passenger door for him. "You get inside. I'll just be a minute. I have to get my purse and I'll be right back."

She closed the door as soon as he was seated in the car, then ran back over to where Jack stood leaning against the fender of his Jeep.

"I'm going to drive him home," she told him, her eyes silently pleading for understanding. "I'm sorry."

"It's all right, Maggie. Some decisions in life are made for us," he said, a note of tender regret in his voice. "I had a wonderful evening." Then he brushed his lips over hers and said, "I'll call you about the reunion."

She nodded, and reluctantly released his hands to reach inside the Jeep for her purse. She was halfway across the street when she remembered the carnations. She did an about-face and called out, "Jack, wait!"

When she reached his side, she looked beyond him to where the wilted carnations lay in a small heap on the dash. "I forgot my flowers."

He gave her a crooked smile as he handed them to her, and was rewarded with a kiss she softly blew in his face. When she returned to her father's side, she carefully placed the flowers on the seat, making sure they wouldn't get crushed.

"I like your fellow, Maggie," Herb told her as she fastened her seat belt and started the car.

"I like him, too, Pop. He's nice." A little voice in her head repeated, *he is nice*. Funny, that was one word she would have never used to describe him twenty years ago.

DESPITE HER FATHER'S APOLOGY, Maggie had expected living conditions to be awkward around the Stewart home after what had transpired on the Fourth of July. But, except for the fact that everyone seemed to carefully avoid the subject of her father's health, nothing changed. Maggie made a special effort to take her sister to lunch and once more mend fences, but other than Karen admitting to the possibility that their father could have a problem, little was resolved. Like her mother, Karen believed Herb's troubles could be alleviated by his working fewer hours at the store. She also suggested that if Maggie wanted to keep peace in the family, she'd leave her sister and mother to handle her father. After all, Maggie would be going back to Washington when summer was over. They were the ones who would be working with him.

Maggie was not happy with Karen's suggestion, but short of creating tension in the family, there was not much she could do. She also had to accept the possibility that just maybe Karen was right—her father was simply overworked.

Maggie thought it was rather ironic that after her own personal experience with exhaustion, she was having such a difficult time accepting that her father's problems were work-related. She had come home this summer looking for peace and quiet. The last thing she had expected was to get caught in an emotional tug-of-war with her family. Dr. Walker would not be pleased if he were to find out about the added stress in her life. So instead of sitting around worrying about her father, she concentrated on putting together the reunion book, a job that was much more time-consuming than she had anticipated.

With each passing day, she found herself spending more time dwelling on memories of the past. It was interesting to read the questionnaires and learn what had become of her old classmates, and she often found herself flipping through the yearbook trying to match what she knew about the present day person to the face from twenty years ago. Invariably, she'd end up staring at page forty-six where Jack's graduation photo seemed to stand out like a sore thumb in the grid of senior pictures.

A week before the reunion, Sheila dropped off a tattered but intact copy of the final issue of their highschool newspaper, *The Quill*, so that Maggie would be able to incorporate some of the old news into the reunion book. Included in the final senior issue was the class prophesy, in which some of the graduates had listed what they hoped to be doing in twenty years.

Maggie quickly scanned the list for Jack's name, but it wasn't there. Nor was it in the section devoted to the class will, where students bequeathed to the junior class such items as the remains of a frog dissected in the biology lab and the chemical equation for stink bombs. Next she came to the senior favorites, where the results of the senior class poll were announced. Her eyes did a quick survey of the cutest couple, the most athletic seniors and the best dancers until she came to what she knew she would eventually find. Beneath the caption "Biggest Flirts" was a photograph of Jack and one of the cheerleaders Maggie had no trouble remembering—sexy Suzie.

Had Jack really been a big flirt? She tried to remember an occasion when he had behaved like a Romeo, but she was drawing a blank. Other than the rumors she had heard about his conquests and the comments she heard other girls make, she had no reason to suspect that he was any more fickle than any of the other guys in school. But there had been plenty of rumors. And now she found herself wondering just how many of them had a grain of truth to them. It was because of a rumor that she and Sheila and Judy Karner had fixed the Snow King contest. And now it was that same rumor causing doubts in her mind as to her feelings for him.

He had come to Duluth on several occasions since the Fourth of July, and each time they were together, Maggie found herself falling a little bit more in love with him. It was the last thing she had expected would happen to her when she had come home for the summer, but now that it had she realized how lonesome she had been with nothing but work in her life. She had forgotten what an intoxicating experience falling in love could be, and she found herself practically floating as the reunion drew near and she finished her work on the alumni book. For the first time in months she felt healthy and full of excess energy. When Jack told her he would be staying at the hotel the night of the reunion, she knew that even though she had made arrangements to share a room with Sheila, she would probably end up spending the night with him.

The thought brought a flush to her cheeks as she packed a black wispy negligee into her overnight case the morning of the reunion. On her bed was the royal-blue dress she had spent a small fortune on simply because Sheila had convinced her everyone else would be dressed to the nines. As she held the ruffled bodice against her skin, she wondered for the umpteenth time if she hadn't picked the wrong shade. Despite what her color analysis had revealed, she felt pale in blue.

Sheila had also said the dress made her look sexy. The thought brought another flush to her cheeks and Maggie quietly moaned. She zipped the dress into her garment bag, snapped the lock shut on her overnight case and willed her jumpy nerves to relax as she gathered her belongings together and went to wait downstairs for Sheila's arrival.

Staring out the kitchen window, she mentally berated herself for allowing her nerves to turn her into a frazzled mess. At first she had thought that it was simply the reunion and the idea that she hadn't seen many of her classmates in twenty years. If she were truly honest with herself, she had to admit that the bulk of the butterflies centered around Jack.

Everything had been fine when it had only been the two of them. But now she was going to be on a date with him in front of practically her entire graduating class! And Gina Loring was going to be there, not to mention several other of Jack's old girlfriends. Soon she would be confronted with Jack's past. Would she discover the rumors were true or false? Would he discover she had helped keep him from being Snow King? She put a hand to her chest. Heart palpitations! If she kept on like this, she wouldn't make it through the welcoming ceremony, let alone the program.

When Sheila's van pulled into the driveway, Maggie hurried out, dragging her garment bag and overnight case as though they were chains shackled to her.

"You want me to open the back?" Sheila asked, getting out of the van.

"No, this is all I'm bringing," she said, stuffing her things in the back seat.

"What about the reunion books?"

"I had them sent directly to the hotel."

"Then I guess this is it," Sheila announced, and immediately launched into an off-key rendition of *The Way We Were*, which brought a giggle from Maggie.

"Aren't you in the least bit nervous?" Maggie asked, marveling at her friend's bubbly disposition as she maneuvered the van through the light city traffic.

"I'm too tired to be nervous. Besides, I don't know what could possibly go wrong. We've double-checked and triple-checked everything that could possibly need checking."

"You really have done an outstanding job with this whole thing," Maggie complimented her.

"I can honestly say it was fun."

"But a lot of work."

"True, but the work is done. Now it's time to party with a capital *P*. Why don't you put a cassette in the tape player?" she instructed her friend. "I've got some of those golden oldies in that case on the floor. That ought to put us into a sock hop state of mind. Or at least prepare us for the music we're going to be dancing to this evening."

"Do people really dance at these things?" Maggie asked cynically, then cussed mildly when she dropped a taped cassette on the floor.

"Of course they do. It'll be fun." She cast a sideways glance at Maggie, who was fumbling with inserting the cassette into the tape player. "Boy, you really are tense over this thing, aren't you? I don't know why. You're one of the few people who has fulfilled a class prophesy. You were voted the girl most likely to succeed and you did. You know what happened to the boy voted most likely to succeed?"

"No, what?"

"That's precisely my point." Sheila giggled, then said, "Reunions have a way of bringing out all of our old teenage insecurities. It doesn't matter that we've gotten married, had children and had wonderfully successful careers. The minute we contemplate going to the reunion, we revert to that high-school mentality where all that mattered was whether or not you had a date for the prom."

Maggie moaned. "Did you have to bring that up? I didn't."

"Didn't what?"

"Have a date for the prom. No one asked me," she said with a halfhearted pout.

"The way you're going to look in that blue dress tonight, there will be some heavy sighs of regret. I can guarantee it."

"That dress is part of the reason for my anxiety. I can't believe I let you talk me into buying it. I can just imagine what people are going to say when Miss Goody-Two-Shoes walks in with a dress split to her navel."

"See! There you go—calling yourself Miss Goody-Two-Shoes. I bet there isn't a single person in Washington who would dare to put such a label on you. And that dress is not split to your navel. It has décolletage because you have cleavage. Lucky you." There was envy in her voice.

"Lucky me," Maggie parroted sarcastically, but Sheila didn't pay any attention, for her eyes had spotted the hotel parking lot.

"Look." One recently manicured fingernail pointed out the front windshield to the vehicle parked under the entrance canopy. "Isn't that Jack's Wagoneer?"

"You're right, it is," Maggie said, the knot in her stomach tightening.

"He must be checking in," Sheila stated, parking her van directly behind his Jeep.

Maggie's anxiety threatened to turn to panic, and she gripped the door handle tightly. "I suppose this means we're going to run into him in the lobby."

"He *is* your date tonight," Sheila reminded her wryly, reaching for the box of file folders in the back seat. "If you don't want him, I'd be happy to take him off your hands. Do you suppose he'd mind being a proxy for a missing husband?"

"You told me you were happy Tom got called out of town on business."

"Don't want to share your heartthrob, eh? Come on, let's go in," she said, opening her door. When Maggie made no move to get out, Sheila leaned back in and asked, "Are you coming in to register or do you want me to take care of it?"

"I'm coming," Maggie responded weakly, mentally making a list of all the reasons why she shouldn't be nervous about seeing Jack.

None of the reasons mattered once she stepped into the lobby. The fear she hadn't wanted to name materialized right before her eyes. As though she had timed it perfectly, she arrived just in time to witness him running into Gina Loring in the lobby. Their greeting was anything but detached; he wrapped his arms around her and hugged her tightly. Maggie's heart nearly stopped at the sight of the two of them embracing, especially when she heard Jack say, "Gina! I wish I had known you were coming!"

Maggie wished the floor could open up and swallow her, not that it would have been necessary. Jack was too engrossed with Gina to notice her gawking at him like an adolescent. Fortunately the hotel manager did notice Sheila, and ushered her into his office to clear up a few last-minute details. Maggie went along, like a child following her mother. By the time the details were disposed of and Maggie and Sheila returned to the registration desk, Jack and Gina were gone.

Maggie didn't see Jack again the rest of the afternoon. While she hung crepe paper streamers and filled balloons with helium, her imagination conjured up images of what he could be doing. Was he swimming in the indoor pool with Gina? Having a drink in the lounge with Gina? Reminiscing about old times with Gina? It was such thoughts that had her forgetting about the balloon she was filling with helium until it burst with a loud bang, startling Maggie as well as half a dozen others who had volunteered to help decorate the ballroom.

By the time she returned to her room to shower and get dressed, Maggie was sorry that she hadn't sat down with Jack and talked about their past. She wished she would have confronted him about the rumors that had circulated when they were in high school, and more than ever, as the reunion program neared, she wished she had told him about the Snow King balloting. Now all she could do was wait for an opportunity to present itself.

"Well, what do you think?" Sheila asked, flinging her arm around Maggie's shoulders when they had both finished putting the final touches on their makeup and stood poised in front of the floor-to-ceiling mirror. "Could we pass for a couple of seventeen-year-olds?"

Maggie met her friend's eyes in the mirror. "You look terrific."

"I lost seventeen pounds—despite all the chocolate brownies," she boasted.

"Another job well done," Maggie praised her, admiring her slimmed-down figure. "That dress is perfect for you.'' Unconsciously, her fingers tugged at the ruffled V-neck on her own dress.

Sheila's hand playfully slapped hers. ''Will you quit trying to pull that neckline up to your chin? I don't know why you're so self-conscious about that dress. I've seen your closet and know for a fact that you've worn more revealing clothes than this dress.''

Maggie eyed Sheila's classically tailored black dress enviously. ''At least you can wear a bra with yours.'' She turned and primped one final time while Sheila gathered her purse and room key from the dresser.

Sheila put her hands on her hips. ''I can't believe this! You're envying me because I'm wearing a dress that can hide the fact that I'm the mother of two kids and I'm envying you because at our age you can still wear a dress without a bra.'' She grabbed Maggie by the arm. ''Come on. We look great. We're leaving.''

As they waited for the elevator, Sheila opened her small beaded bag and pulled out a pair of badges. ''Here. I picked up your name tag for you.'' She handed one of the badges to Maggie, who groaned and rolled her eyes to the ceiling.

''Good grief! They've got our pictures on them!'' she exclaimed in near horror as she stared at her graduation picture reduced to thumb size. ''Do I really have to put this on? You know what happens when you wear one of these things,'' she told her, pinning the tag to her dress. ''People don't look at your face but your name tag. You get a roomful of people staring at each other's chests.''

''They're going to stare at your chest with or without a name tag,'' Sheila teased, then upon seeing the anxious look on her best friend's face, added, ''Just kidding!''

"I can't believe I'm doing this," Maggie fretted.

"You're going to be happy we're using name tags once you see how many people are here. This way when you don't remember someone's name or worse yet, you don't even recognize them, you won't have to feel embarrassed."

"I think I'm going to feel more embarrassed over people seeing a twenty-year-old picture of me than I would be over forgetting someone's name," Maggie said dryly. "Do you really think people have changed that much we won't even recognize them?"

"You should have been with me when I went down to the registration desk. Remember Dale Ingram?"

"Dreamy Dale? The tall basketball player with sort of a shy grin?"

Sheila gave a sardonic chuckle. "Tall he isn't. I haven't figured out if we grew or he shrunk. Not only is he a shrimp, but Dreamy Dale has got a paunch that would rival my father's and he's trying to mask his baldness by combing all the hair on the back of his head forward. Honestly, Maggie, I wouldn't have recognized him if it hadn't been for his name tag."

Maggie shot her a skeptical look as the elevator doors slid open and they stepped inside. "That may be the case with a few of our classmates, but I still don't see why we need pictures on our name tags," she said with an uncustomary irritability.

"You will," Sheila repeated smugly as the doors slid shut again. She punched the button for the floor where the cocktail reception was located. Maggie was silent until the elevator doors again slid open and they stepped out into a large open foyer filled with people.

"This must be the wrong floor," Maggie murmured to Sheila as she did a quick inventory of the people gathered informally in the foyer. "These people are too old." Then she saw the Welcome Jefferson High Eagles banner that was draped across the registration table and the sinking feeling in the pit of her stomach told her that it wasn't the wrong floor. From one of the groups of old people, Jack came striding toward her, a smile on his face, and looking more handsome than Maggie could ever dream possible.

He was wearing a gray three-piece suit with a crisp white shirt and dark tie that reminded Maggie that he hadn't always been a professional sportsman. Jack the fisherman in denims and plaid shirt was attractive, but Jack the businessman was downright irresistible.

"You look a little stunned, Maggie," he said as he came to her side, a dazzling grin on his face.

"She's just a little overwhelmed by the number of people," Sheila answered for her. "Hi, Jack, you're looking great." She gave him a friendly smile, then added, "I'll leave you to help Maggie get reacquainted with the others. I've got to circulate and make sure everything's on schedule." Then she turned to Maggie, her fingers on her wrist. "If I don't see you again before we're seated for dinner, don't forget you're supposed to be at a front table—you're a committee member."

"That must be why you've got the ribbons," Jack commented when Sheila had gone.

Maggie could feel him staring at her name tag and self-consciously her hand fingered the badge with two blue and orange ribbons dangling beneath it. "Committee members get ribbons." She repeated the obvious.

He steered her over to an isolated corridor behind several large rubber plants where he gave her a thorough appraisal and said, "That's a great dress, Maggie."

No stranger to compliments, she wondered why she felt as though every inch of her skin was blushing at his scrutiny. "Thank you. I like this, too," she told him, running a finger down the lapel of his suit. "Pretty nice threads for a fisherman."

"This was one part of the New York job I didn't mind leaving behind. These things drive me crazy." He adjusted the knot on his tie as though it were choking him. He glanced around and asked, "Are you ready to go meet our classmates?"

Maggie moaned and protested weakly. "Do we have to?"

He groaned himself and gave her an expression of pain. "The way you look in that dress I'm having a hell of a time convincing myself that that's the reason I came to this thing."

"If you keep talking that way I'm going to believe our classmates knew what they were doing when they voted you biggest flirt," she teased.

"The things I got charged with back then..." He trailed off with a shake of his head.

The words were said in a tone of disbelief, which had Maggie wondering if he were thinking about his reputation twenty years ago. She was about to ask him if they could find someplace quiet where they could have that talk she had been postponing for the past few weeks when they were interrupted by a high squeaky voice.

"Well, if it isn't Jack Brannigan and..." There was a pause and Maggie turned to see a skinny little blonde in a strapless red dress and rhinestones around her neck staring at her chest in an attempt to read the name on her badge. "Mag...gie Stew...art," she finally drawled.

"Not the Maggie Stewart who sat behind me in study hall?"

Maggie's eyes quickly searched the woman's bodice—or what there was of it—to learn who this person was standing before her looking like Duluth's version of Madonna.

Before she found the answer the high squeaky voice was saying, "I'm Rita Hastings. Weren't you the goody-two-shoes who turned me in for smoking in the girls' can?"

Maggie knew at that moment that it was going to be a long night.

CHAPTER TWELVE

RITA HASTING'S WELCOME worked wonders on Maggie's prereunion jitters, and soon she was smiling and greeting the other students with an ease she wouldn't have thought possible a few hours earlier. The cocktail reception provided an informal atmosphere in which to get reacquainted with her former classmates.

Putting together the reunion book proved to be to her advantage. Having compiled all the demographic data, Maggie already knew that among her classmates were an exotic dancer, a mortician, and a psychologist whose clients were pets. It also came as no surprise to her to hear the story of the classmate who had moved to Hollywood and made several low-budget movies, but whose greatest claim to fame was the palimony suit she had filed against a popular rock star.

Knowing a little bit about their backgrounds, however, didn't prepare her for the physical changes twenty years had produced. Some changes were more drastic than others, and not even Maggie the diplomat could hide her surprise when the tall, lanky senior who had played Curly in the senior class production of *Oklahoma!* walked in looking like an Orson Welles clone. Unlike the majority of men present, the women looked exactly as she had expected and often times better, and she wondered if it wasn't because all of them had spent the past three months determined to look their absolute best for the reunion.

By the time dinner was ready to be served, Maggie felt as though she were at a party with old friends. She was separated from Jack throughout most of the cocktail hour, but was constantly aware of his presence in the room, and it gave her a tiny thrill every time she caught his eye and he gave her a look only she understood. She kept hearing the seductive "I'll see you later" he had whispered in her ear when they had parted to renew old acquaintances.

The cocktail reception turned out to be a time of discovery for everyone and it was with a sigh of regret that Maggie followed the crowd into the ballroom where dinner was to be served. Despite pangs of hunger fluttering in her stomach, tiny twinges of anxiety stirred every time she thought about what was going to happen as soon as they were finished eating.

As she and Jack made their way to the front of the room in search of the reserved table, she could see that the stage had been decorated for Barb Milton's trip down memory lane. When she sat down beside Sheila, her eyes were on the winter scene painted on one of the sections of the backdrop.

To Maggie's surprise, Sheila had invited Barb and her husband to sit at their table. Maggie managed to stifle her groan when she saw them, but she nearly got up and moved when she heard Barb tell Sheila that since Rob Michaels and Diane Robinson were going to be featured in the program, she had asked them to sit at their table. If it wasn't for Sheila whispering in her ear, "Don't you dare leave," Maggie would have grabbed Jack's arm and bolted for the nearest exit.

Could things get any worse? she wondered to herself, then saw her question answered by Miss Boogstrom, who toddled up to Sheila and asked her in her unforgettable nasal tone, "Is there an extra place by you, dear?"

It wouldn't have done any good for Sheila to say no because Barb Milton was pulling out the last vacant chair at their table for the frail looking Miss Boogstrom and saying, "We'd love to have you join our group."

Maggie and Sheila could only cast sideways glances at each other in silent commiseration. Aware of the looks being exchanged between the two of them, Jack leaned over and said softly, "Is there a problem with Boogie sitting here?"

"Oh, no!" Maggie quickly denied, shaking out her napkin and spreading it across her lap. "It's just that Sheila thought her husband might get back in time to join us for dinner. He's been out of town at a business seminar, but she was hoping he'd be back tonight," she fibbed. "If he isn't here by now, he's probably not coming."

"It's probably better if he doesn't show up. Most of the spouses look pretty bored with the whole event," Jack remarked, his eyes drifting over the crowded room.

Maggie smiled weakly and turned her attention to the spinach salad that had been placed in front of her. As usual, her appetite had vanished, just as it always did whenever nervous tension gnawed at her insides. She forced herself to eat several mouthfuls before pushing the plate aside. Throughout the remainder of the meal, she spent more time rearranging her food with her fork than she did actually eating.

Even though Miss Boogstrom gave her no reason to suspect she knew about the fixed Snow King contest, every time the white-haired lady opened her mouth to speak, Maggie felt her heart move up a notch in her throat. By the end of dinner, however, she was grateful her former typing teacher was at their table. Age, as it turned out, had fine-tuned Boogie's sense of humor, and she proved to be not only interesting and witty, but a balance for the cynical and sarcastic Rob Michaels. Time had done nothing for the once-popular Snow King, other than make him bitter and absorbed in self-pity.

When Sheila suggested to Maggie they powder their noses before the program began, Maggie readily followed her to the ladies room.

"Can you believe that Rob Michaels?" Sheila asked after checking to make sure they were alone in the rest room. "From what I've heard, he's tried to hustle every female in the place."

"I think he's even using the same line on everyone," Maggie answered, studying her reflection in the mirror.

"You mean that bit about you being the one girl he always wanted to date but never had the courage to ask out?" She curled her lip in distaste.

"He used it on you, too?"

Sheila nodded. "He's also been trying to get a few squeezes in with overfriendly welcoming hugs." She applied a coating of cherry red to her lips. "Who would have ever guessed he would have turned out to be such a loser!"

"If he doesn't stop downing those martinis, someone's going to have to carry him up onto the stage for the program," Maggie said, snapping her compact shut.

"It's too bad he even has to go up on that stage."

Maggie's eyes met Sheila's in the mirror and neither one said anything, although they both knew what the other one was thinking. Finally Maggie said, "I'm telling Jack the truth."

"Not tonight?" Sheila questioned anxiously.

She was about to answer when the sound of the door opening had both of their heads turning to see who had come in. Of all the people Maggie didn't want to see at that moment, Gina Loring would have probably topped the list. There was no graceful way she could avoid speaking to the slender blonde, who was beaming a bright smile at both of them.

"I was hoping I'd get a chance to speak to you, Maggie," Gina told her after they had exchanged the usual pleasantries. "With so many people here, I was afraid we might not have the opportunity to talk to each other."

"It is crowded," Maggie agreed, dropping her compact back into her purse before closing it. "Are you having a good time?"

"It's been a pleasant surprise," she said, her voice laced with an East Coast accent that reminded Maggie that Gina had a whole different life now than the one she had had twenty years ago. "Everyone's so friendly." She paused, then added, "I wasn't sure of the welcome I'd get, considering I wasn't really a member of the graduating class."

"You should have been allowed to graduate with us," Maggie told her, feeling the same sense of injustice she had felt twenty years ago. "And just because you didn't go through commencement exercises with the rest of us, doesn't mean you didn't belong in our class, Gina."

Once more Gina smiled. "You really haven't changed, Maggie. You've still got that strong sense of justice. You know, I wish we could have known each other better when we were in high school."

"I would have liked that, too," Maggie told her sincerely.

"I never did get a chance to say thanks to you back then."

"Thanks?" Maggie gave her a quizzical look.

"Yes. For sticking up for me in gym class. If it hadn't been for your protest, Mrs. Flynn would have made me do all those horrible physical fitness tests even though I was pregnant. I was going to call you to thank you properly, but before I knew what was happening I was on a train heading out to the East Coast."

"I still think it's unfair that you had to go to the East Coast," Maggie declared firmly.

Gina shrugged. "At the time I was pretty unhappy about leaving, but things worked out for the best—which is why it was important for me to come tonight. I wanted to tell everybody that I'm happily married with three wonderful kids and to say thanks to a few special people who stood by me during some tough times."

"Well, I for one am glad you came back, and it's good to hear that you're so happy," Maggie said warmly before turning to Sheila to say, "I suppose we'd better get back or we'll miss the program." They were about to leave when Gina reached for Maggie's arm.

"Before you go, I think I ought to tell you something about Jack Brannigan," she said, her expression guarded.

Sheila and Maggie exchanged wary glances. "Why don't I wait for you outside, Maggie?" Sheila suggested, picking up her purse from the vanity.

Maggie was tempted to tell Gina there was nothing she could possibly tell her about Jack that would be of any consequence to her, but she knew she would only be lying, and curiosity had her nodding at Sheila.

When they were alone, Gina said, "Jack told me that the two of you came to the reunion together and that you've been seeing each other."

Maggie's mouth suddenly felt as though it were cotton. "Yes, we have," she said cautiously.

Gina paused, as though searching for the right words. "I don't know whether you ever heard the true story about what Jack did for me when we were in high school."

Cotton mouth and now sweaty palms, Maggie thought to herself, wondering if maybe it wasn't a mistake to be having this conversation after all. If she was going to hear the true story about Gina and Jack, she wanted Jack to be the one to tell her.

"It was such a long time ago, Gina, and it really wasn't any of my business," Maggie said with an uneasy toss of her head.

"Unfortunately certain kids at school had a way of making it their business," Gina insisted in a sad tone. "You must have heard the rumors that people were spreading about me and Jack?" She lifted troubled eyes in supplication.

"I've never been one to pay much attention to rumors," Maggie told her, then immediately felt a stab of guilt. It was because she had listened to the rumors surrounding Gina and Jack that she had acted totally out of character twenty years ago.

"That's what I admired about you when we were in school," Gina went on. "You were probably the only person in our class who didn't judge me. Besides Jack, that is," she hastily added. "When most people were doing their best to avoid being seen with me, you and Jack went out of your way to make things easier for me, and I'll always remember that. Now, when I think of the two of you getting together after all these years, it almost makes me want to cry. You're so right for each other." She reached out to give Maggie a hug. "I'm happy you finally found each other, even if it did take twenty years too long."

Maggie felt more than a twinge of guilt. She felt like a fraud, especially considering her part in the Snow King fiasco. Not knowing just what she should say to Gina, she managed to mumble a thank-you and gave Gina's shoulder a gentle squeeze.

Later, as she sat beside Jack in the ballroom, her thoughts kept returning to that conversation in the ladies' room. Other than Gina telling her that Jack had been someone special in her life, she had neither confirmed nor denied the rumors that had named Jack as the father of her baby. As Maggie sat staring at his strong profile, she suddenly realized that it hadn't been necessary. In her heart she knew that Jack wasn't the kind of man who would have turned his back on his son. Feeling an overwhelming surge of love bubbling inside her, she reached for his hand and was about to suggest they find someplace quiet and intimate when a spotlight engulfed their table in a circle of white.

Maggie's jitters before the reunion were nothing compared to the dread she felt when Barb Milton stood up and made her way to the stage for her trip down memory lane. Maggie looked over at Miss Boogstrom, half expecting her to be wagging a finger in her direction and saying "Shame, shame, shame." But the retired typing teacher was smiling and nodding her head in recollection, her eyes on Barb as she read telegrams and letters from classmates who hadn't been able to attend.

The longer Barb stood at the microphone, the more Maggie found herself wishing that she would simply call the Snow Week royalty up on the stage and get it over with. But as Barb had promised, there were a few surprises lined up for the program, including everyone having to sing the school song while the former cheerleaders in their evening dresses twirled what remained of their frazzled pom-poms. Next Barb read the statistics Maggie had compiled to make sure everyone knew how many classmates still lived within twenty-five miles of school, how many states were represented by the attendees and a dozen more insignificant facts that Maggie now found to be embarrassingly trivial.

When Barb called Miss Boogstrom to the podium, Maggie wanted to crawl under the table. She didn't dare make eye contact with Sheila, irrationally fearing that somehow if she did, her best friend's prognostication just might come true. But to Maggie's relief, Boogie hadn't been called upon to introduce the Snow Week Royalty, but to read the original class will, which drew laughter and applause from the audience. Maggie could only smile wanly, her anxiety escalating as Boogie proceeded to announce the awards for such honors as the graduate with the most children and the one who had traveled the farthest. Again, Maggie avoided Sheila's eyes. Now the irrational fear was that Boogie would have an award for the biggest cheaters in the class. However, Boogie gave no such award, and when she finally returned to her chair, Maggie silently berated herself for allowing her guilty conscience to run wild.

Finally the movie screen was lowered and the slide presentation began. Through the magic of electronics, everyone was transported back to the time when their major problems were what to wear to school and how to get a date for Friday night. Dozens of pictures drew sighs and laughter from the audience, and Maggie, too, was caught up in the memories. When the photos of Snow Week flashed up on the screen, she couldn't prevent her eyes from straying to where Rob Michaels sat. Only he wasn't in his chair. Her eyes made a quick sweep of the room, but he wasn't anywhere in sight.

"What happened to Rob?" Maggie leaned over and whispered in Sheila's ear.

Sheila's head pivoted on her slender neck as she, too, did a quick scan of the room. "Maybe he went to the men's room."

"Barb's noticed his absence, too. She keeps looking over here," Maggie said in a worried tone.

"It's getting close to the finale. What do you suppose she's going to do?" By now, it was obvious that Barb was definitely aware of Rob's absence.

Fortunately the program coordinator was accustomed to having to think on her feet. Rather than inviting the Snow Daze Royalty up to the stage, she simply had them stand in acknowledgement of their names, discreetly allowing for Rob's absence. She smoothly moved on to the athletic highlights, which were followed by a touching tribute to the graduates who had died, which silenced the audience for several minutes.

As soon as Barb's closing words had been uttered, Maggie turned to Jack. "I could use a breath of fresh air," she told him as the quiet crowd slowly came alive again with laughter and conversation. "And I need to talk to you about something."

As they stood, Rob Michaels came staggering back to the table demanding in a loud, slurred voice, "When's the dancing going to start?"

Jack and Maggie exchanged knowing glances before heading for the exit. "It's a good thing Barb changed her mind about having the royalty up onstage," Maggie told him as he guided her through the crowded ballroom, one hand on the small of her back.

"It's a shame that Rob doesn't know when to stop drinking, but I have to confess, I'm relieved we weren't singled out and called up onto the stage. I never was comfortable with that sort of thing." He held the door for her as they stepped out onto the hotel's courtyard overlooking the harbor. "Are you going to be warm enough out here without a coat?" he asked as he led her down the flagstone steps to a large fountain whose dancing waters sparkled with a rainbow of colored lights.

"This feels good," she said, inhaling the fresh air off the lake. The faint sound of laughter and music could be heard echoing across the water and Maggie looked out to see the excursion boat the *Vista Queen* cruise by with a deck full of dancing passengers.

"It does feel good," Jack agreed, loosening the knot on his tie before wrapping his arms around her. "It's also nice to have you alone for a few minutes." Soft lips brushed lightly across hers, sending a warmth tingling through her. "What did you want to talk to me about?"

Maggie knew she wouldn't be able to make her confession with his arms around her, and she gently extricated herself from his hold. She moved over to the rock wall that circled the courtyard and leaned against it, staring out at the pitch-black water of the harbor.

She took a deep breath before saying, "I did something really foolish when we were in high school."

Jack had come to stand beside her, but instead of looking out at the water, his eyes were studying her profile. "You're not alone in that. All of us acted rather foolishly at one time or another. I wouldn't let it worry you after all these years, Maggie."

"But it does worry me. Because it involved you," she said without looking at him.

"Me?" His chuckle was enigmatic. "We didn't even know each other back then."

"No, but I wish we had because if I had known you then the way I do now I wouldn't have done what I did, and I wouldn't be feeling like such a total idiot right now."

He grabbed her by the shoulders and turned her around to face him. "Maggie, what is it you did? Knowing you, I doubt it could be anything serious."

"It wasn't serious, but it wasn't right, either." She closed her eyes and groaned, then met his gaze. "There's no easy way for me to tell you this, Jack, but to blurt it right out. Rob Michaels didn't win the balloting for Snow King twenty years ago. You did, only the three girls in charge of counting the ballots were determined that Rob was going to win." She swallowed with great difficulty, then said, "I was one of the three girls."

For a moment he didn't say anything, but stood staring at her as though completely baffled. Maggie fleetingly wondered if this was how their relationship was going to end.

But then he said, "You? The president of the National Honor Society?" There was an amused tilt to his mouth.

She could only nod in regret. "Are you angry?" she asked softly when another silence stretched between them.

A loud, deep laughter rumbled from inside him. "Angry?" He shook his head in amazement. "If I had known, I would have thanked you. Maggie, getting crowned Snow King was the last thing I wanted at that time in my life. I'm not into stuff like that . . . I never have been and I never will be. In fact, when my name was on the list of candidates, I went to Miss Boogstrom and asked if I couldn't have it removed. Dear, sweet Boogie talked me into staying on the ballot so that Tammy Posten would have an escort during the coronation ceremony."

"You didn't want to be king?" She stared at him in disbelief.

He chuckled. "And have to wear that silly tin foil crown at the sock hop? No way! Believe me, Maggie, you did me a favor."

"Well, maybe I did, but that still doesn't mean that what I did was right," she said remorsefully.

"I still can't believe you did it. How did those other two girls ever talk you into it?"

"What makes you so sure it wasn't my idea?"

Fingers lifted her chin. "I know you," he said softly. "It wasn't, was it?"

She shook her head.

"So why did you do it?" he asked, a curious gleam in his eyes.

"Does it really matter?"

He appeared to be studying every feature on her face, then finally he said, "No, it really doesn't."

There was a short silence, then Maggie said, "If you want to know the truth, we thought we were avenging an injustice to Gina Loring."

"Gina?" he repeated, obviously puzzled.

"We knew what happened to girls who became pregnant in high school. They were the ones who weren't allowed to finish school, yet the guys involved were let off the hook. It didn't seem fair that Gina would be sent away as though she had committed some terrible crime, while you would be reigning as Snow King," she finished quietly.

There was another silence as Maggie waited for him to say something, *anything*.

"You thought I was the father of her baby," he finally said in a sober tone.

"At the time, yes. There were all sorts of rumors circulating..." She trailed off guiltily.

"And I never bothered denying them, right?"

"Why didn't you?" She held her breath as she waited for the answer to that question.

"Because if I had, there probably would have been even uglier rumors being spread around. Maggie, if anyone had learned the true story about Gina back then, she would have suffered even more than she did."

"I don't understand," Maggie said, her brow furrowed.

"Come here." He led her to a small bench in the corner of the courtyard where he pulled her down onto his lap. "Having already seen Gina today, I know she wouldn't object to my telling you what really happened back then."

With his hand resting on her thigh, he quietly began his story. "Gina was one of the nicest girls in our class, yet she was always on the outside looking in, you know what I mean?'' Maggie nodded, and he continued. ''I knew what it was like to be in that position. With my father being in the Air Force, we moved around a lot, and I had to change schools quite often. When I came to Duluth, I was treated like an outsider, too, which is why Gina and I became friends.''

''You knew her quite well, then?''

''Probably as well as Gina would allow anyone to know her. My mother was a piano teacher and Gina's little sister was one of her students. Once a week Gina would walk her over to our house for her lesson, then sit and wait for her to finish so she could take her home again. It was while Gina was waiting one Saturday morning that I noticed she had some nasty bruises on her arm.''

''From what?''

''She claimed that she and her younger brother had been playing football, but I was pretty sure that wasn't where the marks had come from. The better I got to know her, the more I realized that she had more troubles than simply being on the outside at school.''

''I know there were problems in her family. Her mother worked for my father at the store.''

''Then you know about her stepfather?''

''Only that he was an alcoholic and that Gina's mother didn't have an easy life with him,'' she said wryly. ''Was he the one responsible for the bruises?''

Jack exhaled a long sigh that sounded more like a groan of disgust. ''It wasn't only bruises he inflicted on her. Maggie, Gina's stepfather was responsible for her pregnancy.''

''You mean he raped her?'' she whispered in horror.

Solemnly he nodded. ''At first Gina was afraid to tell anyone. Then one day I followed her home after school because I had this strange feeling that something wasn't right. Only she didn't go home, but down by the harbor—you know that place known as suicide leap. I found her slumped over the ground crying her eyes out. She told me what had happened and made me promise not to say anything. You can imagine what that kind of information would have meant to her reputation at school."

"So when rumors started circulating that you were the father of her baby, you figured it would be easier for Gina if everyone believed them to be true," Maggie surmised, a note of wonder in her voice.

"I knew I would be joining the Air Force after graduation, so it really didn't matter to me what anyone in Duluth thought of my reputation. Besides, I was no stranger to rumors. The new kid in town often finds himself the subject of many of them."

Maggie stared at him, an overwhelming surge of emotion blocking her throat. She shook her head in regret, as though she could blot out all the rumors of the past. "I don't know what to say, Jack," she said quietly, her eyes downcast. "What you did was so wonderfully noble, so unexpectedly compassionate considering how young we were and what the consequences were. Now I understand why Gina spoke so fondly of you. I ran into her in the ladies' room and she did everything but give you a halo," she said with a smile.

"I'm no saint, Maggie, and I've never pretended to be."

"Maybe not, but there aren't many senior boys who would have done what you did for Gina. It makes me feel all the more foolish for my part in the Rob Michaels fiasco.''

"I still find it hard to believe you really did it," he said, shaking his head. "But considering the circumstances, you did it for the right reasons."

"That doesn't make it right."

"No, but it makes you human."

Maggie got to her feet and dragged Jack with her. "Come on. I'm going to set the record straight right now." She started toward the hotel door, pulling him by the hand.

"Where are you going?"

"Into the ballroom. I'm going to march up on that stage and tell everyone that you are the real Snow King." She didn't turn around as she talked, but kept striding toward the door.

"Whoa!" Jack said loudly, stopping her in midstride. "Maggie, it's not important."

"Of course it's important! That sleazy Rob Michaels is—"

He silenced her with a kiss. "I don't care about Rob Michaels or the Snow King title or anybody else in that ballroom. If we're going to go back inside that hotel, there's only one place I want us to be—my suite." He kissed her until she was out of breath.

"Does this mean I'm forgiven?" she whispered throatily.

"That depends."

"Depends on what?"

"On whether you spend the night with me."

She ran a teasing finger along the inside of his collar. "Rumor has it that Jack Brannigan can cruise the university campus and pick up any girl he wants. Why would he want a goody-two-shoes?''

Jack pressed himself even closer to her so that she could feel his desire for her and said, ''Because he knows that she can be naughty for the right guy.''

CHAPTER THIRTEEN

MAGGIE AND JACK felt like a couple of teenagers sneaking around to the side entrance of the hotel rather than returning through the plaza entrance. Had any of their classmates noticed them leaving the reunion early, it would have been difficult to not stay until the very end. It was only after they stepped into the elevator and heard the doors slide shut that they were able to breathe a sigh of relief.

"I think we did it," Jack murmured, his hand moving across her shoulder and down the creamy smooth skin exposed beneath her throat.

Maggie felt the heat spread through her as he toyed with the bodice of her dress. Instinctively she moved against his fingers, wanting him to explore the bare flesh concealed beneath the ruffles. As they slowly teased their way inside the silky fabric, she sucked in her breath, his touch kindling her desire until she felt her whole body tremble. When his thumb delicately rubbed against a soft nipple, she closed her eyes and made a helpless little sound.

And then she felt it—the evidence of his need—pressing against her, making her ache with such a longing she shamelessly rubbed her legs against his thighs. Jack groaned, burying his face in her hair as he whispered close to her ear, "Just a few more minutes." Then he was reluctantly removing his fingers from inside the front of her dress and dropping his arm around her shoulders at almost the same time that the elevator doors were sliding open.

He led her down the corridor, his arm possessively clutching her close to his side, warming her, giving her a sense of rightness, as though there were no other place she should be but with him. He stopped in front of the door, and without removing his arm from around her shoulders, managed to reach inside his pocket for the key to open the door.

Within minutes, Maggie found herself standing in the dark, luxurious suite with a breathtaking view of the city. Grasping her gently by the shoulders, Jack turned her around so that her back was pressed against him as they stood staring out the window at the star-filled sky.

Warm breath caressed her cheek as he softly said, "It's hard to tell where the city lights end and the stars begin, isn't it?"

She shivered when his fingers lightly touched the back of her neck. "I had forgotten how beautiful Duluth could be at night," she answered, finding it increasingly difficult to talk as his mouth replaced his fingers, tracing a path across her nape. "And to think I didn't want to come home this summer," she said with a breathless laugh.

Jack's hands, which had been roving lightly over her hips and across her midriff, now found her full breasts, and Maggie felt a hot glow all the way down to her toes. "Ahh, Maggie," he murmured, "I don't know what I would have done if you hadn't." There was such an urgency in his tone, it made her want to touch the powerful masculine body that was causing her own body to weaken with desire.

Unable to resist, she turned into his arms, her hands making their own roving study, sliding up over broad shoulders and down across his back to mold him closer to her. A smile curved his mouth as she slowly lifted her eyes to his and he saw the flame of desire burning there.

Without speaking, she lifted her hands to the knot on his tie while he deftly managed to undo the row of tiny buttons restraining breasts swollen with longing. He paused only long enough to allow her to strip the suit jacket and shirt from his shoulders. Her hands found his naked torso, and she gloried in the feel of the hard muscles she found there. She stopped only to allow the silky blue dress to fall to the floor.

Jack's eyes roamed her form hungrily as the satin slip followed the route of the dress. His hand cupped a bare breast, lifting the ivory flesh until his lips closed around a rosy nipple. With his dark head bent, he nibbled and softly sucked until each of the peaks hardened beneath his lips, while Maggie buried her fingers in the silky thickness of his hair, holding him close. When he slowly lifted his head, she made a soft sound of disappointment, and he quickly planted a long lingering kiss on her lips that had her clutching his shoulders tightly and pressing against him greedily.

He lifted his head and she moaned softly. "Don't stop...."

His breathing was as ragged as hers. "I couldn't if I wanted to." He lowered her to the bed, the feel of her beneath him testing his self-control to the limit. "If there's one thing I'm sure of, it's that I'll never stop wanting you, Maggie," he said before his mouth met hers.

With every caress he gave her pleasure, his touch stealing her breath away. Uttering soft sounds of rapture, she clung to him as his hand slid between her thighs. Every nerve in Maggie's body quivered, yearning for satisfaction only he could provide.

They needed no words, for their bodies spoke of their mutual need. They explored each other with an urgency neither one would have believed possible. When Jack prodded her thigh with his knee, Maggie opened herself to him, melting against him as he swiftly plunged into her warmth. At first she moved gently under him, intense pleasure shuddering through her as her body instinctively matched his movements.

Small explosions began to build inside her, causing her to tighten her legs around his, inviting him to seek the point of greatest pleasure. Moving to his powerful rhythms, she turned her face so that their lips met, and with a groan, Jack relinquished his last bit of control.

When it felt as though he was touching the very center of her, she felt his passion come rushing down with a soft cry of rapture, and ecstasy dominated their world, blinding them with bliss.

Maggie felt as though she were the most beautiful woman in the world in love with the most beautiful man. Locked tightly together, neither one wanted to let go of the power that had consumed them. While hearts slowed, hands gently stroked until with a reluctant sigh, Jack rolled over to his side. He gently kissed her bruised and swollen lips.

"You must have wings, Maggie, for I could have sworn we were flying."

Her fingers reached up to bury themselves in his hair. Her smile was languid, but her eyes still glimmered with passion. "I never dreamed it could be like this," she admitted, realizing only as she spoke the words aloud what they really meant. She had known that her relationship with Brian hadn't been satisfying for either of them, yet until now, she hadn't known just how much had been missing.

"I love you, Maggie Stewart," he said thickly, his eyes burning into hers.

"And I love you, Jack Brannigan," she told him simply, then as if to prove her point, proceeded to show him how much.

"I might need rest. I'm not seventeen anymore," Jack warned her as her fingers traveled across his abdomen and down his thighs, exploring and arousing nerves still tingling from their lovemaking.

"Rest?" Maggie flashed him a teasing smile as her hand found the evidence that sleep was not what he needed at that moment. "I think not."

Jack's laughter echoed her seductive tone, and he watched her fingers work their magic on his flesh. When he could stand no more of the exquisite torture, he succumbed to desire and was about to roll over on top of her when Maggie stopped him. "Uh-uh. You're tired. You just lay back and let me take care of you."

And she did—quite nicely.

WHEN MAGGIE AWOKE the next morning she found Jack's leg holding her captive. She smiled as memories flowed inside her, memories as clear as the bright summer peeking around the edges of the curtains. It seemed so natural to wake up beside Jack, she couldn't help but smile at the sight of his bronzed body beside hers.

"Good morning." She stretched, dislodging the sheet that had barely been covering her breasts.

"After last night it is," he answered, his eyes not missing the flesh exposed by the slipping sheet.

Maggie slid against him, wrapping her arms around him and saying in a low voice, "I still can't believe last night."

He moved, pinning her beneath him. "It's real, Maggie. I only wish it hadn't taken us all these years to find it." He placed several kisses along the swell of her breasts. "Doesn't it make you wonder how different our lives would have been had we dated each other in high school?" He lifted his head to gaze into her eyes. "Do you think we would have fallen in love if we had?"

Maggie looked at his steady blue eyes and honestly couldn't imagine not loving this man. "I guess that's something we'll never know." She sighed, tracing the outline of his lips with the tip of her finger. "Maybe we wouldn't have been ready to fall in love back then. Besides, I didn't date in high school."

"Why not?"

She frowned at the memory. "At the time I blamed it on the shortsightedness of the male members of our class, but now, as I look back, I don't think I was ready emotionally to deal with romance. I've always been an all or nothing type person. I never wanted meaningless relationships."

"Does this mean I have your all?" he asked, his hand sliding down her body and causing her breathing to quicken.

"Yes, it does," she murmured, savoring the feel of his fingers as they traced erotic patterns across her flesh.

"Then we won't think about what might have been," he said, his voice as husky as hers. Her fingers were conveying their own message, teasing him without quite touching him. "It's good between us, Maggie. So good that I can't keep myself from wanting you right this moment even though after last night I can't imagine how I could possibly have an ounce of desire left in me."

"This definitely feels like more than an ounce," she whispered, her hand reaching between his legs.

Jack closed his eyes, shivering with pleasure at the feel of her hands on him. "Maggie." It came out sounding like a plea for mercy and produced lightning-quick results. Just as fast was her withdrawal as the loud ringing of the telephone penetrated both of their senses. With a groan Jack rolled over and reached for the receiver.

"It's for you," he said, handing her the phone.

Before taking it, Maggie mouthed a "Who is it?"

"Sheila," he whispered.

They exchanged puzzled glances before Maggie finally said in a wry tone, "Good morning, Sheila."

"I'm sorry about having to call you, Maggie, but your mother just phoned and said your father's had a car accident."

Maggie shot up like a rocket in the king-size bed, clutching the sheet to her bosom. "How bad is it?"

"He wasn't hurt," she quickly reassured her. "When your mother called she was on her way to pick him up."

"From the hospital?"

"No, the police station."

"The police station?" Maggie's brows drew together. "Why would he be at the police station?"

"She didn't say. She just asked me to tell you your father had been in an accident and that she was on her way to pick him up. I'm sorry I couldn't get more of the details, but she was pretty upset when she called."

"No, that's all right." Maggie smoothed her fingers across her brow. "I'll go over right away and find out what's happened. Thanks for calling me."

Maggie was scrambling off the bed as soon as she had handed the telephone back to Jack.

"What's wrong?" he asked, watching her search for the clothes she'd scattered in the heat of passion.

"It's my father." She relayed the brief message she had received from Sheila, then groaned as she snagged her nylons in her haste to put them on. "Damn. I should have gotten my suitcase from Sheila's room," she said, dropping the stockings in frustration.

"I'll get it for you," Jack offered, pulling on a pair of jeans. "And then I'll drive you to the police station."

She could only nod her head gratefully, relieved to have someone take charge for the moment. Even though Sheila had insisted her father wasn't hurt, Maggie couldn't help but wonder if he hadn't done something criminal. Such thoughts haunted her as they traveled across town in Jack's Jeep.

She breathed a sigh of relief when they pulled up in front of the police station just as her father was coming down the steps with Delores and Karen on either side of him. Before Jack could even turn off the engine, Maggie was out of the car running up the steps to meet them.

"What happened? Are you all right?" she asked her father, her fingers wrapping themselves around his arm.

"I'm fine. I don't know what everybody's making the big fuss about," he snapped irritably, shaking off Maggie's hand.

"He went through a red light over on Seventh Street and smashed up the car," Karen explained.

"It wasn't red," Herb contradicted her.

"Pop, there was a cop right behind you and he said it was red," Karen told him.

"Shh! Do we have to discuss this on the front steps of the police station?" Delores pleaded, glancing around uneasily.

Maggie raised a hand to her temple and sighed. "Mom's right. Why don't we wait until we get home?"

Karen looked over to where Jack sat waiting for Maggie. "I have to pick up the girls from Sunday school. Is it possible for you to take Mom and Pop home?"

"I'm sure Jack won't mind," Maggie answered. "You go on. We'll be fine."

Karen shot her a glance that told her she didn't believe that last statement. "As soon as I've picked up Erin and Nicole, I'll be right over. I think we'd better have a family meeting."

Herb glared at her, but Karen didn't back down. Mumbling to himself, he followed Maggie and Delores to the Jeep. All the way home, conversation was stilted, and Maggie was grateful the police station was only a ten-minute drive from the Stewart home. Jack dropped them off at the door, and Maggie said goodbye to him, saddened by the thought that this was not how she had planned for their weekend to end.

They talked about the informal picnic to be held that afternoon at Minnesota Point for any of the graduates still in town. Although it didn't seem likely that she would be able to join in the fun, Jack told Maggie he would call her later to see how everything was going.

"You don't need to cancel your plans because of me," Herb told her after Jack had driven away.

"I didn't," Maggie assured him. "Jack had to see to a few things and I wanted to come home and change clothes," she lied, pouring herself a cup of coffee from the pot that was still warm.

"Have you had breakfast?" Delores asked her daughter.

"I'll get myself something, Mom." She waved a hand at her mother who was slipping an apron around her waist.

"I'd better put a coffee cake in the oven if Karen and the girls are coming over."

"There's no need for them to come over," Herb said irritably, raking a hand through his thinning gray hair. "If they're coming here with the idea that we're all going to sit down and have some useless meeting, they're wasting their time."

Maggie faced him squarely and said, "Pop, we're concerned about you."

"Well I don't need anyone's concern. Not yours or your sister's!" he shouted, then stalked off in the direction of the basement.

Maggie called after him, but he ignored her, retreating to the game room. When she would have followed him down the stairs, her mother's arm on her shoulder stopped her. "Just let him be."

"I hope this doesn't mean he's going to hide away down there while Karen's here." Maggie picked up the mug of coffee and carried it over to the table.

Delores sighed and shook her salt-and-pepper curls. "With your father, who knows?"

Maggie patted the chair beside her and said, "Come sit down and tell me about the accident. How did it happen?"

Her mother sank wearily onto the chair. "We were all set to go to church this morning when I remembered I'd forgotten my watch upstairs. So I went up to get it and when I came back down, your father was gone."

"Gone? Where did he go?"

She shrugged. "He had said something about there not being enough gas in the car, so I assumed he must have decided to run and get some before we went to church."

"Is that when he had the accident? On the way to the gas station?"

She nodded. "When he didn't come home, I began to get worried. I called Karen because I knew she would be coming over this way to take the girls to Sunday school. By the time she arrived, the police had called to tell me to come pick up your father."

"Was he charged with a criminal offense?" Maggie asked as she lifted the coffee mug to her lips.

"Oh, no," she was quick to say. "They only gave him a citation for not stopping at a red light."

Puzzled, Maggie frowned. "Then why was he at the police station?"

"Apparently the officer who saw him go through the red light had been following him for several blocks and had been about to pull him over when the accident occurred," Delores explained quietly, her eyes on her hands clasped together in front of her.

"What do you mean?" Maggie's eyebrow lifted suspiciously. "Why was he going to pull him over?"

"He thought your father was a drunk driver. That's why he brought him in to the police station and called me to come get him." She paused to wet her lips before saying, "According to the officer on the scene, Dad was incoherent and slurring his words when he got out of the car."

"But he wasn't drunk, was he?" Apprehension edged her words.

"Of course not!" She gave Maggie a "You should know better than to ask" look. "They ran a couple of different tests on him, all of which proved he hadn't had anything to drink.''

"If that's the case, Mom, why was he behaving as though he were? Doesn't this tell you that there must be something seriously wrong with Pop?"

At that moment, Karen and her daughters arrived, the two little girls bursting into the kitchen with giggles and squeals of delight. They greeted their grandmother with hugs and kisses.

"Oh, my! Here you are already and I haven't even put the coffee cake in the oven yet," Delores said, rising to her feet.

"It's all right, Mom. We don't need any coffee cake," Karen insisted.

"Do you have any chocolate chip cookies?" six-year-old Erin asked, her bright eyes looking hopefully at her grandmother.

"You know Grandma always has chocolate chip cookies," Delores answered, moving over to the ceramic pig cookie jar on the counter. "Why don't you go find Grandpa and see if he wants to have cookies and milk with you?" she suggested, and both girls went scrambling for the stairs.

"How is Pop?" Karen asked, pulling out a chair beside Maggie.

"Belligerent," Maggie replied, getting up to refill her coffee cup.

"Maggie!" Delores's tone was censorial.

"Well he is, Mom." Maggie shot her mother a defensive look, then said to Karen, "He's taken refuge in the basement. After shouting at me because I suggested we were concerned about him, he told us he didn't want to be a part of any family meeting. We might need a stick of dynamite to get him upstairs."

"Maybe Erin and Nicole can soften him up a bit," Karen said hopefully. "Did Mom fill you in on all the details of the accident?" She looked over at Delores who was nervously arranging cookies on a plate.

"Enough of them for me to know that Pop has a serious problem." Maggie sat back down at the table. "Both of you do see that now, don't you?" Her gaze moved speculatively from her sister to her mother.

"Obviously you were right, Maggie. It's not simply a matter of Pop being overworked," Karen agreed, a note of apology in her tone.

"He didn't sleep well last night," Delores interjected as if it could be a reasonable explanation for his behavior.

"Mom, you heard what that policeman said," Karen replied, then seeing Maggie's quizzical look added for her benefit, "One of the officers at the station hinted that Pop might not be competent enough to be driving."

"And that's ridiculous," Delores insisted, unable to keep the irritation out of her voice. "Your father's only sixty-four years old. He's more cautious than those young kids who drive as though they were on a race track."

Maggie looked at her mother and felt an annoying ripple of exasperation. Then she saw the fear lining the normally serene face and her voice softened. "Mom, something isn't right with Pop. You can't keep denying there is anything wrong with him. Whether it's physical or mental, we won't know until he goes and sees a doctor."

"Maggie's right," Karen concurred soberly, much to Maggie's relief. "Pop needs to see a doctor."

"You think he has something horribly wrong, don't you?" Delores said apprehensively.

"It might not be as serious as it appears to be." Karen pushed back her chair and went to stand beside her mother. "Lots of things can affect a person's mental state."

"That's true, Mom," Maggie spoke up. "I've been doing some reading about senility—"

"Senility?" her mother interrupted, a look of horror on her face. "Your father is not suffering from senility!"

"At his age, he shouldn't be, but something is causing him to be confused," Maggie stated evenly. "The first thing that came to my mind was Alzheimer's disease—"

"Alzheimer's disease?" her mother parroted, sounding even more horrified. "Oh, no, he couldn't have that!" She began wringing her hands nervously.

"Chances are he doesn't," Maggie reassured her. "There could be any number of physical reasons for what Pop is experiencing. Maybe he has a thyroid disorder, or he could be anemic. That's why I want you to get him to a doctor. Once he's had a thorough physical exam, we'll be able to pinpoint just what it is that is causing him to behave so uncharacteristically."

"That's right, Mom," Karen said in support of Maggie's statements. "It could be something as minor as an infection or a nutritional disorder that is easily treatable with medication."

Delores appeared to be contemplating their words. "He's not going to want to go to the doctor," she warned them.

Just then both Erin and Nicole came bouncing into the kitchen. "Who has to go to the doctor?" Erin demanded, tugging on her mother's shirtsleeve.

It was Delores who answered her. "Grandpa."

"Is he sick?" Four-year-old Nicole gave her grandmother a saucer-eyed look.

"We don't know." Delores reached for the plate of cookies and set them in the center of the table. "You know how you have to go in for your checkup every year around your birthday so the doctor can see that you're healthy?" Two little heads nodded. "Well, Grandpa needs to make sure he's healthy, too."

"I don't need a doctor so you can quit making plans for me," Herb announced in a stern voice as he made his entrance into the kitchen.

"But Grandpa, don't you want to go for your checkup?" Erin asked. "They give you Garfield bandages to stop your prick from bleeding."

"My what?" he barked, startling Nicole so that she moved closer to her mother.

"Your prick on your finger." Erin bravely held up her small index finger. "Where they sample your blood— you know, to make sure you're not sick."

"Well, I'm not sick," he squawked in such a sullen manner that even Erin sought refuge at her mother's side.

"See what I mean?" Erin spoke to her mother from behind her shoulder. "Grandpa's scary sometimes." Nicole began to cry and four pairs of eyes glanced at Herb.

Maggie saw the expression on her father's face soften. She watched as he bent down beside Nicole and placed his hand gently on her golden head.

"There's no reason to be afraid of Grandpa," he said quietly, then looked over Karen's shoulder at Erin and waved a hand in her direction. When she came into his outstretched arm, he hugged her tightly. Nicole lifted her head from her mother's lap and moved into the crook of his other arm. "If you two think Grandpa should go see the doctor, then Grandpa will go see the doctor."

"And get your finger pricked?" Erin asked.

"Only if I can get a Garfield bandage," Herb said, ruffling her curls. "Now let's get your mother and your aunt out of our chairs so we can have those cookies and milk your grandmother promised us."

Maggie and Karen willingly gave up their chairs, retreating into the family room where they dabbed at their eyes with tissues and made plans to spend the afternoon together.

DURING THE NEXT TWO WEEKS Maggie saw little of Jack. After their night together, she had hoped they would be seeing a lot of each other. But with her father undergoing extensive testing, she had promised her mother she'd be there since Karen was needed at the store.

After a complete physical exam and extensive lab tests, the doctors had determined that Herb was not suffering from anemia, cardiovascular disease or any metabolic disorders. Maggie was almost saddened that the doctors hadn't found an infection or some physical ailment, because the next steps were the neurological and psychiatric examinations. As the physical causes for Herb's mental confusion had eventually been eliminated, Maggie's worst fears had begun to take shape. It wasn't, however, until the doctor actually confirmed her suspicions that she was able to accept that her father was suffering from Alzheimer's disease.

Unlike her daughter, Delores did not want to accept the doctor's diagnosis and immediately made arrangements for Herb to see another set of specialists at a different clinic. Although Maggie believed the doctors hadn't misdiagnosed her father, the desperation in her mother's face was all that she needed to agree to go along while her father saw even more doctors. Again, the results were the same, and it was a solemn, weary group that sat around the Stewart kitchen table after the final examination.

Neither Delores nor Karen seemed able to cope with the feeling of helplessness the diagnosis had left them with. This time the anger that was in the air emanated not from Herb, but from the women of the family. For weeks Maggie had been deluding herself into believing that the anxiety they had suffered over not knowing what was wrong with her father was worse than whatever the doctors might discover. Now she could see how wrong she had been. The unknown was known and now anxiety about Herb's condition consumed them.

After several family meetings, Maggie could see that it was going to be a difficult, if not nearly impossible, task. How did one accept the fact that there was no cure for her father's slowly deteriorating state of mind? Trying to remain optimistic in the face of adversity, Maggie put all of her strength into helping the rest of her family come to grips with what the disease meant in emotional terms for all of them.

Despite appearing to be a rock for her family to cling to, Maggie felt as though she were crumbling inside, and it was only with Jack that she was able to let any of her true emotions show. When she was with her family, she needed to be the strong and stable one, but when she was with him, she could be the one seeking strength.

As soon as he had heard about her father's condition, he had come rushing to her side. Sensing her inner turmoil, he had taken her to what now was one of their favorite spots along the North Shore, a sweeping curve of beach that was as rugged in appearance as the ocean's coast. There, amid the wave-splashed rocks they found a relatively dry boulder where they sat and watched the wisps of morning fog slowly dissipate over Lake Superior.

"Why did it have to happen to my father, Jack?" she asked him, staring out at the water. "It's bad enough knowing that he's dying, but to lose himself in the process..." She trailed off, emotion choking her voice.

He sat behind her on the large rock, his hands gently smoothing the shoulder muscles taut with tension. "How much time are you talking about?"

"That's something the doctors couldn't say. He could live five, ten, even fifteen years." She shook her head. "But what good is it to live at all if he doesn't even know who he is? He's not simply dying, Jack. He's losing bits and pieces of his memory, his ability to communicate and even his thoughts. He's slipping away from us and as much as we love him, we're powerless to stop his slide."

"What is the doctor's prognosis? Is there any medication to slow the progression of the disease?"

She shook her head. "They can give him drugs to treat his depression and anxiety, but other than that..." She ended with a hopeless shrug, and Jack pulled her head close to his chest, his fingers smoothing her windblown curls affectionately. Disconsolately, she added,

"You'd think that in this day and age there would be something."

"Maggie, if you think it's unthinkable, imagine what it must be like for your father," he said quietly.

"Oh, Jack, it's so sad." She swallowed with difficulty, but her voice still broke. "He's going to have to retire." Then she could no longer prevent the tears that had been building inside for such a long time. She turned into his chest and allowed all the anger and emotion she had been trying to deny during the past few days to be released.

Jack wrapped his arms around her, murmuring soothing words in between the kisses he planted on her bent head. "It's okay, Maggie, go ahead and get it all out," he whispered, not sure whether she heard him or not.

When the sobbing subsided, she looked up at him, her face blotched with red marks, her eyes smudged with mascara. Her words came out unsteadily. "If there's one thing my father's always feared, it's retirement. But I think he's even more worried that my mother will want to sell the store."

"Do you think that will be necessary?" he asked, his thumb catching one last teardrop that had trickled down her cheek.

"I'm going to try to talk her out of it if she does. Karen is perfectly capable of taking over for Pop. And as long as there's a Stewart running the place, it'll still be his store. I think it'll be better for him if he can ease into retirement, gradually spending less time there as the days go by."

"How are your mother and sister taking all of this?"

"It's been a little rocky. Even after hearing the doctor's diagnosis, I don't think my mother really believes it. The doctor suggested we contact the Alzheimer's family support group that meets in Duluth.''

"And how do you feel about that?''

"I think he's probably right. Right now we need to talk with other people who are feeling the way we are. I also think it might help my father feel less isolated socially. Despite the doctor's reassurance that his social behavior will remain fairly well preserved for quite some time, I know he's worried that he's going to do something that will embarrass us. Seeing and talking to other patients with Alzheimer's might help.''

"Your father's lucky he has you for a daughter,'' Jack said lovingly, kissing her fingers.

"It seems so strange to think of how I hated the idea of coming home for the summer.'' Maggie looked down at her fingers entwined with Jack's. "Now I realize how important it was for me and for my family. It's taken my father's illness to make me see how preoccupied I've been with money, achievement and constant activity. What gave my life meaning seems so inconsequential now. A job can be replaced, but relationships are priceless.''

"Yes, they are, which is exactly how I feel about ours.'' He kissed her, a long lingering kiss that had passion stirring in both of them.

"Oh, Jack, I need you so much,'' she told him, her sigh saying more than her words.

"I know things are rather unsettled right now with your father's condition, but I want us to have a weekend together. If you want, I'll come to Duluth or you can come to Lake Magda.''

"I'll come to you,'' she told him and saw his eyes smolder. "Next weekend.''

CHAPTER FOURTEEN

JACK FELT LIKE a little kid waiting for the ice-cream truck to round the bend as he glanced for the hundredth time at the dirt road in search of Maggie's car. He looked again at his watch. Three-thirty. She had said she would be arriving between three and four. He wished now that he had gone to Duluth to pick her up. He would have—in fact he had suggested it—but she had insisted she drive herself. "I'm a big girl," she had told him. "I can manage."

"Big girl," he mumbled to himself, squelching the urge to get in his Jeep and go look for her. True, she was accustomed to traveling all over the world on her own, but that didn't make him feel any less protective toward her. It seemed rather ironic that one of the things he admired most about her was her independent streak, yet at the same time he wanted to cherish her and not let her out of his sight. Ever since the night of the reunion he had been able to think of little else.

At first he had attributed his attraction to her as a reawakening of his libido. Ever since Jill's death, he had put his emotions in cold storage, unwilling to accept the possibility that he could find happiness in a commitment to another person. And until he had met Maggie, he hadn't even wanted to try. But just as the early-morning sun had burned through the curtains of fog draping the lakeshore, she had penetrated the cold haziness surrounding his heart.

His thoughts strayed to the memory of the hours they had spent intimately discovering each other in the king-size hotel bed, and a wave of longing washed over him. He had never expected to find such an intimacy with anyone. Nor had he expected that his feelings would be so intense. It made what he had shared with Jill pale by comparison, yet he knew that his relationship with his wife had been anything but pallid. It was just that now it seemed so...distant. In two short months Maggie had been able to do what he hadn't been able to do in a year and a half—make him forget that Jill wasn't lying beside him when he woke up each morning.

He shook his head in amazement. Two months ago he had been living one day at a time, waiting for time to do what everyone kept telling him it would—ease his pain. But Maggie had been able to work the magic that time had failed to perform, and now he found himself planning for his future—a future that suddenly was full of promise.

He wandered into the garage, looking for an old bicycle pump to inflate the extra large rubber raft he had purchased at the surplus store. A smile lifted the corners of his mouth as he imagined what kind of water games they could play with the shiny plastic floating device. As he reached into an obscure corner for the pump, his eyes caught sight of the wooden sign Jill had had made for him in celebration of the ground-breaking of their new home. It said Brannigan's: Where Jack Takes Care of Jill.

Jack lifted the redwood sign and sighed. Unlike Maggie, Jill had always needed someone to take care of her. She had been just as compassionate and sincere as

Maggie, but she had never really had to stand on her own two feet. Maybe that was because John and the rest of her family had always doted on her, given in to her every whim.

If it had been Jill's parent who had been diagnosed as an Alzheimer's patient, she wouldn't have been able to pull her family together the way Maggie had. She was always the first one to fall to pieces at even the slightest hint of bad news. Funny, but until he had met Maggie, he hadn't realized how dependent Jill had always been on the men in her life.

Immediately he felt a twinge of guilt. Jill had been a good wife and he had loved her, but that part of his life was over. So many things had changed since her death—*he* had changed. Whether or not Maggie was responsible for that change didn't matter. Maybe he was fortunate that she had come along when she had. He might not have been ready for her any earlier in his life.

But now, everything felt right, and if one could say there had been anything positive to come out of Herb's illness, it was that Maggie had realized how important her family was in her life. For weeks he had been wondering what was going to happen to their relationship once her leave of absence was over. Now the question facing him was how long should he wait before discussing marriage. If the weekend went as he expected, they would be having that discussion very soon.

ONLY AS MAGGIE TURNED OFF the main highway onto the dusty gravel road leading to Lake Magda did she finally feel the tension easing from her body. Throughout her journey she had been preoccupied with trying to mentally arrange her life so that she could spend time with her father yet return to her job in Washington. It had been one more source of anxiety—the realization that her leave of absence would soon come to an end and she would once more be a long-distance daughter. Her request for a two-week extension had been granted, but sooner or later she was going to have to return to Washington, and the thought was one she didn't want to confront just yet.

She didn't want thoughts of her father's illness or her job in Washington to intrude on the weekend ahead of her. It was going to be a wonderfully romantic weekend, a time for her and Jack to concentrate on each other. She thought about the peach satin teddy she had purchased and a smile spread across her face.

Then she glanced at the bag of groceries on the front seat beside her. This was going to be her chance to show Jack her culinary skills and pamper him a bit. It had been a long time since she had had anyone to cook for, and the thought was appealing. She would bring him breakfast in bed. And lunch in bed. And maybe even dinner in bed. She chuckled. Well, maybe they could have a couple of meals out on the deck overlooking the lake.

At any rate, she wanted it to be a weekend of romance, not reality. The last few weeks had been too sobering, too realistic. What she needed now was to retreat into the arms of her lover.

Her lover. The thought brought a warmth to her skin despite the car's air conditioning. She had always done everything by the book. When she had married Brian she had been a virgin, and during their ten-year marriage she had never been unfaithful to him, not even when she knew that he had had several affairs of his own. There had been no one-night stands in her life, no lovers—not even a near affair. Now, for the first time in her life, she was thinking with her heart, and it felt so right.

That's because he is right for me, she reminded herself. She chuckled when she thought of what her co-workers in Washington would say when she told them she was in love with a professional fisherman. It didn't matter because he was exactly the kind of man she needed in her life. Unlike Brian, who had felt threatened by her success, Jack understood the demands and pressures of her job, yet he never made her feel guilty for wanting such demands and pressures. He was secure enough with his own identity that he would never attempt to try to control hers, whereas Brian had nearly killed himself trying to compete with her.

A small frown puckered her brow. She wouldn't think about Brian. He was her past, just as Jill was Jack's past. Or was she? Maggie wondered. Thoughts of Brian evoked little emotion in her other than pity. But then a divorce was not the same kind of loss as the death of a spouse. She was definitely over Brian, but was Jack over Jill?

It was a question that had been nagging her more than she cared to admit, which was why the first thing she did when she arrived at the cabin was to follow Jack as he carried her luggage into his room. When he deposited the suitcase on the floor, her eyes flew to the nightstand where she had last seen Jill's picture. The only item on the wooden table was an alarm clock.

Maggie's eyes met Jack's and she knew that he had seen her looking for the photo. He crossed the short distance separating them and pulled her into his arms.

"I think it's time we leave all the memories where they belong—in the past," he told her. "If there's one thing your father's illness has taught us, it's that people don't consist of memory alone. They have feelings, imagination, desires..." He trailed off as his hands sought the curve of her breast.

She inhaled sharply as his hand worked its way between the buttons of her sundress. "That's true," she murmured, although right now her memory was reminding her of the intense pleasure his hands could evoke.

He kissed her slowly and very thoroughly, his hands sliding down her body producing a familiar warmth that made her want to melt into him.

"I'm glad you came, Maggie Stewart," he whispered against her lips, his breath warm and sweet.

"I'm glad you invited me, Jack Brannigan." She spread her fingers over his chest, savoring the feel of hard muscle beneath his knit shirt. "It's going to be a wonderful weekend."

"And this is just the beginning." He reached up and stilled the hands that could reduce him to jelly, kissing her fingertips. "And the first thing on the agenda is picking."

"Picking?"

"Umm-hmm. Blueberries. They'll taste wonderful on our pancakes tomorrow morning." He started for the door, pulling her by the hand. When they reached the garage, he handed her one of the two plastic ice-cream pails he had uncovered earlier.

"You ever been blueberry picking?" he asked, taking the other pail for himself.

"Do pine trees shed cones?" she retorted, an impish glint in her cat-green eyes.

"Somehow I knew you were no stranger to blueberry picking," he said, an amazed slant to his mouth.

"So what kind of picker are you? Fast and dirty or slow and clean?"

"Which do you think?" she asked, her fingers provocatively tickling the flesh protruding from his short-sleeve shirt.

"Slow and clean," he said with exaggerated disappointment.

"Don't make it sound like a crime," she replied with mock indignation. "I suppose you think it's better to dump all the twigs and bugs and dirt in with the berries and clean them later?"

"We fast-and-dirty pickers know that there's always plenty of time to clean them," he argued lightly, his mouth twitching into a grin. "We also know that at this time of year and with the amount of rain we've been experiencing, mosquitoes can be mistaken for hummingbirds."

Maggie grinned. "Then in that case I'll work fast and dirty."

"I don't know about that." He rubbed a hand thoughtfully across his jaw. "Trying to change from slow and clean to fast and dirty can be like trying to change political parties."

"Then I know I can do it," she proclaimed and shoved her arm through his. "Take me to your berries."

They didn't spend much time gathering the midnight-blue berries, for as Jack predicted, the mosquitoes, although not the size of hummingbirds, were abundant. As soon as they each had half a bucketful, they scampered out of the blueberry thicket and back onto the dust-blown gravel road. Jack carried both of the pails so that Maggie could gather a bouquet of daisies from the field of wildflowers behind the pasture. After stopping to feed Dixie a handful of oats, they returned to the cabin where they sat outside at the picnic table cleaning the fruit.

"I feel as though someone should be pulling the grass and twigs from me and dousing me with cold water," Maggie commented, wiping the back of her hand across her damp brow.

"Want to clean up? We have several options—the lake, the shower or the sauna." He paused, then added, "I recommend the sauna. You'll never feel cleaner and more refreshed, I guarantee."

"Are you going to join me?"

He stood and reached for her hand. "Come. I'll show you where it is."

Even though she didn't remember seeing a sauna when he had given her a tour of the house, Maggie had expected him to take her inside. Instead he led her through a narrow opening in the trees and down a winding path until they came to a small cedar building built close to the lake.

"You mean a real sauna!" she proclaimed in delight.

Jack grinned. "My Finnish neighbor wouldn't have ever spoken to me again if I had built it inside." He nodded toward the cabin.

"Does this mean we have to beat ourselves with switches off the birch trees?" she asked with a grin.

"Only if you want to." He held up his palm defensively. "I take it you're familiar with the Finnish sauna?"

She sighed wistfully. "One spring when I must have been around seven or eight years old, my father took us to visit one of his cousins on the Iron Range." She smiled in recollection. "All I can remember is putting on our boots and heavy clothes to trample through the snow to the sauna, which turned out to be delightfully warm despite the miserable, damp cold outside. My father went first with the men, while my mother, my sister and I waited to go with the women.''

"As you can see, I do have separate dressing facilities," Jack said, grasping the handle of the women's changing room. "But there's no need for you to wait until I'm finished before you come in," he added with a lazy grin as he held the door open for her.

"Good. Because I prefer steaming with a friend," she told him, her voice far more seductive than her words.

"I was hoping you'd say that." A flash of desire flickered in his eyes before he quickly averted his gaze and said, "Towels are on the shelf. I'll see you inside."

She nodded, then stepped into the tiny room, which, although illuminated with a pair of bulbs over the mirror, seemed dark in contrast to the brightness out-of-doors. In a matter of seconds her eyes had adjusted to the dimness and she quickly stripped off her clothes, setting them on the long wooden bench lining the wall. Grabbing a thick towel from the shelf, she paused in front of the mirror, wondering if she should use it as a cover-up or simply walk in naked.

"This is no time for modesty, Maggie," she chided herself, wondering why she should suddenly feel self-conscious about Jack seeing her in the flesh after everything that had happened between them the night of the reunion. Memories of that night had her flinging the towel over her arm and marching into the steam room with a decided spring in her step.

Jack was already inside, looking like some glorious calendar hunk, a sheen of perspiration glistening on his bronzed skin. He sat on the middle tier of wooden benches, his elbows supporting his upper torso as he indolently leaned back, his eyes fixed on the entrance to the women's dressing room. As Maggie walked over to him, he sat motionless, scrutinizing her flawless beauty, an ardent message in his gaze.

"Hot, hotter or hottest," he said, gesturing first to the lowest of the tri-leveled benches, then patting the middle and upper seats with his palm.

"I think I'd better try hot," she told him, dropping onto the lowest bench.

When Jack got up to throw a pail of water on the pile of rocks surrounding the cast-iron stove, she took advantage of the opportunity to study him as he had studied her only moments before. When he noticed her bold scrutiny, he smiled, and Maggie felt a familiar stirring deep inside. Between the heat of the sauna and the smoldering look in his eyes, she thought for sure she would melt when he sat down beside her. She knew that he was as hungry for her as she was for him, yet he made no move to touch her—not until they were both drenched with moisture.

Then he reached for a bar of soap and filled a small pail with water from one of the large barrels. "Want me to do your back?" he asked with a sheepish grin, offering her the soap and water.

"I'd rather have you do my front," she said, catching him off guard, and was rewarded with a glowing gaze. He ended up soaping all of her—an exquisite torture. Her limbs, already weakened by the heat, felt as though they were dissolving under his touch. Then she returned the favor, sudsing his entire body, her fingers moving over his firm muscles caressingly so that the only sound to be heard was that of their heavy breathing.

When Maggie thought she would not be able to stand for one more moment, Jack rinsed them both with water from the second large barrel, then said, "Are you ready for that swim now?"

She groaned. "I don't know if I'm brave enough."

A corner of his mouth twitched. "To jump in the cold water or to go skinny-dipping?"

"Both," she admitted.

"Come on, Maggie. Take a chance with me," he said cajolingly, reaching out and wrapping his fingers around her wrist. "You're going to love it. The lake water feels like silk after being in here."

"All right," she finally agreed, and he took her by the hand and led her out through the men's dressing room, grabbing two dry towels as they exited. It was only a short distance to the water, and they went streaking across the grass and straight into the lake like a couple of children, screaming and giggling as they submerged themselves in the crystal-blue water.

"You're right—this does feel like silk," Maggie told him as she floated on her back, the water sloshing across her bare skin as she gazed up at the thin white clouds in the summer sky. "This is heavenly."

"Yes, it is," Jack agreed, but Maggie could tell by the huskiness in his voice that he wasn't referring to the refreshing sensation the lake provided.

When she lifted her head to glance up at him, he was standing, his eyes riveted to the parts of her gently bobbing in and out of the water. He had looked at her with the same hungry gaze when they had been in the sauna, but this time she knew there was no enervating steam to impede his desire. She let her feet sink to the sandy bottom until she was facing him. When he started wading toward her, she felt a tremor deep in her stomach.

"Jack we can't…" she began as he dived for her and began planting kisses all over her trembling flesh.

But he didn't pay any attention to her; his lips found every sensitive bit of skin on her body.

"Here in the water?" she asked breathlessly when he wrapped her legs around his hips and began moving her into deeper water.

His skin was hot to her touch where her fingers clutched his shoulders, and her body rode weightlessly in his arms.

"How can you possibly…" She never got the chance to finish her question, because he silenced her with a fierce kiss. Her fingers dug in deeper as he showed her exactly what he could do.

Waves of pleasure washed over them as passion joined them and once again they found their own private ecstasy.

Later, with their arms wrapped around each other, they staggered out of the lake over to the spot where Jack had dropped the fluffy towels on the grass. He reached for one of them, and began to dry her off. As he bent down to do her legs, she played with the wet hair on his head, noticing how the sunlight glistened in its thickness. When he had finished, he wrapped the large towel around her toga style, his fingers lingering longer than was necessary as he secured the ends.

When he would have begun drying himself, she reached for the other towel and said, "Let me."

He gently eased the towel from her fingers. "I think it's best that those hands of yours stay away from this aging body of mine—at least until after dinner." He quickly wrapped the towel around his waist then slipped his arm around hers. "I think we need clothes and food—and in that order," he told her as they walked back to the cabin.

"All right, I'll keep my hands off that wonderful body of yours but only if you allow me to put them to work in the kitchen. I love to cook and I told myself I was going to be the one pampering you this weekend. So far, it's been the other way around." She paused on the wooden deck.

"You mean it's going to get better?" he asked, his eyes dancing.

"We definitely started the weekend off on the right foot, but yes, it is going to get better." She slipped a finger inside the towel around his waist and grazed his bare flesh. "You'll see." Then, flashing him an impish grin, she slid inside the cabin.

And it did get better. After dinner, just before dusk when the lake was mirror smooth and the only movement on the water was the occasional plunge of a loon, Jack took her out in his canoe, and they circled the lake so they could watch nature prepare for night. Then, in the path of the sparkling moon, he built a campfire on the beach, where they sat and talked until they could no longer deny their need for each other. Then, for the first time, they made love in his bed, again and again, until she wondered how two people could find so much pleasure in each other's arms yet still find something new and exciting with each exploration.

It was a glorious weekend of sharing and loving, and when Sunday afternoon came, Maggie found she had to fight back the tears at the thought of leaving. Jack was grilling fresh walleye they had caught earlier that morning while she put together a pasta salad. Both were lost in their thoughts. He was wishing that this was the way the rest of their lives could be—just the two of them in their own private world. She was wondering how she was going to bear being away from him, knowing that even if she did come home from D.C. on the weekends, she would need to spend part of her time in Duluth.

Dinner was rather quiet, with neither one speaking much, but it wasn't an uncomfortable silence. When Maggie served Jack a piece of the blueberry pie she had made Saturday afternoon, he grabbed one of her hands and said, "It's amazing what those hands of yours can do. They bait a hook—"

"As long as it's not a leech," she interjected.

Jack grinned. "And they make great blueberry pie." His fingers toyed with hers. "And they make wonderful music."

"Music?" She shot him a quizzical glance. "They don't make music—unless you call punching the buttons on your tape player making music."

He pulled her down onto his lap and brought her hands to his lips. "You're wrong. They make my skin vibrate until it feels as though a melody is zinging right through me—a melody I can't forget long after the music is over." He looked again at her hands. "Oh, yes, these are wonderful music makers, Maggie. They make my heart sing."

"Oh, Jack!" She was so touched by his words she couldn't speak. She bit down hard on her lip to stem the threatening tears, then finally whispered, "You do the same thing to me. This has been the best weekend of my life." She turned her face into his shoulder and sighed. "I can't believe it's almost over."

He buried his face in her neck, trailing kisses up to her ear. "I don't want the music to stop—ever," he said seriously.

"Me, neither," she said huskily.

"Then marry me, Maggie." He said it so easily, as though he were asking her out on a date.

She stiffened. "What?" She thought she must not have heard him correctly.

"Marry me," he repeated. "I love you and I want every day of the rest of my life to be like these past two days were." He saw the uncertainty in her expression and he said, "Maggie, we're right for each other. You must feel it."

"I do, but . . ." She trailed off.

"What is it? Am I rushing things?"

When she slid off his lap and walked over to gaze out at the lake, he didn't stop her, but leaned back in his chair staring at her.

"Have I misread what this weekend has meant for us?" he asked quietly.

Maggie could only shake her head, her mind searching for the right words that would explain what a shock his proposal had been.

"Then what is it?" he demanded to know.

"It's just that I wasn't expecting a marriage proposal. In this day and age, women have come to expect the big question to be 'Will you move in with me?' not 'Will you marry me?'"

"I want you to be my wife, Maggie, not simply a lover who drops in on convenient weekends." He stood and came to stand beside her. "This isn't a rash decision on my part. I've thought about it a lot. Aw, hell, I've thought of nothing else this past week. If I had my way, we'd be off to the nearest justice of the peace and spending the rest of our days and nights right here in this cabin."

"But what about my job?" she asked, meeting his gaze.

"Your job?" This time he looked perplexed.

"Yes, you know, the one the government is holding open for me in Washington?" she reminded him with more than a hint of sarcasm. "The one I'm supposed to return to next month."

"But you said you were leaving Washington."

"Leaving my job?" she exclaimed, staring at him in amazement. "What ever gave you that idea?"

"You did. Right after your father's illness was diagnosed," he said evenly. "You told me that you realized what a mistake it was to get so caught up with money and success. You said you were going to concern yourself with values—family values—because you couldn't build solid relationships from a distance." He gave her an accusing glare. "Or was that emotion talking?"

"No, it wasn't emotion talking!" she retorted. "I meant every word of it. It's true that I allowed my job to keep me so preoccupied I didn't have time for any relationships, but that situation can be resolved without my quitting my job."

"So how *do* you plan on resolving that situation?"

"Until now, my whole life has revolved around my career. That's all going to change," she assured him. "For one thing I'm going to come home more often."

"You know as well as I do that once you're back in Washington, the trips home will be few and when you do come home, you're going to have to spend some time with your family." He voiced the same concerns she had been worrying about only minutes before.

She sighed and smoothed the wrinkles from her brow. "And what would you have me do? Quit my job and move here? Jack, what would I do all day long?"

"I was hoping you were sincere when you told me you wanted children."

Children. Marriage. Choices. For the first time in her life the choices weren't black-and-white. So many changes had occurred this summer, changes deep in her soul. How could she explain them to him when she didn't understand them herself? How could she admit she was frightened of what the future held?

When she didn't respond, he said, "Do you want children, Maggie?"

"Yes, I do," she told him candidly. "But it's not simply a matter of wanting children. Everything is happening so fast."

"I know." He cupped her face in his hands. "I never thought I'd fall in love again so easily. But I have, Maggie, and it's the best thing in my life right now. I want you to be a part of my life always."

She closed her eyes momentarily, then opened them and asked, "Do you want me to leave my job in Washington?"

"Only if it's what you want to do." He dropped his hands, shoving them into his pockets. "I've never regretted dropping out of corporate America."

"Does that mean you wouldn't reconsider going back?"

"Is that what you want me to do? Take a job in Washington so we can be together?"

"We could still have this place for a weekend getaway."

He shook his head. "After having the life-style I've had for the past eighteen months, I don't think I could go back to the hectic world you live in, Maggie."

"Will you at least come visit me and see what you think?" she asked hopefully.

"It sounds as though you've already made plans to return."

"My boss has already granted me a two-week extension on my leave. I can't ask for another one."

"So where does that leave us?" he asked.

"Rather than come home every weekend I thought I'd take two long weekends every month. That way I'll be able to spend time in Duluth and time here," she explained.

"From what you've told me about your job, that might not be a very realistic expectation," he warned, a skeptical frown covering his face.

"It can be," she said, trying to sound positive. "I've changed my priorities, Jack. That's what's important. Before I was willing to put in long hours. I brought a lot of the stress upon myself." She moved closer to him and wrapped her hands around his neck. "I do want to get married and have children, but I can't deny that my career is important, too."

"So what do you want me to do?"

"Be patient until I figure out a way that I can have it all—marriage, children and a career."

"And what if you discover you can't have it all, Maggie? What goes?"

Maggie never did answer the question.

CHAPTER FIFTEEN

MAGGIE PACKED HER SUITCASES knowing that saying goodbye to Duluth was not going to be easy. It had been four weeks since her father had been diagnosed with Alzheimer's disease and during that time she felt they had made considerable progress with understanding and accepting his illness. Yet she couldn't prevent the feelings of uneasiness that haunted her concerning her decision to return to Washington.

The Alzheimer's Family Support Group had provided a forum for talking out feelings and frustrations, and Maggie felt comforted by the thought that the support group was there for her family. Hearing how other Alzheimer's patients and their loved ones coped with the disease had helped the Stewart family retain a sense of hope for the future.

They had also learned a few practical things such as how color coding the bathroom and kitchen helped alleviate Herb's tendency to forget where things belonged. They also suggested he start keeping a journal, a simple task that would enable him to write down his daily routine and give him a feeling of self-worth. Most importantly, the group helped them to understand the value of everyday activities—activities that didn't require memory, such as eating together, listening to music and taking long walks.

Maggie thought it was rather ironic that the reason she had originally felt like an outsider was now the same one that had drawn her closer to her family than she had been in years. There was a sense of belonging, an intimacy she hadn't felt with her family since she had been a child. Now she was leaving it all behind and going back to what? An empty apartment in D.C. that she barely spent any time in because she was either out of the country conferring with international trade officials or being entertained by some visiting diplomat who hoped to persuade her to change her position on import quotas.

"Need any help?"

Maggie looked up from her packing to see her sister standing in the doorway, her hands behind her back.

"I come bearing gifts." Karen pulled her hands out from behind her and proudly produced two watercolors for Maggie's inspection. "Erin and Nicole wanted you to take these wonderful pieces of art back with you. These are what are known around our house as refrigerator art."

Maggie couldn't help but smile at the stick-figure drawings presented to her. "How sweet. I see they take after the Stewart side. These are quite good considering the ages of the artists," she commented as she studied the pictures.

"Spoken like a biased aunt. How's the packing coming along?" Karen asked, peeking over Maggie's shoulder at the piles of clothing still sitting on the bed.

Maggie carefully set the art on the walnut desk she had used as a student. "I'm slowly getting everything done. I'm not sure I'm going to be able to get this thing closed, however," she told her, pressing her palms down on the top of a suitcase bulging with more clothes than it was designed to carry.

"I've got an extra bag you can borrow," Karen offered.

"Mom's already given me one of hers. I think I'm going to have to ship some of this back." She put her hands on her hips and looked at the clothing still needing to be packed. "I can't believe I bought so many things. It must have been because I had so much time on my hands. I bought more clothes this summer than I did in the last five years in D.C."

"That's because in Washington you spend all of your time working. You didn't have any clothes for just loafing around and having fun in," Karen told her, holding up a one-piece romper. "Do you think you'll ever wear any of these things back in Washington?"

"I suppose I could leave some of it behind," Maggie said, shaking out the bottoms of a teal-blue jogging suit. "I am going to be coming home regularly."

"Are you?"

From her sister's tone of voice, Maggie knew Karen was doubting her statement rather than asking a question.

"Yes, I am." She met her sister's inquisitive gaze. "I know that in the past I haven't exactly been the dutiful daughter. And I know that you've always been the one to shoulder the everyday problems that have arisen over the years, but I want you to remember this: you've had Pop for all those years that I was away. You were the one sharing Sunday dinner with him, cheering him on when he played in his curling tournaments and laughing at all the funny anecdotes he always had to tell. You were there for the good times and the bad. All I have are the memories of coming home for special occasions.

Twenty years of short visits." There was self-recrimination in a voice steeped with emotion.

"Pop is so proud of you, Maggie." Karen's voice softened. "You should hear the way he talks about you to customers in the store. He's always bragging about you—what a success you've become. I think your job is just as important to him as it is to you."

Maggie shook her head, her eyes downcast. "Funny, but it doesn't seem so important now."

"What is important to you, Maggie?"

Maggie walked over to the window overlooking the backyard, her eyes finding the old tire swing her father had hung from an oak tree when she was only five years old. "Until this summer, I thought I knew the answer to that question."

"Is it because of Pop's illness or Jack Brannigan that you don't know the answer?" Karen asked, coming to stand beside her at the window.

"It's because of a lot of things—Pop, Jack, even me." She sat down on the padded window seat. "You saw the shape I was in when I came home this summer. I had worked myself sick. I always thought my career was the most important thing in my life, but that was because it was the only thing in my life that was working properly. Now I know there's more to life than work."

"Isn't that what we've been telling Pop these past few weeks?" Karen squeezed in beside her sister on the window seat. "Yet you know as well as I do that as long as Pop's capable of performing even the simplest of duties at the store, he's not going to be happy at home. Isn't that the way it is with you, Maggie? Could you be happy away from Washington?"

It was a question Maggie had been asking herself for the past month and she still didn't know the answer. With troubled eyes, she appealed to her sister. "I was this summer."

Karen patted her hand as though she were a small child needing comfort. "I know."

"But maybe that's because I knew that come fall I'd be going back." Confused, Maggie closed her eyes and gently shook her head. When she opened her eyes, they were drawn once again to the tire swing swaying in the brisk autumn breeze, looking lost and abandoned. She remembered the day her father had brought the tire home and fastened the thick rope to the largest oak tree in the yard. He had warned her to sit inside the circle of rubber and not to try standing up. But she had seen the neighbor boy swaying to and fro in a standing position and had been determined to give it a try. For her bravery she had been rewarded with a nosebleed and a tear in her favorite dress.

"What are you staring at?" Karen asked when Maggie grew silent.

"Our tire swing. Doesn't it look lonesome?"

"There are a lot of memories in that old swing," Karen reflected wistfully.

"Yeah—like the time Stevie Dawes kept spinning you and wouldn't let you get off even though you were screaming."

"And you hit him in the stomach and sent him home crying."

"And his mother called Mom accusing me of attacking her innocent little lamb."

Both smiled in recollection. "You were a pretty neat big sister," Karen said, her eyes glinting with affection. "I know I probably never told you that when we were kids, but I was feeling it in here." She patted her chest with her fingers.

Maggie reached for a tissue on the desk. "You shouldn't say such sweet things on a person's last day in town," she gently chastised her, dabbing at her eyes.

"I'm really happy this summer happened, Maggie. Not Pop's illness of course, but I'm glad you came home. For the first time in my life I feel as though I've finally discovered what sisters are supposed to mean to each other. Ever since I can remember I've felt as though we've been competing with each other. Only this summer did I realize how wrong I was about that."

"I felt the same way," Maggie admitted. "Now, as I look back, it seems so ridiculous. Why didn't we have this conversation ten or even fifteen years ago?"

"Maybe because whenever we were together we were still behaving like Mom and Pop's kids rather than two adult women. I was only thirteen when you left for college. At the time I felt as though you had abandoned me. From then on I think I acted like that thirteen-year-old every time you came home—never forgiving you for leaving me when I needed a big sister."

"I wasn't much better," Maggie admitted with a sigh. "I expected you to listen to every word I said as though it were the gospel. When you told me you weren't going to college, I took it as a personal insult. Then, when I came home to visit and saw that you were perfectly happy being a wife and mother, I still didn't want to admit that I didn't know what was best for you."

"We didn't want to let ourselves be different, did we?" Karen mused. "I would harp at you about having children before your biological clock ticked away and you would harp at me about finishing college."

"But we are different and it's okay," Maggie said with a smile. "I really admire the way you've taken over at the store for Pop, but more than that, I admire what you're doing with Erin and Nicole. Being a mother is such a tremendous responsibility."

Karen regarded her thoughtfully. "Maggie, haven't you ever thought about having children?"

"Of course I have. Doesn't every woman? I just didn't think they'd be a part of my life."

"Why is that?"

Maggie suddenly realized that she hadn't told her sister about her problems with her ex-husband. "Karen, Brian was sterile."

A look of disbelief had her gaping. "Why didn't you tell us? My God, Maggie, I wouldn't have made all those comments about your having children if I had known."

"I probably should have said something, but Brian didn't want anybody to know. He preferred to let people think we had chosen not to have children. His ego just couldn't handle the fact that he was the reason we couldn't have a biological child, especially when he was already having to deal with feelings of inadequacy because he didn't make as much money as I did."

"But you could have adopted children."

"With the problems we had to work out in our marriage, I figured it was better if I pushed all thoughts of motherhood from my head and put all of my energy into my career."

"And now?"

"Now I find myself confronted with choices I never thought I'd have to make." She paused, and a smile erupted on her face. "Jack wants to get married."

Karen reached out and hugged her. "Congratulations! That's wonderful." Then she pushed her away and studied the face that now was lined with worry. "It is wonderful, isn't it? You do love him, Maggie?"

Again, Maggie's face softened into a smile. "Yes, I do love him. But it isn't simply a case of loving him. He wants to live here in Minnesota. He also wants to have children. Until I met Jack, I never even thought I'd want to get married again. Now I find myself faced with decisions I feel totally unprepared to make."

"Do you want to get married?" she asked candidly.

"I don't want to lose what we have going for us."

"That's not what I asked you." Karen studied her sister's pensive face. "What do you want—marriage or an affair?"

"If Jack would come with me to Washington I wouldn't have any trouble giving you an answer."

"But he's going to stay here in Minnesota and you're going to go back to Washington. So where does that leave the two of you?"

Maggie frowned. "Apart. Except for the weekends I come home or whenever he can manage to come to Washington for a few days."

"So you're going to have one of those long-distance relationships that are so vogue nowadays." There was a hint of disapproval in her tone, but Maggie didn't mind. How could she when she felt the same way?

"After living in Washington I've certainly seen enough of them—some successful, others not so successful." She sighed and pushed her bangs off her forehead. "I just wish I felt more confident that ours was going to be one of the successful ones." She glanced again at the tire swing outside. "And I wish it wasn't so

hard for me to leave this place.'' She had to swallow
hard to clear the emotion blocking her throat.

"Maggie, if you don't want to go back to Washington, why are you leaving? Is your job that important to
you?''

She gave her an uncertain smile. "I guess that's why
I'm going back—to find out if it is.'' She reached for
Karen's hands. "Wish me luck?''

Karen squeezed her hands in reassurance. "Of course
I do. But I have to confess, I'm on Jack's side for purely
selfish reasons. I'd like to have you living here. This
summer has made me realize how much I've missed
having my big sister around.'' She hugged her tightly,
then reached for the tissues, passing another one to
Maggie as well.

"I'm going to be coming home so often you won't
even realize I've left,'' Maggie said, dabbing her eyes
once more.

"Do you need a ride to the airport tomorrow?''

Maggie shook her head. "I've asked Sheila to take
me. Now that we have Pop's daily routine structured, I
didn't want to confuse him with an unnecessary inter-
ruption.''

"This probably won't make you feel any better, but
if it's any consolation at all, I think you're doing the
right thing,'' Karen told her.

Sheila didn't share Karen's sentiments and told Maggie so as they waited for her flight to board the next
morning. "You can still change your mind and stay
right here in Duluth.''

"Is it that obvious that I don't want to leave?'' Maggie asked, trying not to frown.

"I keep expecting Jack to come storming in here like a knight on a white horse and carry you off to the woods," Sheila said, glancing around the airport.

Maggie smiled weakly. "He wouldn't do that."

"I think you wish he would, though, don't you?"

Maggie clicked her tongue. "Of course not. Look, Sheila, it's hard enough for me to leave. Do you think we might change the subject?"

Sheila raised her eyebrows and shrugged. "Did I tell you the latest postreunion news?" When Maggie shook her head she said, "Yours wasn't the only romance to blossom because of our great get-together. It seems that Vicki Dolson has left her husband and moved in with Andy Nester."

Maggie's face registered her disbelief. "Vicki and Andy? Weren't they the ones who went steady all through their entire senior year only to break up after they were photographed as the cutest couple for senior favorites?"

Sheila nodded. "Yup, and they're definitely a couple again. Only now she has three kids and he has two, plus they have one on the way."

"She's not pregnant?" Maggie's mouth dropped open.

"Umm-hmm. I ran into her at the dentist's office last week where she filled me in on all the details—and I do mean *all* the details of her experience at what she called the reunion party of a lifetime," Sheila drawled sarcastically.

"Wasn't her husband with her that night?"

"I remember her telling me at the time he didn't want to come because he thought nothing exciting ever happened at any of these things." She rolled her eyes heavenward. "If you and Jack hadn't left so early, you would have seen her dancing with Andy. It was rather obvious from the way they were rubbing up against each other on the dance floor that they weren't simply reminiscing about the good old days.''

''I guess it shouldn't surprise us. It looked as though there were several people at the reunion who were hoping to rekindle past romances.''

''All of us were probably trying to relive a little bit of the past,'' Sheila stated philosophically. ''Overall, I'm really happy with the way everything turned out. I've received so many wonderful letters with all sorts of nice comments on the evening. And we've already got a committee formed for when the twenty-fifth anniversary rolls around.''

''Haven't I always said you have excellent organizational skills?'' Maggie reminded her with an ''I told you so'' grin. ''I could use someone like you in my office.''

''Don't tempt me. You might find yourself with a runaway mom on your doorstep.''

Maggie sighed. ''We make quite a pair, Sheila. You'd like to be flying off somewhere and I'd like to be staying here. We both want what we can't have.''

''But you can have a life in Duluth if you really want it,'' Sheila corrected her.

Those words haunted Maggie as she watched the city diminish in size as her plane climbed higher and higher until all that was visible below were masses of fluffy white clouds.

IF MAGGIE HAD ANY DOUBTS about feeling awkward at work after such a long leave of absence, they were quickly forgotten. Within a few days of being back in Washington, she felt as though she hadn't been away at all; returning to D.C. had felt like putting on an old pair

of shoes. However, she couldn't forget that she had
tried on a different pair in Minnesota, shoes that had all
the magic of a glass slipper. By the end of her first week,
she was almost ready to believe that her summer in Duluth had been a dream. But her heart wouldn't let her
mistake it for a dream. Nor would her memories. They
intruded often, both at home and at work.

Even during her busiest times at the office, she'd find
herself glancing at her watch and wondering if her father had remembered where he was supposed to be. But
the worst time was at night, when she would return to
an empty apartment and loneliness would settle all
around her, just as the dew drenched the sleeping grass.
When she had first moved back home, she had found it
difficult having to share her living space with two other
adults. Now that she was alone, she found herself listening for the comforting sound of her father humming as he padded around in search of his pipe, and
sniffing for the aroma of cinnamon and apples that
permeated the air whenever her mother baked one of
her coffee cakes.

It was a loneliness she hadn't experienced previ-
ously—not even when Brian had moved out after their
marriage had failed. She told herself she'd get used to
it, but the trouble was she didn't want to get used to it.
Thinking activity would make the days pass more
quickly, she filled her social calendar and renewed her
membership at the local health club. But no matter how
busy she kept herself, she found herself wishing away
the time in anticipation of her trips back home.

There were two such trips in October—both hectic,
but worth the effort and the hassles they created in her
life. She spent part of the time with her parents in Duluth and the other part with Jack at Lake Magda. By the

time November arrived, Maggie knew that half a weekend twice a month was not enough time to be with the man she loved and she convinced Jack to fly to Washington to spend a few days sightseeing in the nation's capital.

Unfortunately the trip had to be postponed because Maggie learned that she was going to have to travel to Geneva the week they had scheduled for his visit. She found the meetings in Geneva less than satisfying, especially when she knew she should have been showing Jack the Lincoln Memorial rather than arguing with negotiators over removing food import restrictions.

She finally did manage to cut her trip short, and flew back to Minnesota only to discover that Jack, unaware of her change in plans, had traveled to the Gulf Coast to enter a fishing tournament. By the time December arrived and Maggie had only seen him three times in three months, she knew that their long-distance relationship was definitely not without problems.

As more time elapsed between visits, Maggie felt the frustration building in both of them, and she wasn't certain how much longer their relationship would last under the strain. When they were together, their world was filled with laughter and love, and when they were apart, it was littered with tension and solitude.

Even though Maggie had cut down on the number of hours she worked, she still felt fatigued almost every day. Worried that she might experience a relapse of the exhaustion that had sidelined her during the summer, she shortened her workday even more—by several hours—and took extra care to make certain she had enough sleep. But the fatigue persisted, and even seemed to worsen. When she experienced several days of nausea as well, she made an appointment with Dr. Walker.

After a complete examination and several lab tests, Maggie watched as the doctor's bald head bent over his desk while his fingers scribbled on her medical chart. When he was finally finished writing, he snapped the cap back on his fountain pen and rested his palms on his knees as he faced her.

"I hope you're not going to chew me out," she warned him. "I've done everything you've told me to do and there's no reason for me to have a relapse of this—"

"You aren't having a relapse," he interrupted, lifting his hand. "You're pregnant."

"I'm what?" she nearly shrieked.

"You're pregnant. As in going to have a baby."

"But I had my period." She paused with her mouth agape. "Is that why it was so light?" she asked tentatively.

"It's not uncommon for a little bleeding to occur during the first missed period. My guess is you're barely two months along. That's why you've been so tired and feeling a little queasy."

"I'm pregnant," she repeated, still in shock.

Dr. Walker asked cautiously, "I take it this isn't something you planned?"

"No, it isn't. Obviously I didn't use the best method of birth control," she stated dryly.

"The only foolproof methods I know of are sterilization and abstinence." He pulled open a drawer and withdrew several pamphlets. "We're going to have to get you started on some vitamins, and here's some information I want you to read." He handed her several glossy booklets that Maggie looked at with widened eyes.

"'Pregnancy and You,'" she read aloud. "'Nutritional Guidelines for Pregnant Women.'" She stopped and looked at the doctor. "This is for real, isn't it? I'm going to have a baby." Her voice was filled with awe.

"Yes, Maggie, you are," Dr. Walker confirmed, then nearly fell backward as Maggie jumped off the examining table and grabbed him in a bear hug.

"Thank you, Dr. Walker. If you hadn't sent me home to recuperate this summer, this wouldn't have happened." She did a wobbly pirouette, then dropped into the leather chair beside his desk and shoved her head between her knees.

"Are you all right, Maggie?" the doctor asked, placing his arm around her shoulders.

After a few moments she sat back up. "I'm wonderful. Just answer one question for me?"

"What's that?" he said, concern in his voice.

"Am I going to feel this rotten the entire nine months?"

MAGGIE SOON DISCOVERED that she didn't feel rotten all the time—only when she first woke up in the morning. And right before she went to bed at night. And whenever someone stepped into the elevator wearing a heavy perfume. And when she tried to make a pot of coffee, the aroma nearly laid her out flat. As soon as she had left Dr. Walker's office she had gone to the bookstore and purchased every book in stock on the subject of pregnancy. Then she had gone home and started to read them, but had fallen asleep before finishing the first chapter of the first book.

An unusually busy week had her coming home at night too tired to even think about the decisions she needed to make now that she was expecting a baby. When her boss called her into his office to offer her a promotion that meant extensive traveling to Japan, she knew that she could no longer postpone making decisions about her future and booked a flight to Duluth.

After being snowed out of the Duluth airport on Friday night, Maggie's plane was finally able to land early Saturday morning. Having told no one of her plans to come home, she took a taxi from the airport and surprised her father who was eating breakfast when she arrived. He sat at the kitchen table with his plaid flannel shirt on inside out, a hot dog in his hand.

When he saw Maggie walk in and shake the snow from her felt hat, he said, "I thought you weren't coming back until Christmas?"

She kicked off her shoes and padded over to give him a kiss on the cheek. "I missed you." She shrugged out of her woolen coat, draping it over the back of a chair.

"Still snowing?"

"Just enough to keep the roads slick. Where's Mom?"

"Her turn at the store this morning. I'm just having myself some breakfast." She noticed that his journal was beside him as he ate.

"Is the coffee hot?"

"I just made a fresh pot. And there are muffins in the bread box."

Maggie poured herself a cup then sat down across from him. "How are you feeling?"

Herb smiled and gave her a wink. "I feel great. Must be the medication the doc gave me."

"You look great," Maggie said sincerely. A dab of mustard slipped off his hot dog and trickled down his flannel shirt. She reached for a napkin and swiped at the spot. "Mustard will stain. Maybe I should get a wet cloth."

Herb glanced down at the front of his shirt, then grimaced. "What the—" He broke off, as though suddenly conscious of his mistake. "Did I put this on—" He fiddled with the buttons.

"Inside out." She supplied the words for him when he had difficulty finishing his sentence. Then she bestowed a lovely smile on him. "It's okay, Pop."

"Look at it this way. You could have been here last week. Mother says I came down to breakfast buck naked." There was a silence, then gradually he began to chuckle until they both were laughing out loud. When Maggie had to reach into her pocket for a tissue to dab the moisture from her eyes, Herb said, "The doctors tell me the ability to laugh at oneself is therapeutic."

"I'd say they're right," she agreed.

"I know one thing. You're much prettier when you're laughing." He lifted her chin with his forefinger. "You want to tell me the true reason you're back home and don't tell me it's because you missed your father." He winked as he wagged his finger at her. "You having trouble with your fellow?"

Maggie couldn't prevent the smile. Some things never changed. "I'm going to have to make some decisions, Pop. I've been avoiding them for several months now thinking that with time they would become easier to make."

"Are you talking about personal or professional decisions?" he asked, his face growing serious.

"Both." She sighed. "I'm in love with Jack, Pop. There's no point in denying it, nor do I want to. I want to be with him."

"Does this mean I'm going to be gaining a son-in-law?" He raised both eyebrows eagerly.

"That's where the problem comes in. Jack's life is here in Minnesota. He's happy being a professional fisherman."

"And that isn't enough for you?" He shook his head. "I've never known you to be pretentious, Maggie."

"I'm not," she denied. "If he's happy, then yes, it's enough for me. But what about my job, Pop? I love Jack but the thought of leaving my job and moving to a small town in Minnesota is frightening."

"So what's the alternative?"

"The alternative isn't making any sense. When I left in September, I thought that Jack and I would be able to manage a long-distance relationship. But it's not going to work. Another snag has appeared, too."

"What's that?" He looked at her with interest.

"I've been offered a promotion, which means I'd be traveling even more than I am right now."

Herb whistled through his teeth. "Another step up the ladder, eh?" His smile was one of pride, and it warmed Maggie's heart.

"I should be happy. Six months ago it was exactly what I had been hoping for. Now I don't want it, yet I feel guilty about not wanting it. I'm really confused, Pop."

"Maggie, my dear, let me show you something." He reached across the table for her hand, then led her into the hallway where a long beveled mirror adorned the wall. He positioned her in front of the mirror, then stood beside her. "Do you know that every morning when I wake up, the very first thing I do is look in the mirror and ask myself, 'Who am I?' Because, you see, I know that one day I'm going to wake up and I'm not going to know the answer to that question."

Maggie's eyes held her father's in the mirror. "Oh, Pop." Her voice was choked with emotion, unshed tears in her eyes.

"It's part of the disease and I've accepted that. But look," he stared into the mirror. "See that man in there. As long as I do know who he is, I'm going to make sure the rest of the world knows, too." He gently placed his hands on her shoulders and urged her to step in front of him. "I think maybe you should look at that woman in there and ask yourself the same question. Do you know who you are, Maggie?"

CHAPTER SIXTEEN

WHEN MAGGIE AWOKE the next morning, the first thing she did was rush over to the dressing table and gaze into the mirror. She did know who she was. She was a woman in love who also happened to be expecting a baby—a baby she wanted very much. Although there had never been any doubt in her mind about that, the actual realization came only as she had climbed out of the double bed she had spent more than half of her life waking up in each morning. Only this morning was like no other one in her entire life.

She looked down as her hand found her abdomen and gently massaged the area she knew would soon be swelling with a new life. Today she was going to drive to Garrison and announce to Jack that their long-distance affair was finished. She could just imagine the look on his face when she arrived on his snowy doorstep demanding that he make an honest woman of her. A smile slowly spread across her face as she contemplated the scene in her imagination.

If it hadn't been for the inclement weather, she would have been at Lake Magda by now. But even though the snow had diminished in the city, the highway patrol had advised motorists not to travel in the rural areas of the state, as strong winds had left the highways hazardous. Maggie had no choice but to spend the night with her parents and wait for the roads to be cleared. Despite her disappointment, she had found her old room with its dainty wallpaper and lace curtains a haven for her weary body.

It probably was for the better, she told herself as she lifted a corner of the window shade and a bright beam of sunshine caused her to squint. After the twelve-hour delay in her flight yesterday, she had been exhausted and in no shape to drive to Garrison, even though in her present state of mind she probably could have driven to the North Pole if it meant being with Jack. Instead she had spent the afternoon helping her father test the many strings of Christmas tree lights that would adorn the Scotch pine her parents had already purchased from the youth group at church.

Neither of her parents thought it unusual that she not only took a nap before dinner, but retired for the evening shortly after the dishes had been cleared from the table. Maggie would have liked to have confided in her mother the news of her pregnancy, but she wanted Jack to be the first one to know about the baby, which was why she was determined to get to Lake Magda as soon as possible, even if it meant she had to go by dogsled. She was excited about this baby and she wanted to tell the world that she, Maggie Stewart, was pregnant!

Despite the queasiness that threatened to send her crawling back to the double bed, she managed to quickly shower and dress, pausing only to try telephoning Jack. After several unsuccessful attempts, she decided that he was probably out on Lake Mille Lacs; he had told her he'd hoped to move the fish houses out on the ice before the end of the week.

Her suspicions were confirmed when she finally reached the gravel road leading into Lake Magda and discovered there was no road, only a massive snowdrift. There was no sign of tire tracks anywhere, and a large bank of snow was blocking the entrance to the private road. It had obviously been deposited by a highway plow that had already cleared the main thoroughfares. She couldn't have traversed the road had she wanted to, so instead of risking getting stuck attempting to turn around, she drove a few miles farther down the highway until she came to a gas station.

Again she tried phoning Jack. When there was no answer, she tried the Blue Goose restaurant and learned that he was out on Lake Mille Lacs. After using the rest room, she purchased a chocolate bar that she munched on as she drove the short distance back to Garrison in search of Jack's fish house. As soon as the frozen surface of Lake Mille Lacs came into view, she saw what a difficult task that was going to be. Hundreds of fish houses were clumped together in what appeared to be little cities with neighborhoods. The only way she would be able to find Jack would be to stop at the Blue Goose and get directions.

Joni wasn't working, but Maggie recognized the man behind the bar as someone she had been introduced to at the sailing regatta. He cheerfully explained the easiest route to take to find Jack, drawing her a map on the back of one of the cocktail napkins.

Maggie was grateful she had the roughly drawn sketch once she reached the shore of the lake, because at least half a dozen plowed paths fanned out from the access point near the highway. Having never driven on a frozen lake before, she was unprepared for the crunch of her car tires as she traveled across the rutted road. At one point a large cracking noise had her reaching for the door handle, ready to jump out should the car plunge through a patch of thin ice. But as she passed a multitude of wooden shacks, many with monstrous four-wheel-drive vehicles parked beside them, she told herself the ice was certainly safe for her small station wagon, despite all the startling popping sounds.

As she drove, she was once again reminded of the enormity of the lake. The scattered clusters of fish houses grew farther and farther apart until they finally disappeared and Maggie felt as though she were in the middle of a white wilderness. She experienced a momentary sense of panic when she wondered what would happen if she developed car trouble in the middle of nowhere with a temperature of about fifteen degrees outside. Then, in the distance, she saw the faint outline of more wooden shacks, and she breathed a sigh of relief.

As she drew nearer to the group of fish houses, she noticed that at least a dozen of them were all painted the same periwinkle blue as the Blue Goose restaurant and she knew that she had located Jack's little city. There, amid the cluster of small wooden shacks, she found the gray Jeep Wagoneer parked beside one of the rectangular-shaped buildings.

Suddenly nervous, Maggie pulled down the visor mirror and grimaced. She had borrowed her mother's down jacket, which, although warm, was horribly out of fashion besides being a dull green that made her skin look even paler than it already was. She wished now that she had worn earmuffs, because the woolen ski cap her mother had insisted she wear had flattened her hair to her head, and not even vigorous finger brushing could give it any life. To top it off, the chocolate bar she had eaten had given her indigestion and despite the time of day, she was feeling queasy again.

She rummaged in her purse for a lipstick and blush, only to remember they were in the makeup bag that now sat on the dressing table in her old bedroom. Shoving her sunglasses back in place, she sighed, inhaled deeply and climbed out of the car.

The air was brittley cold, and Maggie gratefully allowed the wind to sting her cheeks, hoping it would add some color. Her booted feet crunched in the snow as she tucked her chin into the collar of her jacket and trampled over to the fish house. When she reached the door, she pulled off her mittens and rapped with her bare knuckles.

A warm rush of air greeted her as the door opened and a familiar voice called out, "Maggie?"

"Jack?" she answered, removing her sunglasses to squint into his handsome face.

"Maggie, Maggie, Maggie!" he repeated, sweeping her into his arms and twirling her around, down jacket, clunky boots and all. He kissed her thoroughly before putting her down.

The twirling motion was enough to cause the already queasy Maggie to weaken at the knees, and she nearly collapsed against him, her creamy skin going pale. "Jack, I think I'd better sit down for a minute."

Noticing her pallid complexion, he led her over to a folding chair and helped her unbutton her coat. "What is it, sweetheart. Are you ill?" he asked, a tender concern in his voice as he helped her out of her outer garment.

Maggie closed her eyes for just a moment, then did the last thing Jack expected her to do. She started to cry.

Jack knelt down beside her, pulling her head to his shoulder as he wrapped his arms around her. "Tell me what's wrong, Maggie? Is it your father?" he asked gently as his hand affectionately stroked her red tresses while she sobbed into his shoulder.

"No, he's fine," she mumbled into his plaid flannel shirt. "It's me, Jack." She lifted her head and made an effort to smile but failed miserably. She bit her lower lip, then, with a hiccup, said, "I'm preg . . . nant."

"You're pregnant," he repeated, his face expressionless. He was too stunned to do anything but stare at the tearstained face of the woman who had come to mean the world to him. Why was she crying—unless she was distressed because she was going to have his baby. Had she come all the way out here to tell him she didn't want to have his child? Unconsciously a frown marred his features.

Maggie waited anxiously for him to smile and rejoice at her good news. Instead he gave her a look that had her wondering if maybe he wasn't having second thoughts about their relationship. She had thought he would have rained kisses of joy all over her face at her announcement, but he was as silent as a stone wall.

Finally she could stand it no longer. "I thought you would be happy," she said, choking back a sob of disappointment as her eyes unknowingly pleaded with his for sympathy. "You told me you wanted to get married and have kids and stuff," she said unevenly as hiccups laced her words.

"I *am* happy!" he declared, his eyes staring at her in amazement. Then he flashed her a grin, a proud grin that stretched across his unshaven jaw.

"Oh, good," she said, a smile breaking out on her splotchy red face as she swiped at the few lingering tears with the back of her hand.

"Good?" he repeated tentatively, studying her face with undisguised interest.

She laughed, then gave him a big hug. "Better than good. It's wonderful." She sniffled, then added, "I'm happy, too."

He pushed her back an arm's length. "You're happy? Then why are you crying?" He gave her a baffled look.

"Because I feel so awful. My stomach's queasy, I'm tired all the time and I wanted it to be romantic and wonderful when I told you the good news. So what do I do? I walk in here and burst into tears and blurt it out."

He circled his arms around her and drew her close into a big hug. "Just the very thought that we're going to have a baby *is* romantic and wonderful," he told her, his voice husky with emotion.

"It is, isn't it?" she said in awe, suddenly feeling as though someone had given her a million dollars.

"It is if it means you want to get married." His blue eyes probed hers for an answer.

"I do," she said softly, love written all over her face.

"I have to tell you, I'm old-fashioned when it comes to marriage. I think husbands and wives should live together under the same roof," he warned in a husky voice.

"I want that, too," she admitted. "This long-distance stuff isn't working very well. I hate being away from you, Jack."

"And I hate being away from you. So what are we going to do about it?"

"I'm leaving my job. I turned in my resignation two days ago."

He hugged her again, kissing the skin below her ears. Then he lifted her chin with his finger and gazed into her eyes. "Are you sure about this? I know how much your career has meant to you."

"It was my whole life until a few months ago. But that's why it was so important. Jack, I had nothing in my life but work. And now as I look back, I can see how empty my life was." Her fingers caressed his cheek. "I want this baby and I want to be your wife."

"And a career? A few months ago you told me you wanted all three," he reminded her.

"I'm not saying that I won't ever want to go back to work," she warned him. "But for right now, the only job I want is that of wife and mother."

He nuzzled her close and exhaled an appreciative sigh. "Do you know how much I've wanted to hear you say those words?"

"They're true, Jack. I've finally realized that the things I value most are all right here in Minnesota."

"You know, we don't have to live at Lake Magda," he told her. "We could get a place in Duluth and use Magda as a retreat."

"It is a little small for a growing family, but what about your work?"

"That's something I've been meaning to talk to you about." He stood and for the first time Maggie noticed the card table in the corner of the fish house. It had several piles of papers on it plus a lap-top computer.

She gave him a puzzled look. "What are you doing with a portable p.c. in an ice house?" she asked, getting up from the folding chair.

He gave her a sheepish grin. "Would you believe working?"

"Working?" She arched one eyebrow as he handed her a glossy magazine with a walleye on its cover. "Are you writing a story for this?" she asked, flipping through the pages absently.

"I'm publishing it," he said, watching her reaction carefully.

She was surprised. "You own this?"

"My lawyers are still ironing out all of the details, but as of last week, I became sole owner and publisher."

"But what about your fishing?"

"I'm still going to be a professional fisherman," he assured her. "I'll probably have to cut back on the amount of time I spend as a guide, but I was planning on doing that anyway. With this—" he reached for the magazine "—I hope to put to use a few of my entrepreneurial skills as well as improve the quality of the magazine, which just happens to be about my favorite subject—fishing."

"Looking for a bit of challenge, are you?" she teased with a knowing grin.

"I hadn't been until a certain redhead entered my life," he said, pulling her into his arms again.

"Are you sure you really want to reenter the business world?" she asked, loving the feel of his arms around her.

"About as sure as you are that you want to leave it," he confessed with a grin.

"This business you just purchased, it isn't in New York, is it?"

"No, St. Paul. It's been a family-run operation for the past four years, but now they're all moving on to other things so I pretty much have to find an entire new staff. I could move headquarters to a more suitable area."

"Not up here?" she looked around the inside of the fish house and raised her eyebrows.

He grinned. "No, but I could publish it in Duluth," he told her. "That way you'd be near your family and we could still use Magda on weekends and during the summer.''

She looked pensive. ''Or you could keep its headquarters in St. Paul and use Magda on weekends.''

''Would you want to live in St. Paul?''

''Right now all I want is to live with you, whether it be at Magda or in Duluth or St. Paul.'' She ran her fingers over the dark stubble lining his jaw. ''How long have you been in this place?''

''Not as long as it might appear,'' he answered, pulling her fingers from his two-day growth of beard and kissing her fingertips. ''John let me bunk down at his place last night because the snowplows hadn't been out to Lake Magda yet.''

''Does that mean we'll have to spend the night here?'' She lifted her eyebrows suspiciously.

''It's not such a bad place,'' he said, feigning hurt feelings. ''It's warm and you've got carpet beneath your feet—''

''With a hole in every corner,'' she interrupted, glancing at the round ice holes used for fishing.

''And there's a TV and refreshments . . .''

''Refreshments?'' she cut in again, looking over at the cooler sitting against one wall.

''During the day you can even get the local pizza place to make deliveries,'' he told her. ''Ice fishing is a lot more relaxing than summer fishing.''

''And where do we sleep?'' she asked coyly. ''In my delicate condition I need lots of sleep.''

''I do have a couple of fold-out cots,'' he teased. ''Or would you rather go back to Magda?''

''Can't,'' she stated simply. ''The road's not plowed.''

"No problem. While I take you to lunch at the Blue Goose, I'll have Fred from the service station go over with his four-wheel drive and open up the road for us."

"And then we'll be able to return?"

"Umm-hmm. We'll build a fire and have a cozy evening for two with candlelight and soft music," he murmured into her hair. "I'll feel like a king with my queen in my castle."

"Oh, Jack. You've always been a king in my eyes," she said with a grin.

EPILOGUE

Twenty years later

"MOM! Wait until you hear Dad's news!" Sixteen-year-old Jennifer Brannigan burst into the kitchen, her auburn hair dusted with huge flakes of fluffy white snow.

Maggie looked up from the pie crust she had been flattening with a wooden rolling pin. "Good or bad?" she asked, her mouth twisting quizzically.

Jennifer had barely had time to kick off her boots before her father came through the door right behind her. "Definitely good news, right, Dad?"

Jack gently shook the snow from his hair and removed his leather gloves. "I'm not so sure I'm happy about this," he answered, his gaze flicking over his wife and daughter before returning to his snow-covered self.

"You're going to be perfect," Jennifer told him, helping him out of his wool-lined parka and hanging it next to hers on the coatrack near the door.

"Perfect at what?" Maggie asked, eyeing her husband and daughter curiously.

Jennifer put both of her hands on her father's arms and led him into the center of the kitchen. "Are you ready for this, Mother?"

Maggie nodded anxiously.

"You see standing before you the next King Boreas Rex of the St. Paul Winter Carnival!" Jennifer's blue eyes sparkled with excitement.

"King Boreas!" Maggie repeated. "I can't believe it!" she exclaimed, wiping her hands on her apron before wrapping them around her husband's shoulders. "What a wonderful surprise!" she exclaimed, then gave him a congratulatory kiss.

"Yes, isn't it," he murmured, his eyes narrowing as they studied his wife's face.

"It's going to be so neat!" Jennifer enthused, unaware of the surreptitious looks being exchanged between her parents. "You'll get to ride in the parade...no wait!" She held both hands up palms outward. "I bet we'll *all* get to ride in the parade...the whole family!" Her face lit up at the thought.

Jack's eyes rolled heavenward and he groaned. "Wonderful," he drawled sarcastically as he practiced his parade wave. His hand moved back and forth like the pendulum on a clock, an action that got Jennifer's tongue clicking and Maggie giggling.

"It's going to be great, Dad." Her father's disinterest didn't dampen her enthusiasm. "You'll get to wear one of those furry robes and a crown—"

"A crown?" he interrupted with an exaggerated ape face.

"Don't be a fuddy-duddy," Jennifer chastised him, affectionately punching his arm. "You're going to have fun. Just think of all those neat winter carnival activities you'll get to preside over. For two weeks you'll get the royal treatment—people waiting on you, following you around like you're somebody important."

Jack rubbed his jaw thoughtfully. "Now that will be a new experience," he said and was promptly rewarded with a glare from his wife.

"I've got to go call Matthew. He's going to want to come home for some of the events, and I know he'll want to attend the coronation ball,'' Jennifer said eagerly, then kissed her father on the cheek before rushing out of the room.

"I'm sure your brother won't want to miss that,'' Jack said dryly, but Jennifer had already disappeared, and the only sound to be heard was her feet racing up the stairs to her room.

"What do you have to say for yourself, Maggie Brannigan?'' Jack said, coming up behind his wife to nuzzle her ear.

She turned into his arms and smiled. "Congratulations, *King Boreas*,'' she said affectionately, amusement dancing in her eyes. "I had a feeling that someday you'd be a king.''

"I just bet you did,'' he said, scrutinizing every familiar feature on her face. "You had something to do with this, didn't you?'' he accused her.

"Now why would you think that?'' she asked, batting her eyelashes innocently.

"I saw the names of those people on the coronation committee.'' He shook his head in amazement. "You've done business with just about every one of them.''

"Jack! I'm a public relations consultant. I do business with lots of people. I hope you're not implying that I would ever attempt to exert any influence on anyone to choose you!'' she said with exaggerated indignation.

"Own up to it, Maggie. You did, didn't you?'' he said in a dangerously low voice, his lips close to hers.

"From all of the men they could have chosen, you are by far the most regal. You're a leader in the business community, you've volunteered innumerable hours on behalf of the city and you are definitely the dreamiest looking man among them all.''

"Dreamiest looking?''

"Umm-hmm. More of a knight in shining armor, I'd say, but king will do for now." She kissed him, a long, slow kiss that he understood better than any words she could ever say. "Maybe we can get you knighted another year." She nibbled on his earlobe. "Did I tell you I might be traveling to London next spring...?"

Harlequin Superromance.

COMING NEXT MONTH

#410 JENNY KISSED ME • Cara West
Sam Grant was flabbergasted when kennel owner Jenny
Hunter transformed his rambunctious fox terrier into an
obedient pet within a few short weeks. Jenny seemed to
have a special relationship with the animals she trained.
Sam sensed depths beneath Jenny's professional
exterior that he wanted to explore, but Jenny didn't
even seem willing to test the waters!

#411 CHOICE OF A LIFETIME • Barbara Kaye
Matt Logan, one of three contenders for the coveted
presidency of the Hamilton House restaurant
conglomerate, finds himself faced with the most
difficult choice of his life: achieving a lifetime goal, or
sacrificing his ambition for the woman he loves....

#412 BLESSING IN DISGUISE • Lorna Michaels
In an attempt to find out who was behind a series of
kidnappings in Houston, investigative reporter Greg
Allen went undercover—as a priest! But his new role as
"Father Gregory" became a frustrating one when social
worker Julie Whitaker insisted on keeping her distance
from a man who was definitely off-limits!

#413 SILVER GIFTS, GOLDEN DREAMS
• Megan Alexander
Brad wanted a condo. Erica wanted a house. Then he let
his mother move in with them, and she wanted their
privacy back. But worst of all, he seemed attracted to
the shapely phys-ed instructor down the block. Erica's
golden dreams lay in tatters. She loved Brad. But would
their silver anniversary be their last?

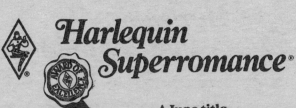

Harlequin Superromance®

A June title
not to be missed....

Superromance author Judith Duncan has created her
most powerfully emotional novel yet, a book about
love too strong to forget and hate too painful to
remember....

Risen from the ashes of her past like a phoenix,
Sydney Foster knew too well the price of wisdom,
especially that gained in the underbelly of the city.
She'd sworn she'd never go back, but in order to
embrace a future with the man she loved, she had to
return to the streets...and settle an old score.

Once in a long while, you read a book that affects you
so strongly, you're never the same again. Harlequin is
proud to present such a book, STREETS OF FIRE by
Judith Duncan (Superromance #407). Her book merits
Harlequin's AWARD OF EXCELLENCE for June 1990,
conferred each month to one specially selected title.

S407-1